For
Better
or for
WOLF

PARANORMAL WEDDING PLANNERS BOOK 4

A E J O N E S

Happy Reading!

aejones

AE Jones: For Better or For Wolf
Copyright © 2019 by Amy E Jones

Publisher: Gabby Reads Publishing LLC

Cover Designer: http://theillustratedauthor.net/
Editor: http://www.demonfordetails.com/
Formatter: http://www.authorems.com

ISBN-10: 1-941871-27-5
ISBN-13: 978-1-941871-27-0

ACKNOWLEDGMENTS

It's hard to believe it's been a year since I spent time in my paranormal wedding planner universe. It's great to be back here to share Connor and Olivia's story. And as always, I have people to thank for this journey.

A shout out to Melissa from the Illustrated Author who created a great cover, especially when she put the wolf shadow on the couch—love it!!

And to Faith, the bestest editor ever! I was a little worried about starting up this universe again after taking a break from it, but you helped steer me down the path. Thanks again.

To my writer pal Becky Lower for keeping me on the straight and narrow. Thanks for your encouragement and all our writerly talks.

And a special thank you to my beta readers: Sandy, Di, and Marin. Thanks for your suggestions, you rock!

Finally to my readers who keep asking me when the next wedding planner book is coming out...this one is for you!

Jordan and Kayla–

To my smart, funny and beautiful twin cousins. It seems fitting to dedicate Connor's story to you since he is a twin as well. There is something so amazing about the twin connection. I hope I captured it correctly in this story. And a special thank you for your amazing support of my writing career. I can always count on you both reading and commenting on my stories!

"Relationship" is not a four-letter word.

CHAPTER 1

Connor Dawson's wolf wanted out—bad. But the hairy dude would just have to wait a bit. Lately his animal side had been getting more and more riled up, and nothing seemed to appease him. But then Connor wouldn't exactly say he had been feeling very *appeased* lately, either.

It didn't help that the sun would soon be setting and tonight was a full moon. Unlike the stereotype, werewolves didn't turn into uncontrollable beasts under the full moon. But the moon did call to his inner Fido rather loudly. And since Connor had a case, Fido needed to chill.

Connor was part of an unofficial law enforcement team tasked with ensuring paranormals didn't kill each other or, at the very least, didn't clue humans in to the fact they exist. And while humans thought vamps and werewolves were cool in the Hollywood sense, in reality there were a lot more to keep quiet about— elves, faeries, nymphs, witches, gargantuans, vampires, gargoyles, shifters, scores of demons—the list went on.

Right now, he stood outside a typical house in the San Diego burbs. On the inside, however, typical was not on the agenda. A philandering husband and a pissed-off witch wife made for a volatile combination.

The wife had been turned over to her coven for punishment and the husband to a healer for...well, healing. Now they were left with the cleanup.

Connor opened the door to the team van as his teammate Giz walked out of the house with a box. Smoke wafted lightly from the top. Which made Connor a little twitchy. But Giz insisted he had muted the spell used on the toaster. Since Giz was a techno-guru and a powerful warlock, Connor would take his word for it.

Sparks shot up from the top. *On second thought...*

"Are you sure you shut down the nastiness?"

"Yes. It won't hurt you. The spell was designed specifically to attack the husband. You definitely don't want to cheat on a witch."

"Female shifters aren't too keen on adultery either," Connor said. And he couldn't blame them. He might like to play the field a bit, but he didn't get involved with married women. Even he had a conscience.

Giz stashed the box in the van.

Connor shut the door. "This is why I won't be getting married."

Giz chuckled.

"What?"

"You won't be getting married because no woman would have you."

Connor bristled. "What the hell does that mean?"

"Except for a few supernatural species, most marriages are based on monogamy. Do you need me to define it for you?"

He knew the definition of monogamy. He just never got into a situation where he had to practice it.

Relationships were not his modus operandi.

"Very funny. Don't tell me you've been drinking the happily-ever-after Kool-Aid."

Giz grinned. "It's hard not to thanks to all our teammates catching the lovebug."

Lovebug, hell. It was more like love fungus or bacteria, or black mold. Connor and Giz were the only two of their five-man team who hadn't succumbed. Which was more than fine with him.

Love made his brother and his friends more than a little stupid. And, Connor reluctantly had to admit, a lot happy. But he couldn't imagine how he would ever find that kind of happiness — not that he was looking. He hoped for their sakes their happiness would last, but he'd never seen love work out over the long haul.

Of course he and Giz were handling this case while his teammates were spending time with their significant others. And after Connor and Giz wrote up their notes to send to the supernatural Tribunal and disposed of the magically toxic toaster, they would go back to the house, where they lived like a couple of overgrown frat boys, and stare at each other over pizza and beer. Which didn't sound very appealing.

At all.

Nope, on second thought, he needed to go out and find a little no-strings companionship.

Variety — one. Monogamy — zero.

But then he wasn't one to keep score.

Consult common sense first,
act second.

CHAPTER 2

Olivia Jennings needed a very large glass of wine. The psychiatrist in her knew alcohol was not the answer to...anything, really, but her sessions today had been stressful with a capital S. Whether the full moon beaming brightly through her office window had set her patients off or something else, she couldn't say, but she needed a break. Visions of a glass of chardonnay and her newest cozy mystery danced in her head.

But first she had one more patient to see before her late-night office hours came to a close. Her receptionist beeped the intercom, and Olivia leaned down and clicked on the blinking button. "Send her in, Marcie."

The door across the room opened and Julia Cole walked into the room. Beautiful and smart as a whip, Julia had been widowed far too young when her husband was murdered three years ago. When Julia first came to see Olivia several months ago, she still mourned her husband and buried herself in her work as a defense attorney. She also had surrounded herself with barriers to keep from being hurt again. Now she bounded into the room with a genuine smile on her face.

Olivia smiled back. "Well, don't you look happy."

Julia plopped down on the couch in her normal spot and crossed her legs. "I am happy."

"Tell me all about it," Olivia said as she scooped up her notepad and pen.

"Jack's been acting weird."

Olivia's eyebrows rose and she admonished herself for showing a reaction. "Jack, your boyfriend? And it makes you happy?"

Julia chuckled. "Don't write it on your notepad. It's not as strange as it seems."

"Further explanation is required before your doctor can refrain from taking notes."

"Well, he's been being secretive, and the other day I caught him in a lie."

Olivia uncapped her pen and poised it over the notepad. "Not feeling your joy over that announcement."

Julia uncrossed her legs. "Okay, even I know it didn't help with the explanation."

"I'm giving you to the count of three and then ink is hitting paper."

"He's going to ask me to marry him!" Julia blurted.

Olivia set her pen and paper down. "You're sure?"

"Yes. He's been asking me ridiculous questions. Like have I ever been in a hot air balloon. He's trying to plan something really romantic when all the silly man has to do is ask me. I don't care where it happens."

Olivia waited a couple of beats before asking her question. "And you think you're ready for this next step?"

Julia nodded. "I'll always love Thomas and miss him. But Jack is my future, and you helped me realize I have the capacity to love again."

"Yes, you do."

An hour later, Olivia sat in the corner booth of a crowded restaurant bar waiting for her friend Elena to finish her assistant manager shift. Normally she wouldn't have said yes to meeting at the bar, but Elena called her when Olivia had just finished her session with Julia, and she wanted to celebrate because one of her patients was moving forward and not letting fear stop her.

Olivia wanted that for all her patients. Every success was a validation for her that life could be good, in spite of what she had experienced in her own past.

Olivia ran her hands along the bun securely fashioned at the nape of her neck. The pins were starting to dig into her scalp, but she could leave it up for a while longer. Hair up, glasses on when in work mode. The persona she showed the world...or rather, allowed the world to see. In reality, she never was out of work mode unless in her apartment. Alone.

Even the bar served as an opportunity to study interactions and mating practices. She watched the people milling around. Anticipation percolated beneath the surface for both the women and men. The question, "is he or she *the one*?" permeated the air. Or could it be the wing sauce? Either one caused heartburn in the end.

"What are you thinking so hard about?"

Olivia turned to Elena, who pulled her hair out of her ponytail and sat down in the booth across from her.

"I'm thinking adults aren't much different from their child selves, needing attention."

A burst of high-pitched laughter drew her attention. "Like the fake laugh. The woman is acting like the guy talking to her is hilarious, but it's coming across as forced. And now she's draping herself all over him. She's trying way too har—"

Olivia nearly choked when she saw the object of the woman's attention.

Jack.

She'd only met Julia's boyfriend once, but he was hard to forget. He was one of those rugged, good-looking men you'd find in an outdoor catalog, all dark hair and brooding eyes. Tonight he smiled at the hyena-laugher while she ran her fingers down his shirt buttons.

Olivia jerked around and tried to ignore what she just saw.

Elena noticed who she was watching and then shook her head. "You want to stay clear of that one."

"You've seen him before?" she asked, her stomach twisting.

"Oh, yeah. He's a total player. Been in here several times, and always with a different woman."

No. No. No. Was it too much to ask for Fate to give Julia a break? To give them all a break?

Elena frowned. "What's wrong, Olivia? You're pale."

Olivia took a deep breath and pasted a smile on her face. "I'm just tired. Do you mind if I give you a rain check on the late dinner?"

"Of course. Let me go give the incoming assistant manager some instructions and then I'll give you a ride home."

"It's not necessary."

"I insist." Elena stood and held her hands up. "Stay here, and I'll be back in five minutes, tops."

Olivia nodded and picked up her tonic water, turning the cool glass around in her fingers. What was she supposed to do now? She was Julia's doctor. But she couldn't get involved. This was not a professional setting, and she was not Jack's therapist.

But could she just look the other way and not say anything? It wasn't her business. It wasn't—

Another burst of laughter. Every obnoxious, high-pitched, hysterical trill ratcheted Olivia's anger up a notch.

She couldn't stop watching, like a car accident unfolding right in front of her. After another nauseating minute, the woman kissed Jack on the cheek and stood, strolling toward the bathroom with an extra sway in her hips. And...wait for it...yep, she glanced over her shoulder and winked at him.

Before Olivia could stop herself, she was on her feet and on her way to Jack's table. Anger seethed under her skin, drowning out her rational, doctor self. This was not a good idea, but for once her common sense could go stuff itself.

She stopped next to the table and glared down at the man who supposedly had declared his love to Julia. Who Julia thought was lying because he was going to *propose* to her.

"What are you doing?" she demanded.

He looked up at her and blinked. "Excuse me?"

"The question was simple enough. What. Are. You. Doing?"

"Having some fun." He studied her face for a moment before continuing. "Do I know you?"

Of course he wouldn't remember her. "We've met before."

He smirked before leaning toward her. "And did we do something we shouldn't have?"

Olivia picked up the fruity, electric-blue cocktail

drink sitting on the table and threw it in his face, then blinked down at the empty glass in her hand and up to his dripping face. *Oh God. Now I've done it.*

"What the hell?" he sputtered.

"I can't believe you would do this to Julia. You're supposed to be in a relationship, Jack."

He stood, pushing back the chair with a loud scrape. Loud, because everyone else in the previously raucous bar had stopped talking to watch the show she was putting on. She was always the observer of the train wreck, not an active participant in it. She made sure of it. Until tonight, that is.

He shook his head like a wet dog, scattering sticky drops off his face and hair and hitting her glasses.

"There's a first time for everything," he drawled.

"I can't believe you've never had a drink thrown in your face before." She barely managed not to slap her hand over her mouth. Who was this woman spewing sarcastic remarks?

He wiped his face. "Oh, I've had a drink thrown in my face, all right, but not for something I didn't do."

Fear started to crack her righteous indignation and her voice lost its strength. "What do you mean?"

"The statement was simple enough, but let me spell it out to you. I'm. Not. Jack."

Dots swam in front of her eyes. "Not Jack?"

"Nope."

"Julia introduced me to you."

"It wasn't me."

Dear God. Was he telling the truth, and she'd just accosted a stranger? The crowd leaned in closer, as if eager for first blood. "I…I'm sorry. I should never have done that. I thought you were Jack. You look just like him."

How could she make amends? She could pay his bar tab and give him money for a new shirt. Maybe, just maybe, she could get out of here without explaining too much and hope to maintain a shred of her dignity.

"I look like him because I'm his twin brother, Connor. And who, exactly, are you?"

Twin? Blood pounded in her ears like a bass drum. Dignity had officially left the building, followed quickly by self-esteem and professional integrity.

This was what happened when you told common sense to go stuff itself.

Always pay attention to the little voice in your head.

CHAPTER 3

Connor's wolf clawed to get out. What the hell had gotten into him lately? He promised the hairy beast he would shift and go for a run in the woods later, but right now he had to deal with the irate woman in front of him.

She had approached him like an avenging Fury. Suit, glasses, and dark hair pinned up in a bun, she had a surprisingly sexy librarian vibe going on. Until she let him have it.

And instead of taking a step back, he had poked the lion. How many times had his even-keeled twin told him *not* to poke the lion? But that's not how Connor rolled. And now fruity-smelling, fluorescent-blue liquid dripped off his face onto his shirt.

His senses told him the female in front of him was human, but that didn't mean she shouldn't be taken seriously. Although after he announced he wasn't Jack, her indignation had disappeared, quickly replaced by embarrassment, exacerbated by the crowded but silent bar hanging on their every word.

She stood there frozen, as if she hadn't heard him ask her name. Well, he had no trouble repeating the question. If she got to throw a drink in his face, he at least deserved to know her name.

Before he could ask her again, one of the female restaurant managers he'd seen before walked over to them, followed by two large bouncers. The spectacle was about to turn into a circus.

"Are you okay?" the manager asked the woman.

"I'm fine."

Her? She attacked *him*.

The manager turned to him. "It's time for you to leave."

The bouncers stood on either side of him.

Connor frowned. So much for asking him what happened.

His attacker shook her head. "Wait—"

The manager interrupted her. "It's okay. Let me take care of this."

Oh no, this was not how it was going to go down. Time to set everyone straight on who should be thrown out of this bar.

Then his cell beeped from its spot on the table. And the tone had him reaching for his phone regardless of the craptastic situation he found himself in.

It was the tone he had assigned for text messages he received from Devin, their team leader. Which meant they had a case. Devin's timing was impeccable, as always.

Connor took a step back, giving the woman who'd started this one last look. "I'm going." And he strode out the door and into the parking lot before he could say anything else.

After getting his go bag and a bottle of water out of his SUV, he yanked off his drink-soaked shirt. Then he opened the bottle of water, pouring some into his hand

and quickly wiping his face and hair to get rid of the stickiness. He used the back of the soaked shirt, which hadn't been doused with fluorescent drink, to quickly dry off before putting on a clean shirt from his bag. After tossing the ruined shirt in a nearby dumpster, he jumped into the SUV and peeled out of the parking lot.

Connor reached out to his brother through what they called their twinspeak link.

You there, Jack?

Yeah. Did you get the message?

Connor turned a corner. *Yes. I'm on my way to the team house. Where are you?*

On my way. Devin said Sullivan called him.

Connor's nerves went on high alert. If their alpha was calling in *their* team, something bad had happened or was about to happen. Besides Jack and Connor, their cross-supernatural team included Devin, an elf, Charlie, a nymph, and, of course Giz, the warlock.

Do you know what happened?

No.

Connor signed off and sped up. The pack generally kept to their own, but Connor and Jack were an exception to the rule. While many in the pack, including their father, felt they betrayed the pack by choosing to live outside pack territory, Sullivan, their alpha, was a bit more open-minded. He liked having wolves on the cross-supernatural teams because he wanted representation within the Tribunal.

Whatever happened that caused Connor's alpha to send out the pack equivalent of the Bat Signal was bad. Connor could feel it down to his bones, and his wolf wasn't immune to his anxiety, because he paced under his skin. Or maybe his wolf's pacing was due to the inevitability of seeing his father. Since his father was in charge of pack security, there would be no avoiding the exchange of insults sure to occur. Fingers crossed his father would ignore him the way he normally did.

Connor turned onto the road leading to the team house where he and Giz lived. Even though he'd changed his shirt, he could still smell the cocktail. The last thing he wanted to do was explain why he smelled like pineapple. And to think he'd been soaked in alcohol because that spitfire mistook him for Jack.

He should be pissed, but the more he thought about it, the more he realized her indignation, while misplaced, was in defense of Julia. And while she could have done it in a less messy fashion, he had to grudgingly respect her for standing up for her friend.

Once the pack crisis was taken care of, he would have to question Julia to find out who the drink-wielding Fury was. Because their conversation might have been interrupted, but it was far from over.

Olivia squirmed on Elena's couch while her friend sat gaping at her.

"Say something," Olivia said.

Elena's eyes widened before she blinked. Twice.

"Elena!"

"So, let me get this straight. You walked up to him, yelled at him, and then threw a drink in his face."

Olivia's face heated. "That about sums it up."

"And he wasn't even the right guy."

"How was I supposed to know he has a twin?"

Elena threw her head back and laughed. "Who are you? And what have you done with my friend?"

Olivia's stomach threatened to rebel. "I don't know what I was thinking."

"Who did you think the guy was?" Elena asked.

"I can't tell you too much, due to doctor-patient confidentiality."

"Now you're worried about propriety?"

"Touché. All I can say is, I thought he was my patient's boyfriend/soon-to-be fiancé."

Elena cringed. "I can see where that would have set anyone off."

Except her. It shouldn't have set her off. She was supposed to be a professional. What she'd done was inexcusable.

"Stop."

Olivia looked up at her friend. "What?"

"The self-recrimination. I can see it written all over your face."

"I can't believe I did it. When I think back, I feel like I was a different person. I'm not making excuses. I'm just telling you it was surreal."

"Well, I for one am glad."

Olivia stared at her for a moment before responding. "You're glad I acted like an idiot?"

"I'm glad you actually felt strongly enough about something to go out on a limb. You're normally so guarded, I'm not always sure you have emotions."

Olivia flinched.

Elena's expression softened. "I'm sorry if I sounded harsh. But I worry about you. I had to practically threaten you to get you to be my friend when we first met. Remember?"

"Yes." They both volunteered in a big sister program at the local Y, and Elena had been determined to get Olivia to go out for drinks after their weekly sessions with the girls. Olivia refused at first, but Elena eventually wore her down. "I still don't know why you worked so hard to be my friend."

"Because I saw you with the girls. You're smart, and kindhearted, but never let them make excuses when they weren't trying to succeed. And I also quickly learned that being a therapist is the center of your universe, which was not okay with me. You need to have a life outside of work."

"Now who's hanging up their shingle?"

Elena shrugged. "*You're* sitting on *my* couch right now."

"I'm fine."

Elena's eyes narrowed on her. "I don't think you'd let your patients get away with that answer. So I'm going to call bull."

Olivia managed a smile, even though Elena had landed a little too close to the truth. "A good therapist doesn't browbeat her patients. She allows them to find their own way."

Elena stared at her a little too long before responding. "I guess I'm not cut out to be a therapist, then. But as your friend, I want you to be happy."

"I'm happy," she answered, too quickly.

Again with the staring. "I saw some fire in your eyes this evening, for sure."

Olivia moaned. "Don't remind me. I don't know how I'm going to explain what I did to my patient."

"Maybe you won't need to explain anything. He doesn't know your name, right?"

"I'm sure he's going to say something to Jul—my patient. If I don't own up to things, they inevitably come back to bite me."

"I wouldn't mind him biting me."

"Elena! You told me he's a player and to stay away from him."

"I did, but it doesn't mean he's not a fine-looking specimen. A girl can dream, right?"

"Fantasizing is healthy." And he was ridiculously handsome, even dripping with sticky pineapple juice.

Elena fanned herself. "Then I must be one of the healthiest females on the planet."

Olivia laughed. "Thank you for distracting me. But

I'm going to have to figure out how to deal with this by the time I see my patient again." She thought about his—Connor's—wet face and shirt. And those green eyes radiating challenge. But then for some reason he backed off and left without a fight.

She should be relieved, but the little voice inside her head—the one that was usually right—told her in no uncertain terms that he was not done with her.

Sometimes the best families are bound together by choice, not blood.

CHAPTER 4

It didn't take long for the team to gather at the house. Giz was already at home when Devin sent out the text, and Jack showed up a few minutes after Connor got home. Then in marched Devin and his wife, Alex, along with Charlie and his wife, Sheila.

Connor's eyebrows rose at the group.

"The four of us were out to dinner when I got the call from Sullivan," Devin said as he helped Alex take her seat.

Alex rolled her eyes at him. "I'm not that pregnant yet, husband. I can still sit down on my own."

Devin grinned. "Of course, babe."

Connor had to stifle a sarcastic comment. A classic example of the love fungus rearing its ugly head. Although he had to admit Alex was awfully cute now that she was showing. But he damn well knew better than to tell her. She'd take it the wrong way, and then Devin would make his life hell.

Connor glanced over at Jack, who watched the interaction with a slight smirk...and caught the fleeting image of a velvet ring box. *Damn.* His twin was keeping secrets.

"What did Sullivan have to say?" Connor asked.

Devin moved to the fireplace and leaned against the mantel, his usual spot when they had team meetings. "He wants to meet with the team. He was very cryptic on the phone. Said there are some upcoming negotiations he wants us to take part in. Felt our expertise could be invaluable, whatever that means. Said he would let me know tonight when we could meet."

"Means he's expecting trouble," Jack said.

Devin tapped his fingers on the mantel. "My thought, too. When the West Coast pack leader calls a meeting with a Tribunal team, it can't be anything good."

"And he wants all of us there?" Connor asked. He could feel Jack's stare on him.

Devin's eyes narrowed. "Yeah. Made a point of telling me he already reached out to the Tribunal leader and told him he wanted to work with our team specifically."

The hairs on the back of Connor's neck stood on end, and this time he did glance over at his scowling twin. Their father was not going to like their involvement. At all.

"Tell us more about Sullivan Ross," Alex piped in.

Connor gestured to Jack to explain.

"He's been the pack leader for a little over a year now, since his father, Morgan, died. Morgan was a hard leader."

Connor gritted his teeth at even the mention of the previous alpha's name. "You mean a brutal bastard, don't you, Jack?"

Jack gave a tight nod before continuing. "There was no love lost between father and son. From what I've heard, Sullivan is working to repair relations within the pack."

"And if he's calling us in to help, something isn't going well," Connor said.

Devin's phone beeped and he looked at it. "It's a text from Sullivan. He said he would like to meet with us in a few days. So we have some time before we head to the pack lands. Sorry I interrupted everyone's evening."

Connor stopped himself from groaning. He could have stayed at the bar and had his say with his attacker.

They finished up the meeting a few minutes later, the two couples heading for home, and Giz going up to his room to work on some computer program or other.

Jack apparently wanted to talk some more. Connor grabbed a couple of beers out of the fridge and they sat down at the kitchen table.

Connor took a swig. "My wolf is pacing around in my head right now."

"Mine, too. Jonathan will not want outside interference from the Tribunal."

They had both stopped using the word *father* years ago when it came to Jonathan Dawson. It wasn't something they'd discussed, and Connor couldn't remember who called him Jonathan first, but it had stuck.

"Not our problem," Connor said before taking another drink. "I can't imagine you decided to stick around to talk about Jonathan. Is there something you need to tell me?"

"What do you mean?"

Connor studied his face for a moment. "I saw your thoughts earlier, when you were watching Alex and Devin together."

"Oh."

"'*Oh*'? Is that all you have to say?"

"I was going to tell you. I just got the ring two days ago."

Connor would have expected Jack to take him along to help pick it out, but he wasn't going to say so. "When are you going to propose to Julia?"

"I don't know yet. I'm trying to figure out the best way to do it. I may need your help, if you can keep your mouth shut."

"Absolutely. And you think she'll say yes?"

Jack huffed before responding, "Why the hell wouldn't she?"

Connor grinned. "Because she might realize she picked the wrong twin."

Jack laughed. "I doubt it."

"What's so damn funny?"

"You're a player, Connor. Julia wouldn't touch a player with a ten-foot pole."

"That's a gross exaggeration," Connor said.

"I don't think so. Are you going to tell me why you smell like you bathed in piña coladas?"

"I got a drink thrown in my face tonight."

Jack held up his hands. "See what I mean? Play-yerrr."

Connor set down his beer. "Except the drink was your fault."

Jack settled back after a quick swig of his beer. "This I've got to hear."

"The woman who drenched me thought I was you."

Jack's mouth fell open, and Connor chuckled. "Yep. She thought you were stepping out on Julia and she let you—I mean me—have it."

Jack set his own beer down with a hard thunk. "Holy crap."

"My thoughts exactly."

"Who is she?"

"I didn't get her name. The bouncers came over and offered to escort me out forcibly if necessary, and before I could protest that I was the injured party, Devin's text came through."

"Bad timing."

"A definite understatement. I need to find out who she is. She has to be friends with Julia. She said she met you once, too."

"What did she look like?"

"A sexy librarian."

"Clarification needed."

"Suit, glasses, dark hair in a bun. Uptight but fiery, if that makes sense."

"She could be any one of Julia's lawyer friends."

Connor scowled. "You're not being helpful, here."

Jack laughed. "I'll talk to Julia to see if she can tell us who your attacker was. But I'm warning you now, if I tell her, she'll tell Alex, and —"

"Alex will tell everyone else."

Devin's wife was a great person, but she was always getting into everyone's business. It was for the best of intentions, but was Connor ready to deal with her and the rest of the team giving him a hard time? "Fine. Do it."

"Wow. I dangled the Alex card and you still want to find this woman again. Why?" Jack asked.

A very good question. *Why do I?* He stared down at the table.

"Connor?"

"I didn't get to have the last word, and you know how I hate that." He glanced over at Jack, who had a shit-ass grin pasted on his face.

"What?"

"Nothing. I'll talk to Julia tonight to see if she can figure out who it is."

"Thanks."

After Jack left, Connor's wolf paced under his skin some more, back and forth, back and forth, so he took him on their long-awaited run. He loped along, letting his wolf enjoy the breeze ruffling his fur as his paws hit the earth. There was something so liberating about being in his lupine form. All the craziness and obligations gone. No pack expectations or disappointments. Just doing what you want to do when you want to do it.

Connor ran down along an embankment and stopped to appreciate the clear night, with the moon sitting high in the sky, thinking about Jack's earlier question. He wasn't sure why he wanted to see the drink-wielding Fury again, or what he hoped to accomplish, but he didn't think their conversation was over, not by a long shot.

His wolf howled his agreement at the moon.

Once you confront yourself,
confronting others isn't so scary.

CHAPTER 5

Only eight a.m. and Olivia was already obsessing. As a psychiatrist, she was well versed in the signs. But she couldn't get the confrontation with Connor out of her mind. She replayed the same mortifying scene over and over again, as if she could somehow change it. Not lose her common sense and fling the ridiculous blue drink in his face.

Enough.

What did she tell her patients when they couldn't get over an event in their lives? Confront it. Whether it meant confronting the emotions or the person, even if it included owning up and admitting you were wrong.

Her little voice argued that she didn't need to see Connor again. She'd already apologized to him, after all. But she did in the least need to talk to Julia. By now Connor had probably told Julia what happened and, while he didn't know her name, Julia would eventually figure it out.

Olivia was a professional 99.9% of the time. Unfortunately, the .1% had hosed things up for her. Okay, so she had hosed things up for her own self.

Sometimes she hated being a therapist. Self-actualize this, own up to that, blah, blah, blah.

Olivia opened up her patient database and found Julia's phone number. She stared at it. And stared at it some more. Maybe now wasn't the time to call her. Shouldn't she do this face-to-face?

Olivia pulled up her patient schedule. Julia's next appointment wasn't for another week. She couldn't wait that long. She stared at her calendar again. Maybe she could do something in the meantime. Olivia met with Alex Cole tomorrow. Maybe she should find out what Alex knew first. She was Julia's sister-in-law, and had suggested Julia see a psychiatrist in the first place. If Julia had figured out who accosted Connor, Alex was sure to know.

Olivia took in a deep breath and let it out slowly. She told herself she was not being a chicken, but the little voice started to cluck nonstop.

So she told it to shut up.

The scary thing was, the little voice sounded like Elena. Actually, Olivia shouldn't be surprised, since her friend had said some eye-opening things to her last night. Things that were true, but Olivia didn't want to face. Of course Elena didn't know the truth about Olivia's past. Few people did.

Olivia knew she was a hypocrite. What happened to all her talk about confronting things? To open up and move past the fears holding her patients hostage. Yet she couldn't find a way to manage it herself.

But hers wasn't a normal fear. She didn't have a phobia about flying, or heights, or spiders. There was no word to describe the phobia she had about the glowing-eyed beasts she saw in her night terrors. She would have to schedule another session with Dr. Murphy. Soon.

In the meantime, she wouldn't use Alex as a filter

for speaking to Julia. She would find a time to meet with Julia today if she could. Confess what she'd done.

Connor took a deep breath as he walked down the hall of For Better or For Worse for the weekly staff meeting. Besides working for the Tribunal, the team also covered security for high-profile paranormal weddings. Alex and her grandmother, along with Charlie's wife, Sheila, ran a highly successful paranormal wedding planner business. Even Julia participated when not tied up with her other clients, helping with wedding contracts and prenups. When you were dealing with beings who had been alive for centuries, contracts could get a little sticky.

But when he arrived at the conference room door, his nerves kicked in. He had faced down deranged demons with less trepidation than what he felt now. He needed to suck it up. In other words, be prepared to be ridiculed by his teammates and questioned—aw, hell, who was he kidding?—*interrogated* by the better halves of his teammates over his drink-in-the-face escapade last night.

He turned the doorknob and pushed open the door.

Let the games begin...

Connor's confidence threatened to abandon him when he found everyone already in the room waiting for him. Jack and Julia sat on one side of the long table, with Charlie and Sheila on the other. Next to Charlie, Giz typed away on his laptop, and Devin and Alex sat together at the head of the table.

Everyone smiled at him before Alex gestured for him to take a seat. He sat down in the empty chair next to Jack and waited for the comments to start.

Alex kicked things off. "Grandmother is on the

phone with an anxious client, so she asked me to run the meeting today. We have two high-profile weddings scheduled in a few weeks. One is a pair of vampires, so it will be a night wedding. The other wedding is for avian demons."

Devin spoke next. "Giz and Charlie are already studying schematics for the two facilities, checking for security loopholes." The group spent a few minutes talking about the schematics.

When the conversation quieted, Sheila leaned forward. "I have several new clients who want to look their best for their weddings, so we'll be putting together a diet and exercise program for them, depending on their species and metabolism."

Alex reviewed the notes in front of her. "What about you, Julia?"

"I have one prenup I'm finishing up for a nymph wedding."

"Excellent," Alex said. "Now that the first part of our meeting is concluded, it's time to move on to another business matter."

Connor glanced around the room in confusion. What other business matters? Giz stopped typing on his laptop and stood, walking over to the small table in the corner to pick up a cardboard box, which he brought over and set in front of Connor.

"What is it?" Connor asked, backing the chair away from the table.

"Open it," Alex said.

Connor lifted the flap. He pulled the first item out. A clear plastic poncho with metal snaps and a hood.

Charlie grinned. "Rain gear for the next time you go to the bar."

"And if it doesn't work," Sheila said as she reached into the box and pulled out a small bottle, "here's a stain stick for tough-to-remove drink stains."

Alex pulled out a piece of paper from under her notebook and passed it down the table to him. "And, last but not least, I got you an application for a library card, since there are easier and less messy ways to meet a sexy librarian."

Connor shook his head while everyone around the table grinned and/or snickered, including his turncoat brother.

"I warned you what would happen if I talked to Julia," Jack said.

"You did. But I was expecting some ribbing, not a full-on frontal attack within hours."

"You underestimated us," Alex said, before she, Sheila, and Julia giggled and high-fived each other like teenagers.

"I don't know why I'm the brunt of this joke. The woman thought I was Jack! You don't know who she is, Julia?"

Julia rolled her eyes. "No. A sexy librarian. Really, Connor?"

He shrugged. "I just call it like I see it. Get me a list of your lawyer friends with pictures, and I'll figure out who she is."

Alex blinked at him several times. "I think you're getting a bit obsessed about this. Maybe we should see about getting Connor an appointment with Dr. Jennings, Julia."

Julia's eyes sparkled. "I agree. She could help him for sure."

"You want me to see your shrink? Do I need to remind you...again...I was soaked with a drink because I was mistaken for *Jack*?"

Julia smiled. "Nope. I think it's sweet that someone I know was willing to confront Jack for cheating on me."

"I agree," Connor said.

Julia's eyes widened. "You do?"

"Yep. It's the mark of a true friend. Which is why I want to meet her again and tell her so."

Alex laughed. "Connor Dawson, you want to meet her again because you can't stand anyone one-upping you."

"Not true." Of course he didn't want to tell them the truth. He couldn't get the irate woman out of his mind.

The rest of the team joined Alex in her guffaw-fest. Connor scowled at each of them.

The laughter got louder until Devin held up his hands for quiet. "As much fun as we're having, it's time to get back to work."

Connor couldn't agree more.

*Confessing the truth is as much for you
as for the person you wronged.*

CHAPTER 6

Olivia walked off the elevator and down the hall, stopping in front of Julia's law office door, where she hesitated for a moment.

But it was too late to back out. Olivia had called earlier, and Julia's assistant squeezed her in for a meeting at the end of the day.

Olivia opened the door and stepped inside a waiting room/reception area nicely decorated with blue and teal. It fit Julia's personality. Classy, yet feminine.

A young woman greeted her with a smile. "Dr. Jennings?"

"Yes."

"I'm Tina. We spoke earlier on the phone. I'll let Julia know you're here."

Tina walked over to a closed door, knocked, and walked inside. Olivia pulled on her right jacket sleeve, and then her left, before rolling her shoulders to release the tension. This was the right thing to do, even if her nerves insisted she could still make a break for it. A moment later Tina held the door open for her.

Olivia walked inside and Julia gestured for her to take a seat. Her office resembled the waiting area. Her desk was orderly, with a couple of neat stacks of paperwork.

"Do you need anything else before I go, Julia?" Tina asked.

"No. Have a good night."

Tina shut the door, and Julia gave Olivia a searching glance.

Olivia stopped herself from nervously clearing her throat. "Thank you for agreeing to meet with me on such short notice, Julia."

"I'll admit, you have my curiosity piqued. Are you needing some legal advice?"

Olivia shook her head. "Nothing like that. I'm sorry I've come to your workplace. It's a little unorthodox on my part, but I needed to talk to you. Apologize for something, actually."

Julia frowned slightly. "What in the world would you have to apologize to me for?"

"I—"

A slight knock on the door stopped Olivia's confession.

The door opened and a familiar face popped into the room. "Sorry, Julia. I didn't realize you were meeting with someone."

Julia stood, and Olivia followed suit, even as her nerves jittered under her skin.

"Jack, you remember Dr. Jennings?"

"Of course. Sorry I showed up a bit early to pick you up. I'll let you finish your meeting. We'll wait outside for you."

We? But she already knew who he meant by we. Because Fate always had a way of biting back. And she had told common sense to stuff it. Obviously it hadn't gone over well with Fate.

Jack's mirror image leaned in the doorway, but, unlike Jack, his expression was far from welcoming. Green eyes flared for a moment before narrowing on her with laser-like intensity.

"You!"

And there was the bite.

Julia's eyebrows came together as she looked between Olivia and Connor. "You two know each other?"

"Not really," Olivia said.

"We're not exactly strangers, even if we haven't been properly introduced. Julia, would you do the honors?"

Julia glanced over at Jack, who scowled at his brother. "Dr. Jennings, this is Connor Dawson. Connor, Dr. Jennings."

Connor's eyes widened. "You're Julia and Alex's shrink?"

"Psychiatrist."

He chuckled. "This is too perfect."

"What the hell is going on, Connor?" Jack demanded.

"Dr. Jennings and I..." He turned to her with a small, sardonic bow. "Although don't you think we should be on a first-name basis by now?"

"Olivia," she said through gritted teeth.

"*Olivia* and I met when she threw a drink in my face."

"*You're* the sexy librarian?" Julia asked in a high-pitched voice.

Olivia gaped at her. "The what?"

Pink spread across Julia's face. "Um. That's how he described you."

Olivia turned to Connor. Unlike Julia, he didn't look

embarrassed at all. Far from it. If Olivia had to describe his expression, and she had become an expert at reading unspoken cues, she would say he was loving every moment of this, especially her discomfort. So she wouldn't feed into it anymore.

She lifted her chin and stared into his eyes. "I apologized to you the other night and offered to pay for your shirt."

"So you did, but you didn't tell the bouncers *you* attacked *me* before they kicked me out."

"I tried to, and then you announced you were leaving. And don't you think the word 'attacked' is a bit of an exaggeration?"

"You weren't the one dripping in blue pineapple juice."

Olivia was very much aware of Julia and Jack watching the two of them like they were opponents in a tennis match.

Time to call this circus to a halt.

"Julia, I actually came here today to apologize to you for what I did. Now that Jack is here, I will apologize to both of you. It was both unprofessional and uncalled for of me to react that way. I have no right to get involved in my patients' personal lives in such a direct manner. If you no longer wish to be my patient, I fully understand. I can provide you with a listing of referrals if you'd like."

Julia shook her head. "Completely unnecessary. Apology accepted. Knowing you were sticking up for me is actually sweet."

"Sweet," Connor grumbled.

Olivia turned to Connor. "I apologize again for my actions." She reached for her bag next to the chair. "The offer still stands for me to pay for a new shirt."

His gleeful expression had gone south. "It's not necessary."

She gave him a tight nod. "I'll just show myself out, then. And rest assured, even though we'll probably never see each other again, if we do, I promise not to—what did you say the other night?—do anything I shouldn't have with you? So I'll try to control myself and refrain from attacking you again. Good night."

Connor watched her walk out of the room like royalty—a queen. Which made him the court jester.

"What the hell just happened?" he blurted before he could control his mouth.

"You just got schooled, brother."

Connor glared at Jack. "Shut it."

Julia laughed. "He's right. You thought you were all high-and-mighty, and then she twisted it so she came out on top. I got to watch it for free, but, boy, I would have paid money for that show."

"What did she mean when she said, 'not do anything I shouldn't have with you'?" Jack asked.

"Nothing." Just Connor's own stupid "player" come-on lines getting thrown back in his face, much like the drink the other night. Only this time he wasn't innocent.

Time to change the subject, even though he had to admit Julia was right. Olivia handled the situation masterfully, in her own uptight fashion. And for some reason his wolf liked the good doctor a lot. But he would need to let it go, since he wouldn't be seeing her again.

And why did the thought make him want to pace alongside his wolf?

*When your reality changes,
you have to change with it.*

CHAPTER 7

Olivia took off her suit jacket and hung it on the hook behind her desk. Depending on the client, she either shed or put on her jacket. She found some patients needed her to look one hundred percent professional, while others were intimidated and needed her to appear more casual.

Alex didn't fit into either category, but she didn't expect Olivia to be buttoned-up. They had worked through many of Alex's anxieties together, and Olivia wouldn't be surprised if Alex someday soon announced she didn't need to meet with her anymore. Although Alex had been a little anxious last session about impending motherhood, but that was common among first-time mothers.

Plus there was the added issue of Alex more than likely knowing by now about Olivia's disastrous meeting with Julia yesterday, and that Olivia was Connor's *sexy librarian*. Good Lord, did the man have no shame?

Marcie knocked on the door and peeked into her office. "Your last appointment is here."

"Thanks. We set for tomorrow?"

Marcie nodded. "Sorry I have to leave before your last appointment is over."

As a matter of protocol and safety, Olivia normally didn't meet with patients in her offices alone, but Alex was not someone Olivia needed to worry about. "No problem. It's not like you would rather get a root canal than stay here. Good luck at the dentist."

Marcie scrunched up her face. "Absolutely not. See you in the morning."

Marcie held open the door for Alex to enter, and she did, with a huge grin.

"Well, don't you look happy," Olivia said.

Alex's grin broadened. "I am happy. For two reasons. First, I can't believe you're the one who threw a drink in Connor's face."

Olivia's face heated. "It was immature and unprofessional of me. I shouldn't have done it. I wasn't even sure if you'd show up for your session today."

Alex dismissed her apology with a wave of her hands. "Are you kidding me? Of course I would. Besides, Connor is a big boy. His ego could use a good soaking every once in a while. And if I know him, he probably said something he shouldn't have."

Time to get a handle on the session. "Why don't you tell me the second reason why you're so happy."

"I've finally stopped vomiting. It's time to celebrate."

Olivia glanced down at Alex's baby bump. "You're in your second trimester, right? Morning sickness still bothering you?"

"Morning, afternoon, evening. It's been an equal-opportunity sickness. But I haven't raced to the bathroom in three days. So, yay!"

Olivia chuckled. "Glad you're being positive about the experience."

Alex sat down on the couch. "We'll see how I feel when my ankles swell and I have to pee every ten minutes."

Olivia picked up her notebook and pen. "Something tells me you'll handle that with flying colors too."

Alex shrugged. "We'll see."

"Where did all your positivity just go? Are you worried about something?"

"I guess I'm starting to realize this is real. What happens if I make mistakes?"

Olivia jotted a note down. Most of her clients wondered what she wrote down on her mysterious notepad, but often it was a word or a doodle. It gave her a moment to collect her thoughts before she replied or offered advice. She studied Alex, who bit the corner of her lip.

"Alex, the one thing I can guarantee is, you are going to make mistakes."

"Aren't you supposed to be supportive?" Alex sputtered.

Olivia nodded. "Yes, but I'm going to tell you the truth, too. You are a human being. No one's perfect, and you will make mistakes. The difference is, the best parents learn from their mistakes."

Alex sighed. "You always sneak in those nuggets of wisdom when I least expect them."

Olivia winked. "Part of my job description. How is Devin handling things?"

"He's good. He'll be a great father. He dropped me off and is coming back to pick me up. I have a checkup after this, and he's coming with me."

"It's so wonderful he's been involved right from the beginning."

"He wouldn't have it any other way. He was overprotective of me before my pregnancy, and now he's a bit over-the-top. I think he'd stay by my side twenty-four hours a day if he could get away with it. Do you have any spare anti-anxiety meds I could mash up in his applesauce?"

Olivia laughed. "Alex."

She sighed dramatically. "I know, but it was worth a shot. Seriously, though, he started talking about me not going back to work after the baby is born, and I almost told him he could stay with Julia and Jack for a while until he came to his senses."

"I'm sure Julia would love that. She and Jack haven't been living together long, and I don't know if having Devin move in with them would be good timing."

Alex ran her hand along the couch arm. "I know. I wouldn't do that to them. I'm so happy for them. Julia seems to be so much better, don't you agree?"

"You know I can't talk to you about other patients, Alex." Olivia shouldn't scold her too much. She hadn't been a role model of professionalism herself lately.

"True, but it doesn't mean I can't talk about her as part of my session, right?"

"You are relentless."

"I think of it more as wanting my friends and family to be happy." Alex jerked upright.

"Are you okay?" Olivia asked.

"Yep. The baby just moved. Surprised me a bit." Alex laid her hands over her growing stomach.

"These are the memories to rememb—" Olivia choked on her words as a small light began to glow beneath Alex's hands. Where was it coming from? Was she holding her phone on her belly?

Alex lifted her hands—her empty hands—and Olivia stood up from her chair, her notebook and pen hitting the floor. The light came from under Alex's shirt!

"Your stomach is glowing," Olivia blurted.

Alex gasped before wrapping her cardigan sweater

over her belly, but the light shone through the second layer as well.

Olivia blinked and then blinked again to clear her mind. When she opened her eyes again, the glow had disappeared. What just happened? Olivia had never hallucinated before. What could have triggered it, and why in the world would it have manifested in a glowing belly?

She needed to remain calm. She didn't want Alex to get upset, but apparently Olivia blurting out that her belly was glowing had scared Alex, who now fumbled in her purse and pulled out her phone. She made a call.

"Devin, I need you here now," she blurted before hanging up and staring at Olivia.

Olivia studied her patient for a moment. There had to be a logical explanation for what just happened. But Alex's stomach had *glowed*. How was that any version of logical or sane?

Maybe the issue wasn't Alex, but Olivia. Alex never said she saw her stomach glowing. And even though she covered up her baby bump with her sweater, was it because her stomach glowed, or because her therapist had freaked her out? First she threw a drink in Connor's face, and now this. Maybe these were all symptoms of a greater mental issue.

Before Olivia could voice her thoughts, a tall, dark-haired man burst into the room and ran around the couch, crouching down in front of Alex.

"What's happened, Alex? Are you okay? Is it the baby?"

Alex bit her lip before responding. "Devin, Dr. Jennings just told me I was glowing."

Devin paused, frowning, before answering her. "And you are, babe. You're beautiful."

Alex rolled her eyes. "I'm not fishing for compliments,

Devin. I was actually glowing. My stomach lit up like the rear end of a lightning bug." She glanced over at Olivia before taking Devin's hand. "Do you see the problem?"

"I definitely do," Olivia mumbled. For some reason her legs didn't feel strong enough to support her, and she plopped down in her chair.

"We'll figure this out. Is this the first time your stomach glowed?" he asked.

Alex huffed. "If the baby had glowed before now, Devin, I would have told you."

Olivia held up her hands. "Excuse me, but are you telling me your stomach actually did just light up, and I'm not hallucinating?"

Alex sighed. "No...umm. We need to explain a few things."

"Are you going to tell me you're an alien?"

Alex straightened and frowned. "Of course not!"

Olivia bit the inside of her cheek to keep from laughing. She wasn't sure why Alex was so indignant. Her stomach had, as she had so eloquently described, "lit up like the butt end of a lightning bug."

"Is someone going to explain how something impossible just happened? Or am I having some sort of psychotic break?"

"You know, that's exactly what I said when I found out," Alex said.

"Found out what?"

"That supernaturals exist."

Olivia opened her mouth and then closed it again, her mind a complete blank.

Alex watched her closely, like she was a science experiment. "You're handling this better than I did when I found out. I passed out when Devin told me."

Devin wrapped his arm around Alex's shoulders. "Actually you didn't believe me when I told you. You said you would get me in to see your psychiatrist."

Alex shrugged at Olivia. "I'd been seeing you as a patient for a while then, and I thought he was crazy."

Olivia tried to keep up, but she was losing ground fast. "But your stomach just glowed, so doesn't that make you..."

"A supernatural? Yes. But I didn't know I was at the time." Alex turned to Devin, who nodded for her to continue. "I'm part human and part faerie."

Olivia glanced at Devin. *Then what is he?* Alex must have seen the question on her face.

"Devin is an elf."

"Faerie. And...elf." Olivia repeated the words, as if saying them would make it more real. But it was impossible. "I'm sorry, but I'm having a hard time believing this."

"Understandable," Devin said. "Do you need more proof?"

More than Alex's glowing belly? Olivia didn't know if her reply should be yes or no. Alex might think Olivia was doing okay, but she wasn't handling this well at all.

Sure, she had heard some truly strange things over the years from her patients, but this? This took things to a whole new level. A level Olivia was pretty sure she wasn't ready for.

Alex patted Devin's arm. "He won't do anything scary. Show her how fast you are, sweetie."

He kissed his wife on the forehead and then he wasn't sitting next to Alex anymore. He was across the room. A moment later he sat next to his wife.

Olivia sucked in a breath. Okay. Okay, she could either accept what just happened or check herself into the hospital. At this point she wasn't sure what the path of least resistance was, so she tossed a coin in her mind and landed on believing them.

"Are...there others like you?"

"Yes, there are different types of supernaturals," Devin said, "but I shouldn't say too much more. I know what we're telling you seems impossible, Dr. Jennings, but it is very real...and very dangerous for us if the truth were to get out."

"I would never divulge what happened in a session unless I feel my patient is a danger to themselves or someone else. You have nothing to worry about."

Devin's eyes tightened on her. "That simple?"

Olivia studied him as he sat with his arm around his pregnant wife, as if to shield her from danger.

"Nothing is simple about what you just told me, but, rest assured, I won't tell anyone. First, because I've seen enough of this world and people's insecurities to be sure humanity wouldn't respond well if they learned that supernaturals actually do exist."

"And second?" Devin asked.

"Second, no one would believe me."

Alex's mouth crooked up. "You got that right. Wouldn't make you appear very stable to your colleagues or your patients."

"Exactly."

Before she could ask any more questions, a voice called out Devin's name from the reception area.

"In here," Devin responded. "After you called me and hung up, I called the team to come too."

The office door opened and Connor rushed into the room—since Olivia's evening wasn't already crazy enough.

"You okay?" Connor asked Devin.

"Yeah. We're okay. The baby decided to show off rather spectacularly in front of Dr. Jennings, here. Where's the rest of the team?" Devin asked.

Connor gazed over at Olivia for a moment before responding. "On their way."

"Can you call and tell them it's a false alarm?"

"Sure." He reached for his phone and walked out into her reception area.

"Here we go again," Alex gasped as her stomach lit up.

Devin put both hands on her stomach. "Does it hurt?"

"No. I didn't even realize it happened the first time until Dr. Jennings said something."

"Holy Fates," Connor exclaimed from the doorway.

Alex's belly went dark again, and Devin scooped her up into his arms. "That does it. We're going to Darcinda's. I want her to tell me it's okay for our baby to be doing that."

Connor nodded. "Okay. I'll stay here with the doc."

Doc? Olivia stood up. "I'm fine. You don't need to stay."

Connor ignored her protests as he held the door open for Devin and Alex. "Let me know what happens."

Alex glanced between Connor and Olivia. "You, too, Connor. Call me later!"

Connor chuckled. Why was he chuckling? And why did he have to be the one who showed up? Olivia thought of herself as a pretty accepting person. She had to be, with her job. But something about Connor Dawson got under her skin and rubbed her the wrong way. He was the last person she wanted to talk to right now.

And then Olivia's heart stuttered. Maybe he wasn't a person at all. Was he a supernatural, too?

Embrace your new reality,
and don't be afraid to ask questions!

CHAPTER 8

Connor stared at the spitfire in front of him. A myriad of emotions—curiosity, annoyance, anxiety—flashed across her face for a moment before her color drained away.

"Why don't you sit down again, Doc? You're a little pale."

"I'm fine." She stared down at the paper and pen lying on the floor as if seeing them for the first time, and bent down to pick them up. When she stood up again, she wobbled, and Connor grabbed her upper arms. "Whoa. Steady. Like I said, let's sit down."

She gave him a silent nod, and he helped her to the couch before taking the paper and pen and setting them on her desk.

"Take some deep breaths."

"I'm fine."

"You keep saying you're fine, but the world you know just got knocked off its axis. Of course you're going to be unsteady after something like that."

She stared at him for a moment.

"What?"

"That was an insightful observation."

He shrugged. "Don't act so surprised. I'm not a horse's ass *all* the time."

Her right eyebrow rose as if to challenge his comment.

Why was that arched eyebrow so damn sexy? "Fine. I'll concede to being an ass some of the time, but not all."

"Accepted."

He sat down next to her on the couch. "I don't know if Devin and Alex got to explain much to you before they left, but if you tell anyone what you saw, you could put them and the baby in danger."

"They told me Alex is part faerie and Devin is an elf. And you don't need to worry, I won't tell anyone."

"I bet this has been the craziest therapy session you've ever had."

"I'll have to think about it some more before I say yes."

"Really?"

"In my job you hear some interesting things. Of course, they don't normally happen to me. I'm an objective listener, not an active participant."

"Until bellies start to glow."

"Exactly," she said after a hard swallow.

"I have to admit it surprised me too."

She turned to him. "It's not normal? I mean...not normal for a supernatural?"

He shook his head. "Nope."

"Why, then?"

"I'd say it's probably because the baby is part faerie and part elf. As far as I know, there's never been an elf-faerie baby before."

She frowned. "Will the baby be all right?"

"Devin and Alex will make sure of it."

Her eyebrows drew together. "I..."

"Just spit it out, Doc. You're thinking too hard."

"I don't know what to ask. Am I allowed to ask about supernaturals?"

"Sure. You can ask, but I might not answer. It's complicated."

"Do they have special powers? Why are they human-size? Can faeries fly? Why doesn't Devin have pointy ears?"

He held up his hands. "Whoa! That's a lot of questions for someone who didn't know what to ask a moment ago."

She bit her lip, and he wanted to reach up and pull it loose.

Instead he settled in the far corner of the couch. "Let's see. Where to begin...? Faeries and elves are high-powered supernaturals. Most can channel energy and some, especially faeries, have magical and healing powers. Faeries do not have wings, and they don't shrink. And elves do not work for Santa at the North Pole. Devin would want me to emphasize the last point. It's a bit of a touchy subject with him."

"Point noted."

She sat up straighter. "Are you a faerie or an elf?"

"Neither. And just so you know, rule number one is, you don't ask supernaturals what they are."

"So you *are* supernatural." Her eyes tightened on him. "Which means there are others besides faeries and elves."

She was a smart thing, but then he wasn't surprised. "That's need-to-know."

"And I don't need to know. Got it."

Her statement didn't match her obvious curiosity, but she let the matter drop. He imagined she would probably try to get more information out of Alex later. "So, are you done for the day?"

She sighed. "Yes. I just need to straighten up and check my calendar for tomorrow before I go home."

"I'll walk you to your car."

She shook her head. "You don't have to wait for me."

"Do you have any idea how much grief I would get from Alex if I don't make sure you get home safely?"

"Actually, I didn't drive to work. I normally take the train home."

"Not tonight, you don't. I'll take you home."

She opened her mouth to protest, and he held up his hand. "Don't make me call the crazy pregnant woman with the glow-in-the-dark baby belly. It could get ugly."

Olivia laughed, and the raspy sound of it suggested she didn't do it very often.

She straightened the items on her desk and sat down at her laptop for a moment, reviewing the screen before shutting it down and taking her purse out of a locked drawer.

She must have read something on his face, since she answered his unasked question. "Unfortunately, it's an occupational hazard. I don't want to give anyone the opportunity to abscond with my money or ID. Most of my patients wouldn't dream of stealing from me."

"But a minority might have sticky fingers. Got it."

Connor escorted her out and waited for her to lock her door and then the main office door before they walked together down the hall.

Other than telling him where she lived, she didn't say much on the quick car ride to her apartment. He wasn't sure if she was trying to digest what had happened or was scared of him. Neither possibility made him happy. As luck would have it, he actually found a parking spot and shut off the car.

He turned to her. "Are you okay? You had quite a shock tonight."

"I'll be fine. Thanks for driving me home," she said as she started to climb out of the car.

"Hold on, Doc. I'll come with you."

She shook her head. "There's no need."

"A gentleman always escorts a lady to her door."

Again with the raised eyebrow. "That's a dating rule. We're not on a date."

Connor got out of the car and jogged around to her side. "I thought you were going to argue about me being a gentleman. Instead you're quoting rules from the dating handbook."

"I can't believe you even know there is a dating handbook. You strike me as someone who makes up his own rules."

Connor couldn't help but grin at her insightful comment. "Jack would agree with you, there. He's the rule follower."

"And you're the rule breaker?"

He walked her to the front door of her building. "I would say risk-taker."

She opened the door and stepped into a vestibule with a key-card lock. She swiped her card and went into the lobby area, where a doorman sat at a desk.

"Good evening, Dr. Jennings." He stood and gave Connor a serious once-over. "You have a guest tonight."

She smiled. "He's not staying long, Sam."

Connor didn't like her quick dismissal. "Actually, I was going to ask you to dinner. I didn't think you would feel much like cooking tonight."

The doorman frowned. *What is his problem?*

"I normally order delivery from down the street."

"Perfect. It's a beautiful night. We'll walk down there instead."

She pushed her glasses up on her pert little nose and frowned slightly. As if she was trying to think of a nice way to say no.

"Come on, Doc. Exercise is good for you."

"Fine."

How could women make that word mean anything *but* fine?

She turned to the doorman. "Sam, I'll bring you your usual, okay?"

He nodded. "Sounds good. And don't forget, extra—"

"Spicy mustard." She finished his sentence. "I'll remember."

Connor waited until they were outside before asking, "Are you and the doorman seeing each other?"

Olivia jerked. "No! On Wednesday nights I order food from the Asian fusion place down the street, and Sam gets something too."

"That's a bit strange."

"What's strange about it? Veronica, Sam's wife, has had some stomach problems and has to watch what she eats. Sam doesn't want to eat foods she used to love in front of her, so when he found out I ordered from there, he asked about it, and we've been ordering food together since then."

He walked next to her. "How do you know all this?"

"Objective listener, remember? It's a powerful tool for understanding people. You'd be amazed at how much you can learn by sitting back and not talking."

"Why does it feel like a recommendation and a slam at the same time?"

"Take it any way you like." She stopped in front of the restaurant. "Here we are."

When they walked in, amazing aromas greeted them in the form of garlic, ginger, and a host of other spices. His wolf senses sat up and took notice. "Smells amazing."

"Wait till you taste it."

He walked toward the dining room.

"Where are you going?" she asked.

"I'm going to sit down so we can eat."

"I thought we were ordering takeout."

He held out a chair for her. "We're here, so we might as well sit down and enjoy it."

She shook her head and sat down. "You're used to getting your way, aren't you?"

He walked to the other side of the table and took his seat, grinning. "What's good here?"

"I order the veggie lo mein."

"And?"

"And what?"

He couldn't believe he had to spell it out for her. "You order takeout here every Wednesday?"

"Yes."

"And you order the same thing every week?"

She tilted her chin up slightly as if preparing for battle. "It's excellent."

"I don't doubt it, but there are probably other excellent dishes on the menu as well. How about trying something new tonight?"

"Fine."

Connor chuckled. He was starting to love the word *fine*. "That's the spirit."

Forty minutes later, Connor placed the chopsticks on his plate and sighed. What an amazing dinner. From the expression on Olivia's face, she had enjoyed it too.

"Well?"

Her eyebrow rose. "I am not going to feed your ego by telling you how fabulous the food was."

He stood and pulled out her chair. "You don't need to. I already know the truth."

Olivia picked up the takeout container for Sam and they stopped at the cash register while Connor paid for their meal.

"Thank you. I didn't expect you to buy me dinner."

He held open the door for her. "Since I convinced you to try different food, it's only fair for me to pay." As they walked back to her building, he said, "You sure know a lot about people. Like our server tonight, for instance."

She shrugged. "It's not hard, really. I've talked to her a few times before."

"I know, you're an objective listener. But you were a pretty active participant the other night when you threw a drink in my face."

She stopped walking. "I'm sorry, Connor. Honestly. I don't know what came over me. Which is a total cop-out, and I would call my patients on it if they said it to me, but when I saw you with the hyena-laugher—"

Connor snorted. "The what?"

Her cheeks pinkened. "Sorry. Totally inappropriate."

He thought about the woman at the bar. "But true."

"If she's your girlfriend—"

"Nope. Don't have a girlfriend."

She tilted her head and looked, really looked at him, her gaze assessing him like a patient on her couch. Had she just flipped into shrink mode?

"What?"

"Why did you say the word 'girlfriend' like it's a disease?"

"I didn't."

"Yes you did. You even curled your lip a little at the end."

"I did not curl my lip when I said 'girlfriend.'"

She wagged her finger in front of his face. "You just did it again!"

He put his hand on her elbow to get her to start walking again. "I think you're reading too much into things, Doc."

"I don't, and please stop calling me Doc."

"What would you like me to call you?"

"Olivia is fine."

Before Connor could decide if it was a victory or not, his phone rang. He glanced at the screen and gestured for Olivia to pause for a moment. "Hi, Alex. How are you feeling?"

"I'm fine and the baby is fine. Darcinda says it's nothing to worry about."

"They're both fine," Connor whispered.

"Who are you talking to?" Alex asked.

"Olivia."

"Olivia who...wait, are you still with Dr. Jennings?"

"Yes."

"Is she okay? She isn't still upset, is she?"

"She's fine, Alex. I've got to go." Connor hung up before Alex's imagination went into hyperdrive.

"I'm glad they're okay," Olivia said as they started walking again.

All too quickly they reached her building. This time when they entered the vestibule, Olivia didn't use her key card. Instead, she turned to face him. Over her shoulder Connor could see Sam watching them quite anxiously. Was he curious to see what might happen between them, or was he just hungry for his pork fried rice and spicy tuna roll?

"Thank you for walking me to my door. I think you've fulfilled your obligation as a gentleman."

"Dinner was fabulous, as was the company." Okay, that might have been a little much, even for him. Connor didn't know where the flattery had come from. Nothing was going to happen between them. He was not the relationship type, and she was definitely not the fling type.

Up went her right eyebrow above the top of her glasses. Was it bad he already had an idea what her facial expressions meant? She wanted to call him out on the line he just used on her. And for some strange reason he actually wanted to hear what she had to say.

Instead she smiled graciously and wished him a good night before leaving him in the vestibule.

Alone.

Which wasn't the usual way Connor ended the evening. But then Olivia was far from typical.

*If you spend all your time in your comfort zone,
it will never grow. . . and neither will you.*

CHAPTER 9

Olivia set her purse on the hall table and locked her apartment door before plopping down on her couch. What just happened?

She'd gone to dinner with Connor. The man was trouble for sure, with his grins and his winks and his baffling ability to get her to agree to things she normally would never do...like allowing him to drive her home from work, and going out to dinner together, and trying new food.

Her defenses had to be down because of the earlier shock of learning about Alex and Devin, right? She sat up from her slouched position. How had she lost sight of the fact that a few short hours ago she learned humans aren't alone on this planet?

Shutting down those thoughts could have been a defense mechanism. She'd seen it often enough with her patients. Instead of dwelling on something that fundamentally changed their world, they would often repress it — push it out of their minds. But she wasn't sure it was true in her case, especially since it came flooding back as soon as she got home. Alone she could think about it.

Not dwelling on it earlier was more likely due to Connor himself.

He was ridiculously handsome. She would have to be dead not to notice, and her body definitely noticed. But her body needed to take a back seat to her brain right now. Sure, he had beautiful dark hair and stunning green eyes, but he was not shy about...well, anything. And he was her polar opposite. A go-with-the-flow guy. So not part of her comfort zone. She reached up and pulled the pins out of her hair, letting the bun unravel, sighing with relief.

Her cell phone rang, and she checked the screen before answering it.

"Hello, Elena."

"Hello. Am I interrupting your veggie lo mein extravaganza?"

Olivia sighed. "I didn't have it tonight."

"It's Wednesday night. Are you not feeling well?"

"Am I so predictable? Wait, don't answer."

"Seriously. You didn't keep your standing dinner date with Sam?"

Olivia hesitated for a moment. "I went out with someone else."

Silence.

"Elena? Are you still there?"

"Isn't Sam working tonight? Who did you go out with? Someone from your book club?"

Good Lord, was she truly this pathetic? "I went out to dinner with a guy."

Olivia yanked the cell away from her ear while Elena squealed, "Hot damn, woman. You better spill, or I'm coming to your apartment right now!"

Maybe Olivia should get this part over with before

holding the phone against her ear again. She took a deep breath. "I went out with Connor."

"Connor who? Is he one of the doctors you met at the boring conference you went to last month?"

"It wasn't boring. It was a symposium about sleep deprivation and its impact on mental illnesses."

Elena chuckled. "I don't even need to respond, do I? Where did you meet this guy?"

There was no getting out of it now. "Um. He's the guy from the bar, the one I doused with a drink."

"No way! Seriously? How in the world did you see him again?"

"I went to see my patient and apologized to her and her boyfriend for what I did, and Connor showed up."

"And he asked you out to dinner?"

"Yes." *Yes* left out the whole supernaturals exist story, but it wasn't something she could tell Elena.

"And you went willingly? No handcuffs involved?"

"Elena! Yes, he offered to drive me home, and then we walked down to the Asian restaurant and had dinner there."

"I thought you said you didn't have the lo mein."

"I didn't. He, ah, convinced me to try some other dishes."

Elena laughed. "I feel like I'm in an episode of *The Twilight Zone* right now."

"You need to stop binge-watching those old shows."

"No can do. And stop trying to change the subject. So how did the dinner go? Are you going out with him again?"

Olivia shook her head, then reminded herself Elena couldn't see her. "It wasn't a date. And we didn't talk about seeing each other again."

Elena sighed.

"What's the big sigh for? You told me he's a player."

"He is. But it doesn't mean you can't have some fun, Olivia. When is the last time you had fun? *Real* fun?"

Olivia opened her mouth to respond and then shut it again. Because she couldn't think of anything.

"Just what I thought. If you had a good time tonight, then why not do it again? If you go into this with your eyes wide open, why not go out with him?"

"That's not what dinner was about tonight."

"Okay. I don't know if I buy it, but I'm going to let you go. Call me if you want to talk about anything, especially sexy men who tempted you out of your lo mein comfort zone."

Olivia laughed. "Good night, Elena."

Finally Olivia changed out of what she called her doctor clothes. She put her suit in the bin where she stored her dry cleaning and pulled on a pair of yoga pants and a T-shirt. Rolling her shoulders, she picked up the mystery novel she started the other day and snuggled down in her comfy reading chair. Two pages in, she had to stop and read the paragraph again. And then again.

She dropped the book on her lap and bounced her head against the back of her chair. How could she settle into her routine when she just found out faeries and elves exist?

And what was Connor? She couldn't tell Elena the truth. Not only were their personalities not the same, they weren't the same species...or whatever the supernaturals called themselves. Olivia needed order and control, and Connor was its antithesis.

It was best to stay far, far away from him, especially with that sexy, dimpled grin and sparkling green eyes.

CHAPTER 10

There were few things Connor backed down from. His brother, Jack, said he was an adrenaline junkie, but it wasn't that simple. Things seldom were.

So when he drove up to the alpha's lodge for the meeting Sullivan scheduled with the team and saw three wolves circling the front building, he was tempted to hang a U-turn in the SUV and drive away. His wolf senses were howling. But then it wasn't often he walked into a pack of werewolves. And since the hairs were standing up on the back of his neck, he knew they were anxious werewolves.

Connor and Jack didn't spend time with other wolves. But since they were treated like pariahs, there wasn't much point in going to the pack barbecues, now was there?

He gave himself a mental kick in the ass and opened the door before walking through the circling, four-legged testosterone. Sniffs of recognition followed by low-level growls greeted him. Connor didn't respond, instead staying on course toward the only two upright pack members.

The two security guards flanked the door leading into the alpha's house. Big Bad Wolf Number One held his hand up, and Connor stopped outside the door. The pair scrutinized him like he was a rotten piece of meat.

"Well, look who decided to honor us with his presence."

Connor managed not to growl. "I'm here to meet with the alpha."

Wolf Number Two scowled. "Not sure why he would want to see you."

A wolf snorted behind him. What the hell? They were laughing at him while in wolf form? Not acceptable.

Connor didn't bother to turn around to see who the hairy culprit was, instead shrugging at the guards. "Not your decision to make. D-E-C-I-S-I-O-N."

"What the hell are you doing?" Number Two demanded.

"It's a big word. I'm spelling it for you so you can look up the definition later. Oh, damn, here I go again. Do you know what definition means? You have to admit it's pretty ironic if you don't know the definition of definition."

Actual growls erupted from the sentries, which had the wolves behind him joining in the chorus.

The front door opened and Sullivan Ross, their alpha, glared at them. "Get inside, Connor, before the fur starts flying."

Connor gave both guards a grin that would make the Joker proud before ambling into the house.

"Did you actually just say 'before the fur starts flying'?"

"Do you have to antagonize everyone?" Sullivan responded, but didn't wait for an answer before striding down the hall toward the rear of the house.

"Yes," Connor replied as he followed along behind

him. Connor glanced around. The house looked like it did when they were pups, when Sullivan's father ran the pack. But it didn't feel the same. The fear, or maybe oppression, didn't pollute the air like smog. Connor took a deep breath because he could.

"Are you going to tell me what's going on, Sully?"

"A potential shit storm, my friend. But then my father was so good at them, wasn't he?"

Connor didn't respond while Sullivan opened the door to a room with a large table and chairs. As pups, Connor and Jack were not allowed to go into this room. It was where the adult pack members had important meetings the young ones weren't invited to. But it hadn't stopped them from sneaking into the room with Sullivan and pretending to hold their own pack meetings.

Now Connor stood in the room staring at the childhood companion who had defied his father by having Connor and Jack as his friends.

Sullivan shut the door and turned to face Connor. "It's about damn time you got here."

Connor gaped at the pack leader. "What are you talking about? You scheduled the meeting for this morning, and I'm here before everyone else."

"I don't mean today. I have asked both you and Jack to come see me several times, and you've given me lame excuses every time."

Connor shrugged. "You have a lot on your plate now."

Sullivan frowned. "I do. Even though Father's been gone for a year now, I still have a lot to repair in the pack. And it includes both you and your brother."

"We're not broken."

"Don't be a smart-ass, Con. There are still a lot of things broken in this pack. I'm working on changing things, and I hope I have your support."

"You will always have my support, and Jack's, of course." Which didn't mean Connor planned to return to the pack anytime soon. While it damn well helped to have Sullivan on their side, it didn't mean the old prejudices would simply vanish.

It hadn't been so long ago when his pack would have banished him if they could. Identical twin wolves were an aberration in the minds of his people. Maybe he and Jack could have fought against it if his own parents stood by them. His father was a high-powered lieutenant in the pack, for Fates' sake. But he'd chosen to stay mired in superstition and old-wolf tales instead of accepting them. Or ever accepting Connor, who was the pup born twenty minutes after Jack and therefore the forgotten son.

Connor shook his head. The whole issue was murky water under the bridge. And he didn't want to stir up the dirt again. Time to get to work. "What's this meeting about?"

Sullivan sighed and walked over to the table. "I'd rather not have to explain the craziness more than once, if it's okay with you."

Connor and his wolf weren't known for their patience, but in this instance he could wait a few more seconds. "Jack is close."

Sullivan's eyes narrowed. "I've always been jealous of the connection you have with your brother."

Surprise rippled down Connor's spine. "That's not the reaction we get from others in the pack."

"Well, I can't help it if they're shortsighted."

Before Connor could respond, the door opened and Jack and Devin walked in, followed by Giz and Charlie.

Devin nodded to the pack leader. "Sullivan."

Sullivan gestured for them all to take their seats. "Glad you all could make it. Let's get started."

"Isn't anyone else joining us?" Jack asked.

"No. I want to discuss this with your team alone first."

Connor's alarm bells weren't just ringing, they were clanging. "What the hell is going on?"

Devin scowled at him. "Connor, take it easy."

Sullivan held up his hand. "It's okay, Devin. I'm used to Connor's tendency to word vomit. He was worse as a pup."

Word vomit? A little harsh, in Connor's opinion.

Actually, word vomit is a nice way to put it, Jack said through their twinspeak.

Can it, Connor retorted.

Sullivan turned to Connor. "I brought you here because I'm getting married."

Connor blinked. He couldn't have heard him right. "Married. You had us meet with you because you're getting married. Do you need help picking out your china pattern?"

Sullivan smirked. "I wish it were so simple. My fiancée is the daughter of the East Coast alpha."

Connor and Jack sat up straight at the same time.

Devin glanced at the twins before turning to Giz and Charlie, who appeared similarly confused. "Elf in the room, here. Someone is going to have to clue me in to the significance of what he just said."

Sullivan tapped his fingers against the table. "Relations between the two packs have been a little problematic of late."

Try the past twenty-five years, Connor thought.

Jack scowled at Connor. *Chill out.*

Charlie leaned forward. "I've seen firsthand the animosity between my own nymph clans, so I hope you don't take offense when I say this. But if you're getting married just to patch things up between the clans, it's not enough to base a relationship on."

"I agree. But I didn't arrange the marriage. My father did it before he died."

Connor groaned.

Sullivan smiled, but it was forced. "Exactly. He's dead and still screwing with my life."

"Can't you get out of it?" Devin asked.

"I can't deny the arrangement outright. It could cause a war. What I have proposed to Alpha Callahan is for us to begin with a courtship to see if his daughter, Maeve, and I are compatible. My hope is we'll come to a calm and rational agreement that we don't belong together.

"In the meantime, I need you guys to be part of the process. I have to show them I'm taking this courtship seriously. There are a number of rituals we need to follow, including an introduction reception followed by other events leading up to the possible wedding." He turned to Devin. "I'm going to use your wife's wedding planner business to handle those events."

Devin nodded. "I'm sure Alex and her grandmother, Lorinda, would be delighted to help."

Something weird was going on. Connor wasn't sure what Sullivan was up to. But before he could ask, Sullivan continued with his line of questioning. "I understand Julia Cole works for the wedding planner business as well."

Jack leaned forward. "What do you want with Julia?"

Sullivan's eyebrows rose at Jack's tone. "I need someone to work on the prenup agreements. Worst-case, I want Julia to review the betrothal contract to see if I can get out of it. I understand she's very good at what she does."

"She's great at what she does," Jack said.

Sullivan gave Jack a long look. "So the rumors are true. You're involved with her. She's human, right?"

"Is there a problem?" Jack growled.

Connor turned toward Jack. *Take it easy, brother.*

Sullivan's mouth flipped up into a grin. "No problem at all. I think it's great if she brings this kind of emotion out in you. Usually Connor's the hothead. It must be serious."

"It is."

"And you all provide security for the wedding planner business's high-profile paranormal weddings as well," Sullivan said.

Connor was done with the twenty questions. "You didn't invite us here to talk about planning your wedding. You could have had the pack secretary call the wedding planner office. What gives?"

"Callahan and his closest advisors will be traveling here in the next few days. When I announce the betrothal to the pack, my official statement will include that your team will be helping with security for the events."

"And unofficially?" Devin asked.

"Unofficially, you will be working to figure out who's trying to kill me." Sullivan pulled the collar of his shirt down and revealed gauze taped over his shoulder.

Connor shoved back his chair with a hard scrape and stood. Jack followed him to his feet a split second later.

"Damn it, Sully. Don't you think you should have led with something like this?" Connor barked.

"Maybe, but I wanted to explain things before you went ballistic. Sit down, both of you."

Jack sat down first, then Connor.

"Tell us what happened," Jack said.

"Two days ago, I changed into my wolf and went for my morning run. When I got near the ridge, I felt like someone was watching me. I ran toward the tree cover when I got hit in the shoulder."

Giz perked up from his slouch in the chair. "Do you have cameras posted throughout your property?"

"I do, but not in the area where I was running."

"I'd still like to review them."

Sullivan made a note.

"And you think this is related to the contract with the East Coast pack?" Charlie asked.

"I think it's too much of a coincidence for this to happen at the same time. Right now I don't know who to trust inside the pack." He turned to Connor and Jack. "I need you both to have my back."

"You don't even have to ask," Connor and Jack said.

Sullivan chuckled. "I see you both still talk at the same time."

"Who knows about the wedding contract?" Devin asked.

"My secretary, Carol, and my two advisors."

Connor and Jack exchanged glances. Their father was one of Sullivan's advisors.

"Who knows about the attempt on your life?" Jack asked.

"No one. I patched myself up."

Connor frowned. "I'm surprised Jonathan isn't here."

Sullivan sighed. "I expect your father here shortly. I'm sure someone has let him know about our meeting by now. He won't be happy about involving your team in pack affairs."

"You're sounding like a politician with your word choices," Connor said. "The truth is, he won't want Jack and me involved."

Sullivan's eyes tightened on Connor. "Then it's a good thing I'm in charge."

It damn sure was a good thing, and Connor would do anything to ensure Sullivan stayed in control. He wouldn't let anyone kill his friend and alpha if he had anything to say about it.

Before Connor could respond, the conference room door burst open and the team jumped up from their seats to protect Sullivan from whatever might be coming through the door.

Speak of the devil...

Jonathan Dawson stood in the doorway, quickly taking in the scene. His eyes lingered for a moment on Jack before his gaze locked on Sullivan. He didn't bother to glance in Connor's direction, which was more than fine with him.

Sullivan narrowed his eyes. "Is there a problem, Jonathan?"

"The guards told me you had unauthorized visitors."

Sullivan leaned back in his chair. "Since I asked the team to meet me here, I would say unauthorized is a bit of an exaggeration."

"Protocol states that security is to be made aware of all visitors."

Sullivan's eyebrows rose. He was acting nonchalant, but the tight grip Sullivan had on the pen he held, told Connor he was anything but.

"Jonathan. I informed your guards that a Tribunal team would be arriving. And they informed you. I think the requirements of protocol have been met."

Jonathan closed his mouth and pressed his lips into a tight line. Connor was very familiar with the expression, having caused it himself multiple times. But unlike his encounters with Jonathan, his father couldn't belittle the alpha. Instead, he cleared his throat. "May I ask why the team is here?"

Sullivan paused for a moment before responding. "The Tribunal needs to be made aware of the upcoming meeting with the East Coast pack."

His father opened up his mouth to speak, and Sullivan held up his hand, effectively stopping it. Connor wished he had the same power.

Sullivan continued. "And while I know you would rather keep all pack matters internal, we cannot afford to keep this a secret from the Tribunal, especially if we face any opposition from Callahan. The Tribunal does not take pack wars lightly."

"Callahan wouldn't come here only to wage war with us," his father replied.

Sullivan sighed. "I have no idea what my father promised Callahan. We'll be proceeding with caution. And it doesn't hurt to have two of our own pack as members of this team."

Connor watched his father's sour expression return. How could someone have a perpetual scowl? Connor was more than ready to leave, but he had to wait until their alpha excused them. As if reading Connor's mind, Sullivan stood.

"I think we've covered everything for now."

Devin nodded. "We'll be ready to help when your guests arrive. And I'll let Alex know to expect a call from you or your staff about the event planning."

"Thank you for coming." Sullivan gestured toward the door. "Let me show you out." He turned to his security chief. "Jonathan, feel free to use the conference room to spend some time catching up with your sons."

Connor couldn't help but notice the emphasis on the s at the end of his sentence. Sully was poking the lion...or wolf...or maybe stubborn ass was a more appropriate descriptor.

Jonathan looked at Jack. "How are you doing, son?"

"Fine."

He continued staring at Jack. Whether he expected him to say anything else, or he was avoiding speaking to Connor, was anyone's guess. Finally he glanced his way. "Connor."

Connor wanted to walk out of the room, but he

wouldn't let Jonathan know he got under his skin. It was better to strike back.

"I'm fine as well, Pops, thanks for asking."

And there was the perpetual scowl. Connor felt right at home now.

Jack stepped up next to Connor. "Sorry, but we have to get going. Tribunal business."

The brothers walked toward the door and out into the hallway. Connor didn't take a full breath until he made it to the main door where their team waited for them.

Sullivan frowned. "That was a short reunion."

Connor shrugged. "Felt like hours to me."

They said their goodbyes and the team went to their vehicles.

Jack turned to Devin. "I'm going to ride back to town with Connor."

"Sure. We'll regroup this afternoon at For Better or For Worse to discuss next steps."

Connor got in his SUV, slamming the door harder than necessary. Jack climbed into the passenger seat.

"I don't need a puppy-sitter, Jack. I'm fine."

"You always haul out your smart-ass banter when you're upset. Don't let Jonathan get to you."

"I didn't."

Jack raised one eyebrow at him.

"Don't go all high-and-mighty on me, *older* brother. I'm not getting a happy vibe off you right now, either."

"Jonathan isn't going to change, and I refuse to let him control any part of my life. You, Julia, and the team are my pack now."

Connor put the car in gear and drove down the pack road leading to the highway. "Agreed. But I also don't want anything to happen to Sully. He's the best thing that's happened to the pack since the hate and bigotry his father perpetuated."

"So we don't let anything happen to him."

"Listen to you, going all alpha. What's gotten into you?"

Jack grinned, which also used to be a rare occurrence but happened more frequently now. "Julia."

Connor pretended to gag, and Jack punched him in the arm. "I'm just kidding. I'm happy for you both. When are you going to ask her to marry you, anyway?"

"Soon. I want it to be perfect."

Connor took his eyes off the road and glanced at Jack. "Nothing is perfect, bro. You should know that by now. Ask her. Or do you need me to do it for you?"

"Not funny, *baby* brother."

Connor laughed as he pulled out onto the highway. He was funny. His brother didn't appreciate his humor.

"On the way here, Devin told me what happened during Alex's session with Dr. Jennings," Jack said.

"Yeah. Since it was a shock for me to see Alex's belly glow, I have trouble imagining what it was like for Olivia."

"Olivia, huh? So what happened after Devin and Alex left last night?"

Connor didn't like where this conversation was going. "I made sure she was okay. She had a hell of a shock, so I drove her home."

"Understandable. Does she live outside the city?"

"No. Why?"

"Devin mentioned Alex called you later and you were still with Dr. Jennings. I'm trying to figure out why."

Connor's wolf started pacing. "Did you expect me to slow down and push her out of my SUV at her door? I got her some dinner."

"And that's it?"

"What else would there be?"

"Good. I just don't want things to get awkward. She's Julia and Alex's therapist."

"Any more awkward than seeing Alex's stomach light up? Just spit out what you really want to say, Jack."

"Fine. Dr. Jennings is not like the women you normally spend time with."

Connor couldn't agree more. She was special. "She's not. You don't need to worry. I won't be bothering Dr. Jennings again."

Connor felt the heat of his brother's stare, but he didn't take his eyes off the road.

He couldn't even be angry at Jack for what he said.

He was trying to protect Olivia, and with Connor's track record, he couldn't blame his twin for warning him off.

Sanity is relative.

CHAPTER 11

Connor watched his four teammates settle around the conference room table at For Better or For Worse while they waited for the women to arrive.

Giz worked on his computer tablet while Devin and Charlie were having some sort of disagreement—contest—to determine which of their wives was the most stubborn. After a few minutes of back and forth, Jack threw Julia's name into the mix as a contender.

Connor thought the more entertaining discussion would be which one of them caved first when it came to these stubborn women, but he didn't say anything. He had learned not to throw his two cents in when it came to their relationships. The mated ones, his brother included, tended to gang up against him if he voiced his opinion.

But just because he was single didn't mean his observations weren't valid.

A few moments later the subjects of said stubborn contest, Alex, Sheila, and Julia, walked in, followed by Lorinda, who ran the wedding planner business with the help of everyone in the room. Devin jumped right into the meeting and recapped everything they'd discussed with Sullivan.

Alex wrote some notes on a pad of paper in front of her before turning to her grandmother. "This is certainly a high-profile opportunity for the business."

"Don't count your chickens, Alex. They probably won't go through with it," Devin said.

"The wedding, no. But Sullivan's secretary already called. When the East Coast pack arrives, they want to host a welcome reception and several other events."

"Do you have enough time to make sure the events are top-notch?" Devin asked.

Lorinda gave him her patented regal nod. "Of course we do. We'll make sure the events run smoothly."

Devin gave Alex a hard look. "If there is one whiff of danger, you and the baby will be leaving, Alex, even if I have to carry you out myself."

Alex patted her growing belly. "And here I thought you were ridiculously overprotective before. It has multiplied by a thousand."

Devin leaned over and kissed her on the temple. "And don't you forget it."

Connor watched Charlie and Jack murmur something along the same overprotective lines to both Sheila and Julia. Both women rolled their eyes at their mates before turning back to Devin. Just as Connor suspected, he was right about who was really in charge in these relationships.

Devin continued. "Giz is already reviewing security weaknesses in the pack compound through a new software program he developed, and Charlie and I will start working on fixing anything he discovers."

"What about me and Jack?" Connor asked.

Devin hesitated for a moment. "You'll be working from the inside, protecting Sullivan."

Connor opened his mouth to protest, but Devin interrupted him. "When Sullivan walked me out this morning, while you were talking to your father, he said he wanted you both there."

This is going to suck, brother, Connor voiced through their twinspeak.

True, but we said last night we would do whatever it takes to keep Sullivan safe.

Julia studied them intently, and Connor cringed. He kept forgetting now that Julia was mated to Jack, she could not only talk to him telepathically, she could also hear their twinspeak conversations. He had to remember to curb his thoughts so he wouldn't upset her.

"Are you up for reviewing the wedding contract, Julia?" Devin asked.

Connor could tell by the determined set of her mouth what she was going to say.

Julia steepled her fingers. "Absolutely. Sullivan's secretary already sent it over to me. If I can find a loophole to get Sullivan out of this contract, I will." She glanced at Jack and Connor. "I'll have questions for both of you about Sullivan and the pack."

Connor saluted her. "Yes, ma'am." Although he felt far from obedient right now. Talking about the pack was like tearing open an old wound. Connor didn't need to engage in twinspeak with his brother to know what he was feeling either, since the tight expression on Jack's face spoke volumes.

Devin leaned forward. "Have you reviewed it yet?"

Julia frowned. "Yes, and I'm not liking what I see."

"Why not?" Connor asked.

"There's a bunch of different criteria Sullivan has to meet to continue to lead the pack. One of the paragraphs refers to his mental stability. One of the stipulations is, if for any reason his mental stability is called into question, he could lose his position as alpha."

"So how do we prevent it?" Connor pushed.

"We have someone evaluate him."

Jack rested his hand on Julia's arm. "No problem. There has to be someone in the pack who can do it."

She shook her head. "I don't recommend using a pack member. The person needs to be unbiased. They can't be associated with either pack."

Alex sat up straighter. "I've got someone in mind."

"No, Alex," Connor said.

She widened her eyes in mock innocence. "What?"

"We are not bringing Olivia into this."

"Olivia?"

Damn. He needed to stop using her first name. "Dr. Jennings. It's bad enough she knows the truth about you and Devin. She doesn't need to get pulled into this pack craziness too."

"I was thinking about calling her myself," Julia said.

"You two tag teaming me now?" Connor asked.

"No," Julia said. "I think we should ask her before you totally reject the idea. It's her decision to make."

"Fine, but I want to be there." Yes, he'd told his brother he would stay away from Olivia, but if they were pulling her farther into their world, he couldn't stand on the sidelines.

Alex and Julia glanced at each other before grinning.

The hairs on Connor's neck stood up. He didn't like the smug expressions on both their faces. At all.

Olivia closed her laptop and straightened her desk. She had just finished her last session for the day and had already shooed Marcie out the door. Julia Cole would be arriving any minute, and Olivia didn't want to risk having Marcie overhear something she shouldn't.

Oliva wasn't sure what Julia wanted to talk about, but she had a hunch it had to do with Alex and Devin. Maybe Julia wanted to confirm that she wouldn't tell anyone about supernaturals. Julia was a lawyer, after all. Was there some sort of legal recourse they could throw at her? Or maybe they were going to make her forget. But could they actually do it?

She'd been too accepting of Connor's non-answers last night. But she had been overwhelmed. Now she had some time to think about it, she wanted to know more. Whether or not Julia would tell her more remained to be seen.

The buzzer sounded at her desk. Marcie would have locked the outside office door when she left, which probably meant Julia had arrived. Olivia walked out to the reception area and could see her through the glass window next to the door.

She unlocked the door and was surprised to find Connor standing outside as well. She beckoned for them both to come inside, and she locked the door again.

"Come in. I've already sent Marcie home," Olivia said as she walked them back to her office.

Julia sat down on her normal spot on the couch and Connor stood behind her as if standing sentry. He appeared far more serious than the night before, which made Olivia's stomach knot.

Olivia sat down in the chair facing the couch. The chair she usually used for sessions, but she didn't feel comfortable. Of course, this wasn't a normal session where she was in control, either.

"You want to talk to me about last night, I assume?"

Julia nodded. "I mostly want to ask how you're doing. Last night had to be a bit of a shock."

"That's an understatement."

"I thought I might possibly answer some questions for you. Within reason."

"So you aren't going to erase my memory?" Olivia blurted.

Julia frowned. "No. Why would we do that?"

"I don't know, because you don't trust me with the truth?"

"Do we need to worry you'll say something?"

"No."

Julia tipped her head to the side. "Do you want your memory erased?"

Olivia opened her mouth to answer...and then hesitated. "Honestly? I thought about it last night. Wondered if it would be easier to go back to the way things were before."

"And?"

Olivia glanced up at Connor's stoic face before meeting Julia's anxious gaze again. "I need to move forward and accept this as my new world."

Julia beamed. "Exactly what I thought when I found out about Thomas."

Olivia blinked. "I didn't think about your husband being an elf, which is silly, since he was Devin's brother."

"No problem. I wouldn't expect you to jump to a bunch of rational conclusions after what you experienced the other night. I'm human like you, and when I found out supernaturals existed, Thomas explained things to me. Since I was already in love with him by then, I wasn't about to walk away from him or the truth."

"So what else do you want to talk to me about?" Olivia asked.

"Can't I just be here to check on you?"

"You could, although you could have done it over the phone. Plus, your demeanor and body language are intense. I bet this is what you look like in the courtroom."

"I sometimes forget I can't get anything past you. I'm here to see if you would be willing to help with something. Besides being a defense attorney, I also review contracts and prenups for paranormals who are getting married. It's a service Alex offers with her wedding planner business."

Olivia gaped at her. "Alex plans paranormal weddings."

"Yes, the business caters exclusively to paranormals now. I'm currently reviewing a contract which stipulates that sanity must be proven before the mating ceremony can take place."

"I've never heard of such a thing before."

"It's not something you see in many paranormal contracts, either." Julia paused for a moment before continuing. "We thought you might be able to help with this. We need someone who's impartial and has no connection to supernaturals. And since you know the truth now — "

"You thought of me."

"Is it something you would be willing to consider?"

"I need to think about it. It's difficult, even for a psychiatrist, to judge someone's mental state through discussion alone. And since in this particular case their reality is different from mine, it will make evaluating them even more difficult."

"What do you mean?" Julia asked.

"Until yesterday, if someone would have told me elves and faeries existed, I would have thought they were having mental issues...hallucinations, perhaps. Today it's a part of my new reality."

"So they might say something you would perceive as crazy because you don't know if they're speaking the truth."

"Exactly."

"Then what would make you more inclined to help us?"

Olivia rolled her eyes. "Wow, I've never seen you in lawyer mode before. It's impressive."

Julia laughed. "Sorry. I'm not trying to convince you to do something you don't want to do."

"I know. If I'm going to consider this—and it's still an if—I would need to know more about the type of supernatural I would be dealing with."

"Totally reasonable."

"I'll tell her," Connor said, his voice low and growly.

Julia glanced up at Connor, and some sort of unspoken conversation appeared to take place before Julia nodded and then turned back to her.

"Are you okay with having Connor answer your questions?"

Olivia studied Connor. His crossed-arms stance didn't convince her that she would get the answers she needed.

"If he's honest with me."

Julia's eyes widened, but she stood as if to finish the conversation. "He will be."

Olivia stood as well, and Julia said her goodbyes, leaving the two of them alone. Olivia walked over to her desk and picked up her pen, twisting it in her fingers while the new, stoic Connor stood watching her.

"Have I done something to upset you?" Olivia asked.

"No."

"Then why did you frown through the entire conversation with Julia? And why are you standing there with your arms crossed?"

Connor dropped his arms and sighed. "I didn't want to involve you in this. It's bad enough for you to know the truth, and now we're sucking you into our world."

"Is it a bad world to be in?"

Connor started to cross his arms again, but caught himself. "It's complicated."

Olivia shrugged. "Every world is complicated, Connor."

"Yes, but it's easier if we can stay in our own lanes."

"Unless we aren't in the right lane to begin with."

He frowned again, and she held up her hand. "I haven't agreed to help you yet. I need some answers first."

"I'll answer what I can."

Olivia nodded. "Let's try it and see if it's acceptable."

Connor's mouth quirked up slightly. "You don't pull any punches, do you?"

"I try to find clear, effective ways to say things without applying a blunt instrument to the head and shoulders."

His slight quirk turned into a full-grown grin, and his ridiculous dimple appeared. "This is your idea of non-bludgeoning words?"

"I'm a little more to the point with you because I think you can handle it."

"Your confidence in me is inspiring."

She smiled back at him. "Are you ready for my questions?"

"Fire away."

"What type of supernaturals are we talking about?"

"Werewolves."

Her mind blanked and she shook her head. Surely she hadn't heard him correctly.

"You've gone pale, Doc. Do you need to sit down?"

"No," she answered too quickly, and then chastised herself. She walked around her desk and took a deep, calming breath. "Why would a wedding contract have a sanity clause? Do werewolves have issues with mental illness?"

"Not any more than humans. Sullivan Ross is alpha of the West Coast pack. He's betrothed to the daughter of the alpha from the East Coast pack. There are a crap-ton of issues between the two packs. This wedding could unite them."

His flat tone told her he didn't buy it. "But you don't think that's the case."

"There's been a lot of animosity between the packs. I don't think marriage is going to solve the issues."

Why was she imagining a werewolf version of *West Side Story*? The music even started playing in her head. "Mr. Ross and his fiancée must think it will," she argued.

"Sullivan and Maeve didn't sign the agreement. Their fathers did."

"Oh. Now there's a recipe for disaster," Olivia said.

Connor rested his hands on the couch. "I agree. But Sullivan can't just back out without possibly causing a rift. So he's agreed to meet Maeve and see if there's any way they can be compatible."

Olivia stopped her pacing. "Are you telling me they've never met before?"

"That's exactly what I'm telling you."

"I spoke too soon. *That's* a recipe for disaster."

"At least we agree on something."

"So why the sanity clause?"

"If it's determined that Sullivan is unstable, his leadership of the West Coast contingent could be called into question."

"And the East Coast could take over?"

"I'm guessing yes."

"Why would Sullivan's father agree to it?"

Connor's eyes took on a hard glint. "The irony is, Sullivan's father was a crazy bastard himself. Of course he was alpha, so no one challenged him."

"Why do I have the feeling you're not telling me the whole story?"

"There are some things I can't tell you."

"Fair enough." Although she wanted to ask him why he was so angry. Every muscle in his body was pulled taught, from his jaw to his forearms. She decided to try another tack. "What powers do werewolves have?"

"They're strong."

"That's it?"

Connor's eyebrows lowered as if he tried to figure out a puzzle. "You mean other than their ability to turn into a wolf?"

This time Olivia actually felt the blood drain from her head in a rush.

A second later, Connor's hands were on her shoulders as he helped her into her desk chair before she fainted. This was déjà vu from yesterday.

"You okay?"

She nodded.

"Don't tell me you're actually surprised to find out they turn?"

She shouldn't be, but she hadn't wanted to face the truth when he first said the word *werewolf*. "You told me yesterday not to believe all the myths about supernaturals. Faeries can't fly and elves aren't small with pointy ears."

"True. But the ability to turn into a wolf isn't a myth."

She asked the question that would help her decide whether or not she could help them.

"When you turn into your wolf, do you have control?"

Connor gaped at her as his wolf leaped to attention for a second. Once again she'd knocked him for a loop. Pale as a ghost one second, asking ridiculously insightful questions the next.

"I never said I was a werewolf."

"You didn't have to. When you were describing the wolf packs your expression and body language spoke volumes. You're invested in them."

He stared at her for a moment. He had planned to tell her about his wolf since, number one, he wasn't ashamed of who he was, and, number two, someone would have let it slip in front of her anyway.

From the tight expression on her face, she did not like his hesitation.

"You aren't going to pull the 'need to know' card, are you?"

Connor couldn't keep the grin off his face. She had a spine of steel. "No."

"Great. Then answer my question." She swallowed hard before continuing. "When you turn into your wolf, do you know what's going on?"

"Do you mean am I a mindless beast? No. I share my conscience with my wolf. I know what's going on at all times. I'm in control when I turn. The moon does call to us, but we don't automatically turn into wolves during the full moon."

She nodded tightly, as if coming to a decision. "Okay. Is there anything else you need to tell me before I meet with your alpha?"

"You've decided to help?"

"Yes."

"Do you want me to tell you about Sullivan himself?" Connor asked.

"No, I don't want to be influenced before I meet him. The fact that he's the alpha and a werewolf is all I need to know right now."

"Thank you for doing this."

Her eyes took on a determined glint. "Don't thank me yet. We'll probably disagree about something during this process."

"I don't doubt it. If you're ready to go home, I'll give you a lift."

"You don't—"

"We've been down this road before, Doc. You know I'm not going to take no for an answer."

She blew out a hard breath, which sounded suspiciously like a huff. But he wasn't going to call her on it. He'd rather get her home before midnight.

He drove to her apartment and parked the car. She opened her mouth, probably to tell him not to walk her in, and he simply tilted his head to the side. She opened her door, and he could have sworn he heard her huff again. Why did the sound make him and his wolf so happy?

He sped up to catch her before she unlocked the door and left him outside. When they walked into the lobby, the doorman got to his feet.

"How's it going, Sam?" Connor asked.

"Good, sir. How are you both tonight?"

Olivia smiled. "I'm good."

"Me too," Connor said, holding out his hand. "I'm Connor, by the way."

Sam shook his hand. "Nice to meet you."

"Is it time to order food again? Last night was Chinese food. Do you have something planned for Thursday nights too?"

Sam chuckled. "No, sir. I brought leftovers tonight."

"Good. I'll see to Olivia's meal."

She waved her hand. "Ah, Olivia is standing right here, you know."

Connor turned to her. "Do you have dinner plans tonight?"

"No."

"Great. Then I'll make you something to eat."

She turned away from him and stomped toward the elevator.

As he jogged past, Connor winked at Sam, who gave Connor a thumbs-up. Olivia didn't block his entry to the elevator, which he took as a good sign, and they rode up to the fifth floor in silence. He followed her to the third door on the right, where she paused to look up at him.

"Come on, Doc. Be wild and crazy. Take a chance. Unless you have no food and live on takeout? Is Thursday night Italian? Greek? Mexican?"

She muttered something that sounded suspiciously like "stubborn mule" while she opened the door, and he didn't waste time following her in. He had the distinct impression that she didn't let many people get close to her.

He glanced around her apartment. It was a newer building, and the unit had an open floor plan. The kitchen was top-notch, and it overlooked a dining and living room with mid-century modern furniture. Sleek and clean, like what you would expect to see on a magazine cover.

Not a thing out of place except the stack of books sitting next to a comfy chair by the window with a view of the city. He had a feeling the chair was where she spent most of her time.

"Your kitchen is amazing. May I?"

She set down her purse and gestured for him to go ahead. He poked around for a couple of minutes in her pantry and refrigerator. "You actually have food."

"If I didn't take advantage of all the fresh fruits and vegetables in this city, I would be missing out. It's one of the best things about living in California."

"Julia would starve to death if left on her own. Her

pantry is like a wasteland. Or at least it used to be until Jack moved in and started feeding her. But truth be told, I'm the better cook."

"Modest too, I see."

"And better-looking."

Olivia shook her head. "Except for your eye color, you two are identical."

He was impressed. "You noticed, huh?"

"Once I saw the two of you together, I noticed."

He pulled out some penne pasta and various spices from the panty before choosing a variety of vegetables from the refrigerator.

He held up a red pepper. "Do you trust me?"

She gave him a long look, and his heart ticked a bit harder before he told himself to knock it off.

"I think either way I answer you, I'm going to be in trouble."

Connor laughed. "I can't get anything past you."

Eyebrow lift followed by a head tilt. She was committed to figuring him out now. It should make him nervous, but it intrigued him instead.

"You're in my apartment right now, cooking dinner. I think you can sneak some things past me."

"So the burden is on me to impress you with my culinary skills."

"Very true." Her gaze ran over the various ingredients he had placed on the counter. "Do you need my help?"

"I could use a sous chef. How good are you at chopping things?"

She opened a cabinet and pulled out a chopping block and a wicked-looking knife. "I can handle it."

"All righty, then. Point me in the direction of your pans and we'll get this culinary show on the road."

The next half hour passed by with small talk as they worked to prep the meal. Conner placed the pasta dish with grilled peppers, spinach, and olives in front of her. He watched for her reaction as she took her first bite.

She groaned.

"That's what I like to hear."

"Good Lord, you weren't exaggerating. You *are* a good cook."

He managed not to let his chest puff up with pride. *What is wrong with me?* Instead he took a bite of the pasta. It was good, sweetness from the red and yellow peppers offset by saltiness from the olives. But it was missing something...

He stood and rummaged through her refrigerator until he found a container of shredded parmesan cheese. He spooned some on his pasta and handed the container to Olivia.

"Even better," she said with a smile.

Connor's heart ticked double time again, and he told it to take a chill pill. Suddenly the food didn't taste as good as it had before. Words seemed to escape him as well.

After a few minutes of silent eating, they finished the meal and Connor stood to take the dishes to the sink.

Olivia held up her hand. "You don't have to do that. You cooked. I'll clean up. It's late, and I'm sure you're ready to head home."

He nodded. "We'll be in touch to schedule your time with Sullivan."

She stared at him for a moment. "Okay. Thanks for dinner."

He walked out of her apartment to the elevator. He felt like retreating for some strange reason.

He wasn't sure why things had changed. Halfway through the meal he'd felt the need to leave. But he forced himself to sit there and choke down the pasta.

He told himself he didn't want to keep involving her in their world. That it wasn't fair to her. She was strong, but he could also sense the vulnerability she worked so hard to hide from everyone. Olivia had erected those walls to keep herself safe.

And that's when the real truth reared its ugly head. He was the last person who should be messing with those walls. She didn't need to be involved with him. He wasn't in the market for a relationship, so he would back the hell off and give her some space. She deserved someone who would appreciate her intelligence and beauty. Someone who would convince her to not be so methodical, to order something different from the menu. Hell, to throw the menu out and start from scratch.

And that someone wasn't him.

Avoiding someone doesn't solve the problem.
It simply postpones it.

CHAPTER 12

Conner was the last to join the team in the field where Sullivan's wolf had been shot.

Devin waved him over to them. "Anything?"

Connor shook his head. "I didn't sense or smell anything."

"Me either," Jack said. "I wish he'd called us in sooner. We might have been able to find something."

"I've checked the cameras, and there's nothing on the recordings," Giz said. "Can't believe they don't have this area wired with cameras."

Devin turned to Charlie. "Have you checked out the other security?"

"As best we can. Giz and I aren't getting a lot of cooperation from the security team."

"I'm sure it's Jonathan's doing," Connor said.

Charlie studied his tablet. "Based on what we've been able to review, the perimeter is pretty well secured, although we found a couple of weak spots that should be dealt with."

"We'll show Sullivan the findings and let him

decide if he wants us to tell his security team or if he wants to do it," Devin said.

Jonathan was not going to like their interference, but Connor was used to pissing him off, so this was familiar territory.

When the team arrived at the alpha's lodge, Jonathan and two security guards met them on the front porch.

"Why are you walking pack land?" Jonathan demanded in lieu of a greeting.

Devin stepped forward. "You know why we're here. We're checking your perimeter security."

"We don't need outside interference. We'll take care of our own."

Connor barely managed not to laugh at the man's hypocrisy.

Jack's voice sounded in his head. *Take it easy, brother.*

I can't stomach him, Connor responded.

Devin frowned. "We're here at the request of your alpha. You may want to discuss it with him if there's some confusion."

The front door opened and Sullivan appeared. "Is there some sort of problem, gentlemen?"

Connor hid his grin. Knowing Sullivan, he had probably been listening on the other side of the door using his wolf hearing.

Devin spoke first. "Just letting your team know we've finished our initial review of your perimeter security."

"Did you find anything we need to be worried about?" Sullivan asked.

"Charlie and Giz have the report," Devin responded.

"Thanks for the fast work. Jonathan, please go through their findings while I talk to the rest of the team."

Jonathan's eyes tightened for a moment before he acquiesced. Charlie and Giz followed him to the small security building adjacent to the alpha's lodge.

Sullivan invited Devin, Jack, and Connor into the lodge. Once again they found themselves in the meeting room. Sullivan shut the door with a decisive click.

"Looks like I interrupted Jonathan's version of a pissing contest. Do I need to be concerned about the security findings?"

"Nothing major," Devin responded, "but I'll make sure we send you the findings as well."

Sullivan gestured for them to take a seat and then sat down next to them. "Did you find anything in the woods?"

Connor shifted in his seat. "We didn't see or smell anything out of the ordinary. You said you sensed something in the woods before you were shot. Did you smell anything? Do you remember what made you realize you weren't alone?"

"My wolf sensed eyes on us." Sullivan closed his eyes. "Did I smell something?" After a few seconds he opened them. "I smelled a slight trace of wolf. Nothing I could definitely recognize, but he or she was a werewolf."

Connor didn't know if that was good or bad news. On the one hand, they didn't need another paranormal species trying to kill their alpha. On the other hand, what did it mean if a werewolf from Callahan's pack or, even worse, someone from their own pack was trying to kill Sullivan?

"Is there someone you've pissed off in the pack?" Connor asked.

Sullivan's eyebrows rose. "Besides your father, you mean?"

Connor nodded.

"I'm sure there are many in the pack who haven't

exactly been happy with me during my first year as alpha. I am not my father."

"Thank the Fates for that," Connor said.

"There are others who wouldn't agree with you. Change is a bitch, both for the ones who want things to stay the same, and for the ones who want change to happen yesterday. You can't please both. And sometimes you can't please any of them."

Devin rested his elbows on the table and steepled his fingers. "You're going to need to give us a list of potential shooters. We'll do some digging."

Sullivan shook his head. "My father was a bastard every day he was alpha and no one tried to kill him. I've been alpha for a year and I'm already being shot at."

"Which makes me wonder what their motivation is," Connor asked.

"It's too much of a coincidence that someone tried to kill me right after I received this surprise contract from the East Coast pack. Someone doesn't want this marriage to happen."

"Because?" Devin asked.

Sullivan stood and paced beside the table. "For our clan, I would think it's the fear of losing control of our pack. Of having Callahan indirectly, through his daughter or any children we might have, influence pack rule. And the same could be said for his pack. I'm sure they would not be happy to have me butting into their business."

"If that's the reason, then the person has to know about the contract in the first place," Jack said. "You said only your advisors and the pack secretary know."

"Yes, Callahan sent it to me, and Carol opened it and then brought it to me. I've told her not to say anything to anyone about it."

"Can you trust her?" Connor asked.

"I believe so. Although it was a shock to all of us."

"What about your advisors? Can you trust them?" Devin asked.

Sullivan stopped pacing and turned to them. "I'd like to think so, but I can't afford to make assumptions when people are shooting at me."

Devin frowned. "So, including your secretary and two advisors, we have at least three suspects in this pack, and who knows how many in Callahan's pack."

Sullivan sat down. "When I spoke to Callahan about it, he said it's not common knowledge in his pack either—just him, his daughter, and his advisors—although he was surprised to learn my father hadn't mentioned anything to me."

"How do we even know if this contract is legit?" Connor asked.

"It's legit. It's signed with the pack crest." Sullivan held up his hand with the alpha's ring. "My father never took it off until the night he died."

Connor leaned forward. "What I don't understand is, why try to kill you to stop the contract? There are other ways to put a stop to it. We need to consider all the options. Maybe this is less about the contract and more about someone wanting to take over the pack. If you die, who's next in line?"

"Since there is no progeny, one of my advisors would step up and rule until a pack vote could be taken."

Connor glanced at Jack and saw the same pained expression on his face that Connor probably had on his own. If Sullivan were killed, there was no way Jonathan wouldn't come out on top to lead the pack. "So we're back to the same set of suspects."

"I think you should let Julia study the pack succession rules to see if it's the only choice you have as a single alpha," Jack said.

"I'll send her the information myself. Speaking of Julia, has she had a chance to review the marriage contract?"

Jack replied, "She did a preliminary read-through, and now she's going to dig into the nitty-gritty to see if there's a way to get you out of this contract without starting a pack war."

Devin spoke up. "The one thing concerning her is the sanity clause."

Sullivan frowned. "She's not the only one."

"Julia wants an expert witness ready to testify that you're not crazy," Connor said.

"And where can we get this expert witness?" Sullivan asked.

Devin responded. "We've asked someone not affiliated with the pack to meet with you."

"Who?"

"Dr. Olivia Jennings," Devin said. "She's a human psychiatrist, and she's very good at what she does."

"How did you find her?"

Devin glanced over at Jack, who nodded. "She's my wife, Alex, and Julia's therapist."

"And she knows about us?"

"Yes. And she's agreed to spend some time with you. I think we should get something scheduled and taken care of ASAP, before Callahan shows up."

"Agreed. But I would like her to come here. I don't want to meet with her in a doctor's office."

Connor wasn't so sure Olivia would like having to come to pack lands, but it was up to her to disagree. He almost wished she would refuse. He didn't like the idea of her being pulled into their mess. And he definitely didn't want her exposed to Jonathan's form of poison. "When is Callahan supposed to be here?"

"Sometime next week. He was close-mouthed about

the exact time. He acts like we're going to attempt to assassinate him if we know his schedule." Sullivan stood. "Since today is Friday, do you think your Dr. Jennings would make a house call tomorrow?"

"I'll call her," Jack said.

They finished their discussion and left. Devin searched for Charlie and Giz, who were riding with him, while Connor and Jack returned to San Diego. Connor stared out the passenger window while Jack maneuvered through the Friday afternoon traffic. Everyone was racing out of the city to spend a weekend somewhere else, only to turn around and race back to start their weekly grind all over again.

He wondered what Olivia did on the weekend. Did she have a special takeout place for weekends? Or maybe she went to the farmer's market in Little Italy on Saturday to pick out fruits and vegetables. Although they were going to mess up whatever plans she had for tomorrow.

Jack changed lanes. "You're awfully quiet."

"Just thinking about the mess Sully's in right now."

"We'll figure it out. Julia is working on things, and Dr. Jennings will help too. Once I confirm the meeting tomorrow, do you want to pick Dr. Jennings up and take her to the pack lands?"

"Actually, I wondered if you could take her. I've got something going on tomorrow."

Jack took the off-ramp and stopped at a light, turning to study him. "Are you okay?"

"Yeah. I don't think we both need to chauffeur her, do we?"

"No, I can take her."

Connor turned his attention to the passenger window. Hell, the last thing he planned to do was tell his twin he wanted to avoid Olivia. But it was the right thing to do. The less time spent together, the better. She would talk to Sullivan, and then he wouldn't see her again.

Which was the best thing for both of them, even if his wolf was pitching a hairy fit.

You can banish your fears from your thoughts but not your dreams.

CHAPTER 13

A scream tore out of Olivia's throat. She sat up, fighting whatever weighed her down. *Blankets.*

Where am I?

She glanced around the room, her eyes acclimating to the dark after a few moments. She was in her bed, not in the woods. She was an adult, not a child. The monsters weren't after her.

They weren't real. It wasn't real.

She kicked the covers off and stumbled to the bathroom. Fumbling for her shower faucet, she turned it on to heat up. She didn't want to turn on the light and see herself, but she couldn't stay in the dark. Monsters thrived in the dark.

Flipping on the light switch, she blinked at the sudden brightness until she could focus again, then looked in the mirror. She was pale, and her hair stuck to her sweaty face and back. She reached up with shaking hands and struggled out of her damp tank top and sleep shorts before climbing into the shower.

The warm water sluiced over her shoulders, and she concentrated on slowing her breathing. Whenever her night terrors struck, a shower usually helped wash away the residual panic. But with the panic gone, it left room for more emotions. Anger because she couldn't seem to stop these terrors. She was a psychiatrist, for God's sake. Why couldn't she figure out what they were supposed to mean?

Who were the monsters?

What had happened to her as a child? It was something so terrifying, so awful, so gut-wrenching that she had turned her memories and feelings into monsters with glowing eyes who were chasing her.

She'd tried numerous things—regression therapy, hypnotherapy, anything—to break through and face her fears. But they wouldn't go away.

Lately she'd been hopeful they were gone since it had been months since the last incident. Why now? In the past she had the night terrors when she faced something new in her life. In the past few days, she discovered that paranormals exist. That werewolves actually exist. Maybe they're what caused the newest terror.

And tomorrow she would be meeting with Sullivan Ross at his estate. Normally she met with patients in her office, where she could control things. But then Sullivan was not the usual patient.

And she wasn't sure if Connor would even be there. Something had happened Thursday night when he made her dinner. They were talking and laughing and, she felt sure, both enjoying themselves—until he simply shut down. She didn't know what else to call it. He went from grins and jokes to finishing his dinner as fast as he could and escaping.

She went over and over their dinner conversation. Had she said or done something to upset him? But she couldn't think of anything. Heck, he was a big boy. She wasn't responsible for his moods.

She turned off the water and dried off before pulling on a fresh tank and sleep shorts. She needed a few hours of sleep before she spent time with Sullivan Ross. Falling asleep during the interview would probably be frowned on.

The familiar black SUV pulled up in front of Olivia's building and her heart sped up. Which was ridiculous. She wasn't going on a date, for goodness' sake. She was interviewing the shifter leader to determine his sanity. Okay, that made her heart speed up again. Why had she agreed to do this?

She walked out of the vestibule and climbed into the passenger seat of the SUV before she looked over at Connor. Only instead of green eyes dancing whimsically, serious blue eyes stared back.

"Hello, Jack."

"Dr. Jennings. Thanks for agreeing to do this for us."

She buckled her seat belt as he pulled away from the curb. She wouldn't ask him why Connor wasn't here. It wasn't any of her business, and really, his presence wasn't necessary for this meeting anyway.

They drove for a few minutes in silence while she fidgeted in her seat. Unlike Connor, Jack was more than happy with silence.

"Is it just the two of us going today?" Okay, she folded like a wet noodle, but at least she didn't point-blank ask about Connor. "I mean, is Julia going?"

Jack glanced over at her for a moment before watching the road again. "Julia wanted to come, but Connor suggested having both you and Julia descend on Sullivan at the same time would put our alpha at a disadvantage."

Olivia watched Jack's profile and saw a slight grin appear. "Did he? And what did Julia have to say about it?"

"After she gave him a piece of her mind, she thought about it for a few minutes and decided she didn't need to interrogate him about the contract because you were already meeting with him."

In reality, it would be better for Sullivan to not be distracted while she met with him. Although it was probably an impossibility, since he was being interviewed to establish his sanity in order to determine whether he could marry a perfect stranger from the rival pack. Great. Songs from *West Side Story* were playing in her head again.

Olivia settled against the seat and watched the world speed by. She wasn't sure how much time passed before Jack slowed the SUV and turned onto a side road leading into a wooded area. Her breathing picked up. Being away from buildings and people unsettled her. The woods especially bothered her. But now was not the time to dwell on her past and her phobias.

Within minutes they had pulled up to the biggest log cabin she had ever seen. Was there such a thing as a log mansion?

A man met them at the double door entrance, and Olivia followed him inside. Was he an actual butler? Did people have butlers in this day and age? The sheer size of the guy made her think his job was more about security than serving, but she was new to the werewolf world. Maybe they all came supersized. Jack and Connor weren't exactly tiny.

As if she conjured the devil by thinking about him, Connor walked toward them.

"I thought you couldn't make it today," Jack said in lieu of greeting.

Connor shrugged. "Things changed." He nodded to her. "Dr. Jennings."

Dr. Jennings? What the hell was going on? Clearly she hadn't imagined the awkwardness on Thursday night. Apparently Connor wanted to keep this all business. Which was fine with her. Business and being a therapist were things she could control.

They were directed into a meeting room with a large table. Olivia carefully placed her briefcase on the shiny wood surface and pulled out her pen and notepad. She would take her notes on the pad and then transfer them later to her laptop.

Connor and Jack stood to the side like twin guards. Before she could ask them if they were going to hover over her, a door on the side of the room opened and a man walked in. Tall, blond, with power literally oozing from his pores, this had to be Sullivan Ross. Following him were two other men, both older. The pack leader stopped across from Olivia.

"Thank you for coming today, Dr. Jennings. I'm Sullivan Ross."

Olivia held out her hand and they shook. "Mr. Ross."

He gestured for her to take a seat. "Since you're going to be spending time in my brain, I think you can call me Sullivan."

"And I'm still Dr. Jennings."

Sullivan might have smiled. And she thought his eyes twinkled. "Noted."

She met the gazes of the men behind him, and they both studied her like a specimen under a microscope.

"These are my two senior advisors, Victor and Jonathan."

"It's nice to meet you gentlemen."

Neither responded, and the tension emanating from Connor and Jack ratcheted up another notch.

"Shall we get started?" she asked.

Sullivan nodded and Olivia barely managed not to roll her eyes. This was not going to work. "I know you're used to having your" — entourage? — "pack around you, Sullivan, but we need to be alone while we talk."

The two advisors behind him started to protest until Sullivan held up his hand, silencing them. There was no mistaking the hierarchy around here.

Sullivan gazed at her for a moment. "If I say no?"

She would not be cowed by him. "Then I don't think this arrangement is going to work."

A few more staring-contest moments before Sullivan finally spoke. "You heard the doctor. Everyone out."

"We don't know anything about her, sir," Jonathan said.

"I don't think I need to worry about my safety." His eyes held a bit of humor. "Do I need to worry about my safety?"

"No. Do I?" she asked.

The spark of humor disappeared. "You're safe here."

The advisors left, and Olivia turned to the twins. "That includes you two."

Connor frowned.

"Do we have to go through the 'am I safe?' questions again?" Olivia asked.

They shook their heads and trudged out of the room.

"Sorry about that," Sullivan said.

"Not a problem. You're their leader, and naturally they want to protect you." Olivia picked up her pen. "Shall we get started?"

"Fire away."

Olivia started with some general questions about his experiences as pack leader, and about his childhood and schooling.

Sullivan answered her with no hesitation. He was

articulate, intelligent, and charismatic, which was probably why he was alpha.

"These are the kinds of questions that will reveal whether I'm crazy or not?" Sullivan asked.

"These questions are helping me get to know you and lay a foundation for further questions."

His lips pressed into a straight line.

She set down her notepad. "What types of questions were you expecting?"

"Do I hear voices, or see things that aren't there?"

"I could ask those questions, except I would imagine in your world hearing voices isn't necessarily a strange thing."

Sullivan smiled. "It is and it isn't. For some of us who are lucky enough to find true mates, we can talk to each other telepathically."

Olivia barely managed not to gape. "And when isn't it normal?"

"Jack and Connor can sense each other and talk to each other through their link."

"Do you think it has something to do with them being twins? Even in the human world, twins have a special connection."

"Yeah. It might be because they're twins, but we have no way of knowing since we've never had identical twins in the pack before."

"Never? It must have been a surprise for their parents."

"You could say that." Sullivan grimaced. "The twins were almost shunned by the pack."

"For what?"

"For being born. Many of our pack's rules are rooted in superstition and prejudice. I'm working to change it."

Olivia picked up her pen again as an excuse to collect herself. As a psychiatrist, she heard horrible things all the time, and it wasn't her place to interject her emotions. Ultimately this was not about her. So she jotted a nonsensical note down on the notepad and then looked up at him once she felt her emotions were back under control again.

"Those are difficult things to overcome."

"Yes, they are. It doesn't help that my father fanned the flames when it came to these prejudices. He was closed-minded and somewhat of a tyrant. I was actually surprised when he didn't agree to the twins being ostracized, which is why they were allowed to stay. Until they left on their own, that is."

"Why would you want to lead a pack that's so broken?" Olivia asked.

Sullivan's eyes flared slightly. "Because there is good in this pack. I can see what we could become as a united pack, and we would be all the stronger for having dealt with the challenges."

"And do you want to unite the West Coast and East Coast packs to help with this?"

"I want to work on strengthening my pack. The animosity between our packs doesn't help things, and I hoped to eventually repair relations."

"By marrying a stranger?"

Sullivan shook his head. "No. Until recently, I didn't even know the betrothal contract existed. But I can't outright reject the contract without further damaging relations."

"Even though your father was the one who signed it?"

Sullivan smiled. "You've done your homework, Dr. Jennings."

"I know why they asked me to come speak to you. Why do you think your father agreed to this contract?"

Sullivan leaned forward, resting his elbows on the

table. "I don't know. I've been trying to figure out why he would be willing to let the East Coast infiltrate our pack. He might not have liked me much, but I just can't imagine him willingly handing the pack over to Alpha Callahan."

"Why do you think he didn't like you?"

"Because I wouldn't bow to his wishes or his twisted way of thinking. As much as I want to make this pack better, my father wanted to avoid change at any cost."

"Which begs the question again, why did he agree to the contract?"

"It's something I'm going to try and get out of Callahan. I don't know how forthcoming he'll be, but I have to start somewhere."

Olivia ran her finger along the clip on her pen cap. "Tell me about your father."

Sullivan's eyes narrowed. "You're getting to the meaty questions now."

Olivia kept her expression neutral, even though it was obvious his father was an emotional trigger for Sullivan. "Am I?"

"If I tell you my father was unstable, would it count against me?"

Interesting question. "Should it?"

"You've got that non-answer therapist talk down to a science."

Olivia set down her pen. "Not really. I just want to hear your thoughts and opinions without interjecting my own. So let's get back to it. Tell me about your father."

Connor stood outside the meeting room, straining to hear what they were saying. Nothing. The room was soundproofed, even against wolf hearing. Not that he wanted to violate Sullivan's privacy. It was more curiosity getting the better of him. What was Olivia like when she was in full therapist mode? He wasn't convinced she ever let herself fully relax. And if her raised eyebrow was any indication, she was constantly trying to get into his psyche.

"Why would you bring a human here?" a voice demanded.

Connor turned to face his father. "Now you decide to talk to me?"

"Answer the question."

"The *human*, as you so eloquently labeled her, has agreed to help the pack. We need an unbiased therapist to confirm Sullivan's sanity."

"This should be handled internally. We don't need your outside interference."

Nice to hear he was considered an outsider, but he wasn't surprised. "I wouldn't throw stones, Daddy Dearest. The mess Sullivan is in right now came from the inside. Morgan signed him up for this mess."

"Alpha Morgan."

"The title of alpha is earned."

Jack walked up to them. "This isn't the time or place for this."

Jonathan stormed away, and Connor took a deep breath.

"Sorry I wasn't here to help deflect him."

"It's not your fault he's...well, who he is." He glanced at the closed door. "How do you think it's going in there?"

"I'm sure it's fine. Dr. Jennings knows what she's doing."

"How can you be so sure?"

"Because both Julia and Alex rave about her," Jack said. "And I sat in on one of Julia's sessions."

"I can't imagine she lets you get away with much," Connor said.

"She's tough, but she needs to be. According to Julia, Dr. Jennings specializes in grief counseling, and also is an expert in anxiety disorders, including phobias."

"Sounds like you're impressed with her too," Connor said.

"I've seen how much happier Julia is now."

"I think a lot of it has to do with you."

Jack grinned. "I hope so."

Connor shrugged. "Although I still think she should throw you back. I'm a much better catch."

"Says the man who doesn't *do* relationships. I was like you, brother."

Connor groaned. "Here we go."

"But then I found Julia, and things changed for the better."

Connor scrubbed his hand over his face. "I agree. But that's what's right for you. I don't want to settle down with one woman. There are too many possibilities out there."

"You forget I'm in your head, Connor. I don't buy this forever-a-player persona you have going on."

Connor frowned. "It's not a game. It's who I am, Jack. Not everyone is meant to have the wife, house in the 'burbs with the white picket fence, and the 2.2 pups. I'm happy for you and Julia. Can't you be happy for me?"

Jack glared back at him. "If you're telling the truth, I can be happy for you, you manipulative bastard."

He was telling the truth. No manipulation involved. He was happy for his brother, but he didn't need a permanent mate in his life. He was good on his own. No relationship meant no disappointment on either side.

The last thing he wanted to do was disappoint Olivia, so it was better to not form any sort of attachment. To step away, for her sake.

Sometimes the best therapy involves friends and pastries.

CHAPTER 14

An hour later...not that Connor had been keeping track...Sullivan opened the door and beckoned for Connor and Jack to join him.

Connor glanced around. "Where's Olivia?"

"Dr. Jennings went to the restroom," Sullivan said. "We're done for today."

"Today?" Connor stepped around the table. "She wants to see you again?"

"Yeah. We're meeting tomorrow as well."

On a Sunday? "So soon? She must think you're actually crazy," Connor pushed.

Sullivan glared at him. "No. Or at least I don't think she does. Although being willing to lead this pack has to be a little crazy, right?"

"Maybe," Jack said.

"No maybe about it," Connor mumbled.

"And what do you think of Dr. Jennings?" Jack asked.

"I think she's smart as a whip and a great therapist."

"From one meeting?" Connor asked.

"I trust my gut. She's impressive."

Connor frowned. "Well she's not your therapist. She's just determining if you're loco or not."

Sullivan narrowed his eyes at him. "I'm very much aware of why Dr. Jennings is here."

Before Connor could respond, the door opened and Olivia came into the room.

Sullivan walked over to her. "Thanks for coming today, Dr. Jennings. What time tomorrow would you like to meet?"

"Same time works for me."

"Great. I'll have some food prepared as well. It's the least I can do since you're taking time out of your Sunday to meet with me."

"It's not necessary, but thank you."

Sullivan nodded to himself. "I find it refreshing when you push back. I don't experience that very often with the pack."

"We'll talk more about why that is tomorrow."

Sullivan chuckled. "Okay." He turned to Jack. "Do you have a couple of minutes to talk?"

"Actually, I'm taking Dr. Jennings home."

Sullivan turned to Olivia. "I don't want you to have to waste any more time here today. Is it okay if Connor runs you home instead?"

Connor shifted his stance. Guess he'd been volunteered for taxi service when he didn't want to spend time with her. He needed to step way away from the spunky therapist.

Olivia glanced at him before responding. "If Connor is free?"

"You're free, aren't you, Connor?" Sullivan asked with a grin.

Bastard.

Connor could tell Olivia all about how Sullivan got his way. But he agreed anyway, and then they started back to the city. Olivia sat ramrod straight as he drove down the long wood-lined driveway. She finally seemed to relax once they made it to the main road.

Connor concentrated on the road and tried not to focus on the awkward silence sucking the air out of the SUV. What was he supposed to talk about? The weather? Why he was such an ass the other night? Hell, he barely knew why himself, other than they weren't a good fit, and he wasn't looking for any type of relationship.

Enough with the silence.

"So how did the talk with Sullivan go? Is he crazy?"

Olivia's eyebrow went up. "Do you honestly think I would or could answer those questions after meeting with him one time?"

"Possibly. Everyone says you're an amazing therapist."

"Hmm."

Connor glanced at her. "What does *hmm* mean?"

"I guess I'm trying to understand where this conversation is going."

He stopped at a red light. "I'm not sure it was going anywhere. But I thought it was better than driving all the way to the city in total silence."

"Sometimes awkward silence is better than awkward conversation."

How in the hell was he supposed to respond to that? He was damned if he said anything and damned if he didn't. "Is this your professional opinion?"

"I don't need a degree to know you're agitated about something."

"I think you're reading into things."

"Really?"

The light turned green and he let his foot off the brake. He didn't have to see her to know what expression was tied to that word.

She shrugged. "Okay, let's continue with the

awkward conversation. The other night at my house, when we were eating dinner, all of sudden you shut down and couldn't get out of there fast enough."

Guess he had been obvious. "Fine. I'm not looking for a relationship."

"And?" she pushed.

"And I didn't want to lead you on."

Silence for a few drawn-out beats, until Olivia laughed. "Wow."

Not the reaction he'd expected.

He glanced over at her, and she laughed again. "Wow, what?"

"You just made an extremely egotistical statement. You assume that, after a couple meals together — which were not dates, by the way — I'm expecting a relationship? And so you decide to stop talking to me and run out of my apartment like I had some sort of contagious disease."

Well, hell. When she put it that way…

"I didn't want any confusion."

Up went the eyebrow again. "Oh, there's no confusion on my part. You were the one who insisted on spending time with me, Connor. Not the other way around."

She was right, which made her words deadlier. He turned onto her street, glad they were getting close to her apartment building. He pulled in front of her building, and she removed her seat belt and opened the door before he had the car in park.

"Olivia —"

"Thank you for the ride," she said, interrupting him. "We may run into each other while I'm working with Sullivan. Rest assured, I'll make sure to control any and all wayward, romantic thoughts if I ever see you again."

As she turned and marched into the building with

her head held high, he realized two things. One, he was an asshat. And two, she had just schooled him again.

Olivia stood in the vestibule searching for her key card. She absolutely would not glance behind her to see if Connor was still there. She had gotten the last word in—quite spectacularly, if she did say so herself—and now she was languishing in her vestibule. The door override clicked, and she thanked Stan, the weekend doorman.

"Your visitor is here, Dr. Jennings."

She turned to the lobby seating area and found Elena perched on the couch with a bakery box. "I'm so sorry! I forgot you were coming over today."

Elena stood. "No problem. I've only been here for ten minutes. Stan and I were catching up."

Stan held up a doughnut. "She brought me a crème stick."

"Well, I appreciate you letting her wait in the lobby even though I wasn't here."

Stan waved them on, and Olivia and Elena got on the elevator.

"I'm so sorry. I was working and I should have called you."

"You already apologized. Stan didn't boot me out when he realized you weren't here, so it was all good." Elena held up the box as they rode up in the elevator. "There is a broad assortment of baked goods in this box. We can eat to our heart's content while you tell me why you're so agitated."

The elevator opened, and they walked down the hall. "I'm not agita— Never mind, I'm not going to finish the sentence since it isn't true."

"Does it have to do with whoever was in the SUV? You practically stomped into the building."

"It was Connor."

"Wait, you were with Connor again?"

They entered Olivia's apartment, and she dropped her bag on the table while Elena took the goodies to the kitchen.

"Sit down, eat an apple turnover, and tell Elena all about it."

Olivia bit into the flaky, cinnamon-coated work of art. Between bites she told her friend about her time with Connor — minus the werewolf parts, of course.

"So then I told him he was egotistical, and promised I would try to control any wayward romantic notions that might pop up if I ever saw him again."

Elena dropped her half-eaten glazed doughnut on her napkin. "You didn't."

She did. She shouldn't have. But she was so thrown by his statement. He had felt the need to distance himself from her? Had she been clinging to him? No. He was the one who insisted they have dinner together both times. He was the pursuer.

But then he backed off. Why? What made him retreat instead of continuing his game? Connor was a player, but only when he was in control of the game. And maybe that was the crux of it. Had she somehow inadvertently changed the rules on him?

She hadn't set out to date Connor, and while he was a gorgeous, funny, and intelligent man, she didn't have an agenda with him. Heck, truth was, he had seemed to be the one with the agenda.

She polished off the apple turnover and then rummaged the box and pulled out a frosted brownie. When she looked up, she found Elena staring at her.

"What?"

"I have never seen you this passionate before."

Olivia set the brownie down and licked her frosting-covered finger before responding. "This has nothing to do with passion. This is annoyance, anger."

"Come on, Olivia. Those are side effects of passion."

Olivia took a large bite of brownie and chewed it slowly to give herself time to come up with a response. What *was* she so upset about? Was it because he was egotistical, or was it because she had been opening herself up to him?

"I'll admit he's good-looking, and he's smart and funny. But I'm not some doe-eyed schoolgirl wearing her heart on her sleeve. He was the one who pushed going out to dinner and then made me pasta the other night. I wasn't expecting this to go anywhere."

"Why not?"

Olivia gaped at her. "What do you mean?"

"I mean, why shouldn't you expect something to develop? This good-looking, smart, funny guy—your words—is paying attention to you. You're allowed to find someone to be with, Olivia. Someone to have a relationship with. Someone to love."

The last brownie bite she took felt like a cement block in her throat. Olivia stood and got a glass of water, taking several sips to clear her throat.

She set down the glass. "I tell my patients something similar."

"But you don't take your own advice."

Olivia sat down again. "I'd like to find someone special, Elena. But in this instance, it's a good thing I didn't get my hopes up, or I would have ended up wondering what I did wrong to send him running after two meals with me."

"Did you pull out a wedding planner book and show him what you want your dream wedding to be?"

"No."

"Did you boil his rabbit?"

Olivia laughed. "I hope that's a reference to *Fatal Attraction* and not some other kinky thing."

Elena laughed. "Nope. All about the movie. I watched it the other night. Glenn Close was wicked scary in the role."

"No rabbits were boiled."

"Okay, then I'm thinking the issue is with Connor and not you. Like I said, I've seen him in the bar before, and he's never with the same woman twice. If anyone has a relationship issue, it's him."

Olivia looked down at the brownie, but it no longer appealed to her. Elena was right. She was allowed to search for someone special in her life, and she shouldn't be sitting around waiting for something to happen. But if she was honest, there was a part of her who had hoped something was happening between her and Connor.

He made her feel, and she hadn't felt much in a long, long time.

*It's amazing how much could be accomplished
if egos weren't involved.*

CHAPTER 15

Olivia clicked the seat belt in place as déjà vu hit her. Jack was her chauffeur again today, not that she'd expected Connor to drive her after what happened yesterday.

Jack pulled away from her apartment building, and they fell into companionable silence, which was more than fine with Olivia.

They drove for a while, and Jack was the first one to speak. "Sorry you have to spend your weekend helping us."

"I don't mind. If talking to Sullivan helps to avoid a conflict between the packs, I'm happy to help."

"You're taking all this very well."

"You mean finding out about the supernatural?"

He nodded.

"I guess you're right. Although I was a little shaky on my feet when I first found out. I don't know if the acceptance has to do with my job. I've heard a lot of surprising things over the years, and I can't get bogged down with them when I'm trying to help people."

"And you do a great job. In fact, I want to thank you for helping Julia."

Olivia could feel her face heat. "Thank you. But I can't take all the credit. You've been the impetus for her to start living again."

Jack glanced over at her and grinned. It transformed his normally stoic expression, and he had dimples, just like his infuriating brother. "Thanks. Truthfully, she saved me too. I'm going to ask her to marry me."

So Julia was right. "Wonderful."

He changed lanes and pulled off the highway. "I'm trying to decide how to make it special, but I'm having a hard time coming up with something perfect."

"Have you asked Alex for ideas? I'm sure she'd be happy to help you."

"Oh, no. Do you honestly think Alex could keep this a secret?"

Olivia shrugged. "Probably not."

He looked over at her. "You won't say anything to Julia, will you?"

Olivia kept a straight face. "Nope. I won't tell her. Do you want my advice?"

"I'd love it."

"Don't overthink this. If your proposal comes from the heart, it doesn't matter how, where, or when you do it."

"Got it. Thanks. Now it's your turn."

"I'm not planning to ask anyone to marry me anytime soon."

Jack chuckled. "No. I meant, you answered my question, now you can ask me some questions about the supernatural."

"Okay…"

"Don't ask everything at once."

"It's a bit overwhelming, and I went blank for a second. I'm not sure if some of it might have to do with the sheer lack of context I have about what it means to be a supernatural. How do you ask questions when you don't know where to begin?"

"How about we talk about one type of supernatural?"

"Makes sense. Let's go with werewolves since you would know about them firsthand. Are you born with the ability to change?"

"We're born human and don't learn to change until we're in our teens, early twenties."

"Does it hurt to change?"

Jack nodded. "The first few times, definitely. As we get older, it's more discomfort than pain."

"Connor said you can control your wolves."

"Yes. It isn't like in the movies where the full moon turns us into raging beasts. We're normally in full control."

"Normally?"

"I should've known you'd pick up on that. Sometimes, if our wolf is under attack or trying to protect someone, it can get a bit possessive. Last year I was almost killed on a case, and Connor's wolf protected me until the team arrived. But it took a bit of persuading to get Connor to back off and let them get near me."

Olivia swallowed around the boulder lodged in her throat. "You two have a very close relationship."

"He's part of me. We totally relied on each other growing up. We used to run around the forest getting into trouble. The pack lands butt up against the Elven Kingdom, so we hung out with Devin as well."

"Sounds like a magical time."

Olivia watched Jack's profile and saw his jaw tighten before he spoke. "Sometimes."

Time to change the subject. She was making Jack uncomfortable, which wasn't the goal of this exercise.

Jack turned onto the road to Sullivan's house, and she immediately tensed at the trees surrounding them.

"Um…is there anything else I should know about werewolves? Can you turn someone into one if you bite them?"

"No. That's a myth. Our saliva will not turn you into a werewolf, even though when we were little Connor used to chase the elven children and tell them he was going to bite them."

"Why am I not surprised?"

Jack grinned. "You haven't spent much time with Connor and you already have him figured out."

Hardly. Especially after yesterday, but it wasn't something Olivia would be sharing with Jack.

"Your brother has a lot of opinions."

"Yes, and he's not afraid to share them. We may look alike, but in some ways we're very different."

"Which isn't a bad thing. You complement each other. Plus, I don't think the world could handle two Connor Dawsons."

He laughed loudly as he pulled in front of Sullivan's house and parked the SUV. "You're right about that."

Jack escorted her to the same room as yesterday and left her alone once he'd confirmed Sullivan was on his way. A few minutes later the alpha walked into the room carrying a tray with food.

"Did you make that?"

He set the tray on the table. "You're not going to make a sexist comment about men not being able to cook, are you?" Sullivan asked.

"No. I know some men who are good cooks." One in particular, who was also a confusing pain in the rear end, but it wasn't something to talk about now.

"Actually, I didn't make this, so I probably shouldn't give you a hard time. Sharon runs the day-to-day of the house for me, and she's an amazing cook.

I hope you like chicken salad and broccoli cheddar soup."

"Absolutely." Olivia sat down and Sullivan put a plate and bowl in front of her. "Thank you."

"Do you mind eating and talking at the same time?" he asked as he took his seat.

"Not at all. The soup smells so good, I can't wait to dig in."

Over an hour later, Olivia finally set her pen down on her notepad. Sullivan stopped talking and looked at her. "What? Have I finally bored you to tears?"

Olivia shook her head with a smile. "Hardly. You're passionate about your pack and about moving forward as alpha. I'll write up my observations and give them to Julia."

Sullivan straightened. "Any hints? Or am I going to have to wait for the official documents?"

"I would say the sanity clause can't be used against you."

"Great. Thank—"

A knock on the door stopped Sullivan's conversation. A woman opened the door and stepped inside. "Sorry to interrupt your meeting, but Callahan has shown up unannounced and insists on meeting with you."

They stood. Before Sullivan could respond, a man marched into the room, followed by a scowling Jack.

"Sullivan," the man said in an indulgent tone.

"Callahan, you're early."

The man smiled, but it didn't reach his eyes. "I am." His eyes narrowed on Olivia before noticing the empty lunch dishes on the table. "Am I interrupting anything?"

"Yes, actually. I'm in the middle of a meeting."

Callahan came closer, and if Olivia wasn't mistaken, she would have sworn his nostrils flared as if he smelled her. Sullivan stepped partially in front of her, and it seemed like some unspoken, testosterone-laden — or werewolf-laden? — communication passed between them.

Olivia often told her patients not to make hasty judgments based on first impressions, but in this instance she didn't take her own advice. She was having an immediate and visceral reaction to the East Coast alpha, and it wasn't positive.

"Could you please give us a moment, Callahan? We need to finish up our meeting."

Callahan looked like he wanted to argue, but at the last moment he turned and stalked out of the room. The woman who interrupted them in the first place still stood in the room like a deer caught in the headlights. Which might not have been the best analogy since Olivia was quite sure she was also a werewolf, but it was all she could come up with right now.

"It's okay, Sharon. Would you take the plates with you when you go?"

Sharon quickly cleared the table before leaving. Sullivan shut the door and faced her and Jack.

"He's your potential father-in-law?" Olivia said before she could curb her tongue.

Sullivan grimaced before nodding. "Sorry you had to be exposed to him. Let's get you out of here before I have to deal with him again."

Jack held out his arm as if to escort her from the room, but her little voice told her not to leave.

"I have another idea, if you're game."

Jack dropped his arm and frowned slightly, but she wouldn't be deterred.

"What is it?" Sullivan asked.

"What if I stay and observe? I can give you my opinions after the discussion."

Sullivan crossed his arms. "Actually, it's not a bad idea. I don't trust Callahan. I'm not sure what his agenda is, and I could use your help. Have an impartial witness to our conversation."

"My thoughts exactly. However, Callahan is probably going to have a problem with me staying."

Sullivan glanced at the door and then at her. "Then it's a good thing he doesn't have any say in the matter. Are you ready to find out what's on his agenda?"

"Yes." Olivia ran her hand over the back of her neck to make sure her bun was still intact. Her doctor persona needed to remain in place. Before Sullivan could open the door, Olivia spoke again. "I think we should just tell Callahan I'm an advisor and not mention me being a psychiatrist until it's necessary."

"Agreed," Sullivan said as he opened the door.

Olivia stood a little straighter and prepared herself for whatever Callahan had to say. She hoped she wasn't making a mistake by getting further involved. Last time she listened to her little voice, she threw a drink in Connor's face, and it hadn't ended well.

Connor ran along the forest edge, letting his wolf set the pace. Even running flat-out, his wolf was not satisfied, as his still-clenched muscles testified.

Connor.

Connor slowed to a jog. *Yeah, Jack?*

Callahan showed up early. He's meeting with Sullivan.

Where's Olivia? Did you get her out of there?

Jack hesitated for a moment. *Not exactly. She convinced Sullivan to let her sit in on the discussion.*

Of course she did. Damn it!

Where are you? Do you have eyes on her? Connor asked.

I'm in the room. Between Sullivan's two advisors and Callahan's two, the room is stuffed full of wolf.

With Little Red Riding Hood smack dab in the damn middle. Connor barely stopped himself from howling.

Can you protect her if all hell breaks loose?

Yeah.

I'm not very far away. Heading there now.

Connor took off, his four legs tearing across the ground as he weaved between the trees toward the pack lands. What was Olivia doing? She shouldn't be involved with whatever dirty business Callahan had planned. Connor was sure the East Coast alpha was up to no good and was going to try and bring Sullivan down. He didn't want Olivia to end up as collateral damage.

And as much as Connor trusted Jack to protect her, it meant there wasn't anyone in the room to back Sully up. Connor couldn't rely on any of their pack right now, so the team would have to make sure nothing happened to Sullivan. Throwing a stubborn woman into the mix was the last thing they needed to worry about.

He made it to the perimeter of alpha land and stopped at one of the clothing caches stashed throughout the forest for the pack to put on once they transitioned to human. Even though wolves weren't shy about nudity, Connor doubted he would be welcome in the alpha's lodge if he strolled in naked.

Connor transitioned faster than he should have, and his bones felt like they were going to burst through his skin. He ignored the pain while he yanked on a pair of sweatpants from the metal box, along with a long-sleeve T-shirt, before jogging to the alpha's lodge. Several members of the security team stood guard at the front entrance, but Connor didn't waste time with niceties. Luckily, they didn't give him any shit before he jogged through the front door and down the hall to the meeting room. Another guard stood outside the door.

"I'm supposed to be inside. Alpha's orders." A lie, but he didn't care, as long as it got him in the room.

The guard opened the door, and Connor slipped inside, standing over to the side so he could quickly scan the room. Callahan's advisors sat on one side of the long table, with Sullivan's across from them.

Jonathan glared at him for a moment, but Connor ignored him. Callahan sat at one far end and Sullivan at the other, and Olivia perched on Sullivan's right with her pen in hand, hovering over her usual notepad. She didn't even glance in his direction, instead watching the East Coast alpha intently. Jack stood behind Sully and Olivia, not-so-subtly standing guard. Good.

Callahan cleared his throat. "As I was saying, we need to move up the timing of the wedding."

Sullivan shook his head. "I'm not going to discuss a wedding before I've met the bride. We agreed there would be a preliminary meeting and time spent together before anything is finalized."

Callahan frowned. "My daughter will not be used as an excuse for you to back out of this arrangement."

Sullivan leaned forward slightly. "Since I didn't know about this 'arrangement,' as you're calling it, until a couple weeks ago, I refuse to be rushed into anything. This isn't just about me. It's about your daughter, too. She needs to agree to this as well."

Callahan waved his hand in a dismissive gesture. "My daughter will agree."

Connor watched Olivia's face. She appeared very stoic, but her eyes flared slightly at Callahan's dismissal of his daughter's feelings. She didn't like the alpha, but then Connor could understand why.

"I would like to speak to your daughter as well.

When can we schedule a meeting?" Sullivan pushed.

"Maeve will arrive here tomorrow evening. I wanted to be sure you're taking this seriously before I brought her here."

Sullivan's eyes narrowed. "I'm taking this very seriously."

Callahan stood, as if he was the one ending the meeting—pompous ass—and his advisors stood as well.

Sullivan remained seated for several seconds, as did his advisors. Callahan's advisors looked back and forth between their alpha and Sullivan, who wasn't going to be pushed around.

After some awkward seconds, Sullivan leisurely stood up, and his advisors followed suit. Olivia got up and stood by Jack while Callahan and his advisors filed out of the room. Sullivan excused his advisors and they left as well, but not before Jonathan scowled at Connor.

A minute later, Connor shut the door and turned to their alpha, Jack, and Olivia...who seemed to notice him for the first time. She took in his clothes and stared at his bare feet, pursing her lips as if she were trying to figure out a puzzle.

Sullivan spoke first. "I want your first impressions, Olivia."

Olivia? When the hell did he start calling her by her first name? Connor's wolf paced under his skin.

Olivia picked up her paper and glanced down at it for a moment, as if to gather her thoughts. "He is egotistical to the extreme. I don't know if he's overcompensating because he's confronting you in your territory, which puts him at a disadvantage, or if he's like this normally. My gut tells me he is normally like this, which he could be a full-blown narcissist.

"He's volatile, and I think if challenged, he will strike out. I have a question. Are werewolves patriarchal? Or do women have a say in things?"

"Absolutely women have a say." Sullivan almost growled the words.

"I thought so from our earlier conversations, but I wanted to confirm it before I gave you my other thoughts. I am very concerned that his daughter is not allowed to disobey her father in any form or fashion. If that's the case, she won't say no to the engagement, which will put you in the proverbial hot seat if you don't agree to marry her."

Sullivan crossed his arms. "That's what I've been afraid of. I still don't understand what he hopes to gain by forcing us to marry."

"Maybe it does have to do with wanting his grandchildren to control the West Coast pack someday."

Jack spoke. "He doesn't strike me as a long-term planner. I think he wants power now."

"I agree," Sullivan said.

Olivia set down her notebook. "I would like to be here tomorrow when you meet Maeve. I can get a better read on things by observing her and how her father treats her."

"I don't think so." Connor had been quiet up to this point, but he was done.

Three sets of eyes focused on him.

Sullivan frowned. "Explain your concerns, Connor."

"I don't think Dr. Jennings should be pulled into this issue any further. We're right, we don't know Callahan's agenda, and we have enough challenges without the added responsibility of protecting her right now."

Olivia stepped closer. "Sullivan has an entire security team to protect him."

"We can't rely on them."

She looked at all three men before turning back to Connor. "What aren't you telling me?"

"May I have a moment alone with Dr. Jennings?" Connor asked Sullivan.

"I think the question should be directed at me, don't you?" Olivia asked.

Wow, she was a spitfire. It made Connor want to throw her over his shoulder and haul her composed little self out of here.

"I would like to discuss this with you in private for a few minutes."

Olivia nodded, and Sullivan and Jack left the room. Connor waited until the door closed before speaking.

"Why are you getting in the middle of this?"

Olivia narrowed her eyes. "You asked me to get in the middle of this."

"No, Julia asked you to interview Sullivan and write up a report, not sit in a room with a bunch of hotheaded wolves and psychoanalyze Callahan. If he's as volatile as you say he is, he might come after you."

"I appreciate your concern, but I'll be fine. I've dealt with unstable people before."

His wolf clawed to get out. "Don't dismiss me with your doctor voice."

"Excuse me?"

"This is not a controlled environment, Olivia. Callahan is not just a person, he's a wolf. I know you're trying to help, but you're out of your league here."

"I think that's Sullivan's call to make."

"Sullivan asked our team to be here to prevent a pack war."

And there went the telltale eyebrow above the top of her glasses. "Isn't it also why I'm here?"

Connor gritted his teeth. "Yes, and you've completed your job."

"I think it would be helpful to your pack if I'm here tomorrow night. I want to see what Sullivan is up against. I'll come for the initial meeting with Maeve, and then I'll leave. Does that work?"

Connor let out a hard breath. He knew with one hundred percent certainty that she would not back down, and would pull Sully over to her side. Hell, Sully was already on her side. Connor was convinced she could talk anyone into anything and make them think they came up with the idea themselves.

"Fine. Tomorrow, and then you're done."

Diabolical and beautiful. A deadly combination, but he couldn't succumb. He would protect her from herself and then get her far away from his world. Keeping her safe. That was his priority.

Observe first, talk second.

CHAPTER 16

Olivia discovered early in her career she could learn a lot about people by standing back and observing them. She had half joked with Connor about her objective listening skills, but they were invaluable to a therapist. The way something was expressed often told more than the words themselves. And mannerisms like tics, gestures, any type of physical reaction gave her an indication of what was wrong even when her patients couldn't tell her or were unaware of it.

And yet she didn't understand Connor at all.

He didn't want to get involved with her—his words—and yet he felt the need to protect her and steer her away from pack craziness, also his words.

She wasn't sure why Connor was so obsessed with removing her from the situation. His protectiveness was sweet in one way and overpowering in another. She had wanted to call him on it yesterday, but she was afraid he would have dug in his heels and prevented her from coming tonight.

Now she stood in the meeting room with Sullivan

and overprotective Connor, waiting for Callahan and his daughter. Callahan had insisted that he didn't want a bunch of Sullivan's men in the room when Maeve arrived. With each additional demand from the East Coast alpha, Olivia worried what she would discover today.

The door opened and Callahan strutted or stomped (*strumped?*) into the room. A moment later he seemed to realize his daughter was not right behind him. He turned and gestured to whoever stood out in the hallway to hurry up.

And then she walked into the room.

Maeve Callahan was one of the most beautiful women Olivia had ever seen. Long, dark brown hair flowed down to her shoulders, and her hazel eyes were so bright they seemed lit from within. She was petite but perfectly proportioned. Maybe Olivia would have been a wee bit intimidated by her if she hadn't also noticed that when Maeve entered the room, she quickly took in her surroundings, as if searching for a possible escape route.

She also placed herself just shy of Callahan's reach. Olivia's little voice wasn't just talking to her, it was screaming in warning.

Maeve didn't look any of the men in the face, which, given the circumstances, was somewhat understandable, but paired with what Olivia had seen already, it concerned her even more.

"Maeve. Come meet your future husband," Callahan ordered as she walked over to the alpha.

"Sullivan. This is Maeve."

For the most part Sullivan kept his composure, although his eyes flared slightly as she walked closer to him. "It's nice to meet you, Maeve."

She stared at the ground while she responded. "It's nice to meet you too."

Callahan cleared his throat.

Maeve looked up at Sullivan. "You have a lovely home."

Sullivan smiled tightly. "Thank you. I'll give you a tour later if you'd like."

"She would like it," Callahan answered for her.

Olivia suppressed a groan. This was incredibly awkward, even for her, an impartial observer. Sullivan and Maeve would never truly get to know each other with Callahan hovering over them, speaking for Maeve.

"I'd like to spend some time with Maeve." Apparently, Sullivan had come to the same conclusion.

Callahan gave him a puzzled look. "You're spending time with her right now."

"Alone."

A scowl replaced his puzzled expression. "You can't be alone with her."

Seriously? They weren't in Regency England, for goodness' sake. "I'll stay in the room with them," Olivia announced.

Callahan acknowledged her for the first time. "I don't know you."

Olivia normally would have counted to ten before responding, but she didn't think subtlety would work with Callahan. "I'm confused by your objection. If you're so concerned about your daughter's welfare, then why did you agree to the wedding contract in the first place?"

Callahan scowled at her. "This is not your concern."

"I'm here to help facilitate this process. I would think my concerns would be your concern as well."

"I will let you stay in here with them," Callahan replied, although it was more like a declaration, "but *he* needs to leave."

Connor's eyes narrowed, but after a nod from Sullivan, he left the room with Callahan.

Olivia smiled at Maeve. "Hello, Maeve, I'm Olivia. I'm going to sit over there so you two can have some time together."

Maeve nodded while her eyes darted around the room like she wanted to be anywhere but here. Olivia's heart went out to the nervous girl.

"Would you like to take a seat?" Sullivan asked, before pulling out the chair for her at the head of the table.

Maeve sat down and watched Sullivan sit down to her right. Olivia was happy to see Sullivan send the unspoken message that he didn't need to be in the head seat. She wasn't sure if he had consciously done it, but she leaned toward thinking he did. From what she had seen so far, Sullivan was very good at reading people.

Maeve stared at her hands, which were clenched in her lap. Sullivan glanced over at Olivia for a moment, and she gestured for him to start things off.

"Okay. I'm not sure how to begin. Is it all right if I tell you I was nervous about meeting you?"

Maeve finally looked up at him. "You were?"

"Yeah. This whole situation isn't exactly normal, even for werewolves. So why don't we do this? Is there something you want to know about me? You can ask me anything."

Maeve's eyes widened, and she opened her mouth…but then shut it before speaking.

Sullivan kept talking as if she wasn't floundering. "All right, I'll start. Favorite food? I love meatball subs and I can't stand lima beans."

She hesitated and then finally blurted, "I love fried chicken and I hate cabbage."

"Favorite movie? I would say *The Godfather*."

"*Never Been Kissed*," Maeve replied.

Olivia closed her eyes for a moment. The irony in

Maeve's choice was not lost on her. Apparently Maeve lived a very sequestered life.

"Oh, I like *Dodge Ball*, too," she said.

Now that was surprising.

Sullivan chuckled. "That movie is ridiculous."

A grin tugged at Maeve's mouth. "Ben Stiller is so stupid in it. I like to watch movies that make me laugh until my stomach hurts."

"Me too." Sullivan sat back a little bit as if he was relaxing into the conversation.

"I don't get to go to the movie theater, so the movies I see are all older ones on TV."

That had Sullivan sitting up again. "Maybe we can watch something together...unless you don't want to spend time with me."

"No. I want to. Did I say something I shouldn't have?"

"Absolutely not. I just don't want to force you to do something you don't want to do."

She studied Sullivan for a moment, like a puzzle she was trying to solve. Why did this make Olivia believe this young woman had never been given a choice before? It made Olivia want to find Callahan and give him a piece of her mind before she punched him in the face. A totally childish, non-doctor reaction, but it didn't make it any less valid.

"What's your favorite movie snack?"

"It's silly. Popcorn with chocolate mixed in."

Sullivan laughed. "That's my favorite too. The chocolate melts on the popcorn, and it's a sweet and salty mess."

Maeve smiled, and Olivia sucked in her breath. If she had thought Maeve was pretty before, she was breathtaking when she smiled.

Sullivan blinked and then blinked again before the alpha seemed to collect himself. The couple continued to talk while Olivia watched Maeve relax a little bit.

The relaxation was short-lived. After a few more minutes, Connor and Callahan came into the room, and the East Coast alpha insisted it was time for them to leave. Olivia watched Maeve retreat into her shell as the two alphas discussed the next meeting.

Olivia walked over to Maeve while the men were occupied. "I'll be here to help you during your visit. I'm available to talk anytime."

Maeve glanced over at her father to see if he was listening, but he seemed too busy with Sullivan to pay them any mind. But Olivia felt someone watching them. Connor stood over to the side, his eyes narrowed on her.

He probably heard what she said, but she wasn't going to back down, even though she was breaking her promise to him.

After what she just saw, she had to help. She would have to deal with Connor, but it was a small price to pay if she could help Maeve.

Connor had always been the laid-back twin. Where Jack was tightly wound and downright grumpy at times, Connor was the one who didn't let things get to him. Until he met Dr. Olivia Jennings. He heard what she said to Maeve, which was the opposite of what she promised him yesterday.

Had she lied to him? He didn't think she would lie. She had been too honest up to this point. But now that he'd spent more time around Callahan, he wanted her far, far away from him. There was no way this was going to end well between the packs.

He clenched his fists as Callahan and Maeve left. As soon as the door shut behind them, Olivia turned to Sullivan.

"What do you think?" she asked Sullivan, surprising Connor.

Sullivan scowled. "I think she's scared."

"Yes. Her actions are similar to many of my patients who have been emotionally or physically abused."

A growl erupted from Sullivan, and Olivia jerked.

Connor started to step in between the two, but Sullivan held up his hands in front of him.

"I'm sorry, Olivia. I didn't mean to scare you."

Olivia straightened her jacket. "It's okay. I know how upsetting this can be. I told Maeve I would be available to help her during her visit. Hopefully, if I can get some time alone with her, I might be able to get her to confide in me."

Sullivan blew out a deep breath. "I had a helluva time letting her leave with him just now."

Olivia's brows drew together. "Sullivan—"

"Don't worry, I don't mean it in a crazy stalker way. She just seems so fragile. I can't help wanting to protect her."

"I know. Me too."

Connor cursed to himself. How the hell was he going to convince her to back off now?

Olivia and Sullivan discussed a few more things before saying their goodbyes. Connor walked her outside and directed her to his SUV.

"I thought Sullivan's driver was going to take me home."

"Change of plans."

They rode in silence for a long while, Connor trying to figure out how to get his point across without having her take it the wrong way.

"I want to thank you for meeting with Sullivan." There, nice and nonconfrontational.

"You're welcome."

He felt her gaze on him, and he glanced over for a moment.

She gave him her raised-eyebrow stare.

"What?"

"I know I told you I would be finished after tonight, but I can't walk away from this."

Connor kept his eyes on the road. "Why? This isn't your problem, your fight. You did what you were asked to. And then some."

"I think Maeve's in trouble. I want to make sure she's safe."

Connor's wolf paced under his skin. "What about *your* safety? Do I need to repeat our conversation from last night about you being in over your head? The one where you promised you were done?"

"I'm confused by this whole conversation, Connor. Why do you think you get to tell me what I can and can't do? We're not friends. We're not anything, really. You made that crystal clear when you told me not to get attached to you."

So much for her not taking things the wrong way.

"Olivia, I'm sorry I offended you the other night. I didn't handle it well at all. But in some ways I was right. You seem to be getting awfully upset, which is exactly why I wanted to avoid a misunderstanding to begin with."

Olivia blew out a hard breath. "You are the perfect case study of the Peter Pan syndrome. The consummate player. Don't let anyone near, because then you may need to open up to them. You're scared to death of relationships and don't want anyone to get close to you. I'm not the one with the issue here, Connor."

Connor gripped the steering wheel, hard. Holy hell, the woman had no problem throwing her shrink-speak around. "I'm so glad you've got me all figured out."

He pulled down her street and double parked in front of her apartment building.

He turned to her. Her cheeks were pink and her eyes were bright. "What about you, Doc?"

"What about me?"

"You could be the poster child for OCD. If you think I'm avoiding relationships, you need to look in the mirror. You are so rigid with your routine and your life, there's no room for relationships. Everything is about control with you. You won't become involved with someone because it would mean relinquishing control, which scares the crap out of you."

"You don't know me."

"No, I think you don't know yourself."

She opened the door and climbed out of the SUV without another word.

Connor watched her walk safely into the building before slamming his hands on the steering wheel.

Damn it! He was a son of a bitch. What the hell had gotten into him? How many times had he been called a player and never let it bother him? But when it came from her, it got past the damn barriers he had built up. Because the more time he spent with her, the more she got under his skin, and what she said mattered to him.

Peter Pan syndrome my ass.

The truth doesn't necessarily set you free.

CHAPTER 17

Olivia stood in front of the mirror and looked at herself. Really looked. She had on her doctor clothes—a suit jacket, pants, and blouse. Her ever-present glasses had slipped down her nose a bit in her rush to get into her apartment building and away from Connor. But her bun was still in place.

Did she wear them because they were professional, or because they were her suit of armor? Another form of control?

Olivia reached up and began pulling the pins out of her hair one by one while she went over her argument with Connor.

Words held power. And words hurt, but words edged with truth cut. Truth was the last thing she wanted to hear. Because it would mean facing what was wrong with her. But wasn't it the crux of almost everyone's problems? Avoid the truth and you could lock the pain of the past away.

But the price of avoidance was foregoing the potential for happiness. Or so she told her patients.

Apparently she couldn't heed her own advice.

Hadn't she used her words to hurt him as well? And she knew better. But she lashed out at him, and he retaliated in kind. Every time she got near him, she couldn't control her emotions or what she said — or herself, for that matter. He was a match to her fuse, and she needed to douse the fire that could easily burn out of control if she let it.

Pulling the last pin out, Olivia ran her fingers through her hair before stripping and dropping her clothes to the floor and then stepping into the shower. With warm water streaming over her head and shoulders, she lathered up her shampoo and washed her hair, letting the steam and lavender scent surround her. Deep breaths. In and out. In and out.

Olivia rinsed her hair and quickly scrubbed her body before leaving the shower and wrapping first her head, and then her body in a bath towel. Then she stared at herself in the mirror some more.

God. She truly was bordering on being obsessive. Oh, who was she kidding? Connor was right. If he was the poster child for Peter Pan, she was the spokesperson for OCD. Everything had to be in its place. And while she might not know what her patients were going to say during their sessions, she ultimately controlled the surroundings and how she was perceived.

And maybe it was why she was so wobbly right now. She was in a whole new world, with supernatural beings who were real, and she had jumped right into their midst. Where was her controlled environment now?

Did she honestly want to continue down this path? It was one thing to meet with Sullivan and have a few conversations. It was another to support Maeve and potentially watch out for her in a roomful of werewolves.

Olivia blew out a hard breath and wandered into her bedroom. She had not been this off-kilter in a long time, but maybe it wasn't a bad thing. There was something to be said for ordering something new off the menu. When it came to helping Maeve, that is, not her feelings—nope, too strong a word—her *thoughts* where Connor was concerned.

Which was why she couldn't agree to step back from this, regardless of Connor's arguments. She might be scared and not in control, but so was Maeve. The young woman was in deep trouble and needed someone to help her. And maybe Olivia saw herself in Maeve. She owed it to herself and, by extension, to Maeve, to see this through.

Connor pulled up to the house he shared with Giz and dropped his head back against the headrest. He had just come from the woods, where he let his wolf take over and almost run him into the ground.

His body ached from the pounding, but his wolf was still not satisfied. He was pissed at Connor for upsetting Olivia. Hell, *Connor* was pissed at Connor for upsetting Olivia.

He climbed out of his SUV with a groan and staggered inside, stopping at the sight of Jack and Giz sitting on the couch staring at him. Even Giz's cat, Monster, narrowed his too-intelligent eyes at him from his perch on the chair. The cat had a chunk of his ear missing and looked like someone splattered him with gray paint. And then there was his less than stellar personality. But now was not the time to dwell on a cranky cat.

From the expression on Jack's face, he had to deal with his grumpy twin instead.

"Where have you been?" Jack asked. "Sullivan said you left his place over two hours ago."

"Went for a run."

"I've been trying to reach you and you blocked me," Jack pushed.

"I needed some time on my own to clear my head."

"Did something happen at the meeting with Callahan today? Sullivan didn't mention much when I spoke to him."

"Not really," Connor said. "Sully met Maeve and spent some time with her. She's beautiful."

Giz and Jack glanced at each other before Jack continued, "Why do you say it like that's a bad thing?"

"Because she is also jumpy as all hell. Olivia thinks Callahan may be abusing her."

Giz set his computer tablet off to the side. "He beats her?" Giz growled. Monster made a low noise in his throat too, as if he understood what they were talking about.

"Possibly. Or it might be verbal or emotional abuse."

"Damn it." Jack stood and faced his brother. "Now what?"

"Olivia is going to try to get Maeve to relax and talk to her."

Jack frowned. "I thought Olivia was bowing out of this after today?"

"She planned to until she met Maeve. I can't get her to back off now."

"Why is it your job to get her to back off at all?" Jack asked.

Connor crossed his arms. "Come on, Jack. Do you honestly think it's safe for her to get in any deeper? Callahan has some sort of agenda we know nothing about, and the bastard probably abuses his own daughter. Olivia doesn't need to be a part of it."

"From what I've seen of Dr. Jennings, she can take care of herself. She might be exactly what Maeve needs."

"Have you forgotten someone tried to kill Sully? This isn't a game, and I don't want her to get hurt."

"So we protect her. That's what we do." Jack squinted at him for a moment. "Why are you getting so worked up about Dr. Jennings? Is something going on with you two?"

"No! Of course not. She's infuriating. She won't listen to anything I have to say." Connor paced. "Besides, I only do casual. I'm not looking for a relationship. And you already know I'm better off on my own."

Jack smirked at him. "The wolf doth protest too much."

Giz made a scoffing noise.

Connor stopped his pacing and wheeled on Giz, who still sat on the couch. "Do you have something to contribute to this conversation?"

Monster jumped off his chair to the coffee table, walking between Connor and Giz.

Giz stood up. "I suspect you don't want to hear my opinion."

"Why would you say that?"

"Because you're not going to like what I have to say."

"Try me."

"I think you're full of shit, Connor."

Connor gaped at his teammate. Giz normally didn't speak up.

"Because?"

"Because you talk about not wanting a relationship. About being a player. But I think the only one being played around here is you. There is more to life than sex. It's great, but what do you think it will be like with someone you love and want to spend the rest of your life with? Stop limiting yourself, and stop running scared."

Connor clenched his fists. "I'm not scared."

Monster let out a deep meow. Even the cat was going to weigh in on this?

Giz glanced from Monster to Connor's hands. "Sure you are. From what little I've heard about your childhood, your parents' marriage was awful. Other than Jack, you had no one to depend on growing up. So it isn't surprising you don't trust in love."

Connor's wolf howled in his head. Jack took a step toward him, and Connor backed away.

He laughed, the sound harsh and rough to his own ears. "Shit, Giz. Are you psychoanalyzing me? I think I've had enough psychoanalysis today."

"No. You asked me, and I'm telling you what I think. I'm your friend, and good friends aren't afraid to give each other a kick in the ass when necessary."

Connor could only nod, because the words were stuck in his throat.

Giz continued. "All I ask is for you to give it some thought. I haven't seen you this invested in a woman in all the time I've known you."

Jack put his hand on Connor's shoulder. "What he said, little brother."

Connor smiled and the tension lessened in the room. "Cut it out with the little brother crap."

Jack grinned in return.

Connor turned to Giz. "You don't say much, but when you do, it packs a wallop."

Giz shrugged. "Just 'cause I don't like to hear myself talk all the time doesn't mean I don't have anything important to say."

"Got it. I'll take what you said under advisement." Connor looked down at Monster. "The same goes for your opinion."

Monster blinked at him before jumping down and marching away, his tail high in the air.

Dismissed by a cat.

Connor sighed. Maybe he was only fooling himself when he said he didn't want a relationship with Olivia, but what he wouldn't say to Giz — or even his twin, for that matter — was, even if he might want to be with Olivia, a voice inside him argued that he didn't deserve to be with her.

Attraction is not logical. It's visceral,
and sometimes overpowering.

CHAPTER 18

Olivia looked around the table at the women surrounding her. She had been invited to a meeting at For Better or For Worse, Alex's family's wedding planner business. A surreal experience before the meeting had even begun, since she felt like she knew the women sitting around the table, even though she hadn't met most of them before today. But she had heard about them in Alex's and Julia's sessions.

Alex's grandmother, Lorinda, sat at the head of the table. She was exactly as Alex had described, a polished, professional woman. On Olivia's right side sat Alex, and then Sheila, a beautiful blond who, according to Alex, ran the healthy bride segment of the business. To the left sat Julia and then Peggy, the office manager and sister to Alex's husband, Devin, and Julia's deceased husband, Thomas. Peggy was as carefree as Alex and Julia had described her, today wearing a floor-length dress in a bold flower print and bright blue glasses.

For some reason Olivia had been directed to sit at the other end of the table. She wasn't sure why she was invited to the meeting, but curiosity won out, and she agreed to come.

Lorinda gave Olivia a regal nod. "Welcome, Dr. Jennings. We're happy you could join us today."

"Thank you, Lorinda. I'll be honest and say I'm not sure I should be here."

Alex frowned. "Why not?"

"Because I'm yours and Julia's doctor. I think spending time here might be a conflict of interest. I have to keep a professional distance from you both if I'm going to continue counseling you."

"We have a simple solution for that," Alex said before nodding to Julia.

Julia spoke up. "We're no longer in need of your services."

Olivia held up her hands. "That's not what I meant. I'm not giving you an ultimatum, and I would not have agreed to help with the packs if I thought it would interfere with our counseling agreement."

Julia cocked her head. "We know. But Alex and I talked about this before you got here, since we had a sneaking suspicion you might have issues with working with us outside our sessions. And we both think we're in a good place now, thanks to you, so we're ready to stop them."

"Unless you disagree with us?" Alex asked.

"No. I think you're both doing fine."

Alex clapped her hands together. "Good. We can definitely use your help with all this."

All what? "I'm not sure what I can contribute here, but I'll do what I can."

Lorinda chimed in. "You've met Callahan and Maeve, which will help us as we plan the upcoming pack events. The first one is the welcome reception happening Thursday night."

"It's in two days," Olivia said. "Can you plan something quickly?"

Peggy typed rapidly on the laptop sitting on the table in front of her. "Absolutely. We already knew the reception was happening this week. The good news is they're having it at the pack reception hall, so we didn't have to book a venue, and we already had a caterer on standby. They have staff who will be bartending and serving at the reception."

"Menu finalized?" Lorinda asked.

Peggy glanced at her computer screen. "Yes. Finger foods, with plenty of meat choices for the wolves."

"Do we have any special restrictions we have to work around?" Sheila asked. "Vampires? Gargoyles? Any demon factions we're concerned about?"

"Vampires?" Olivia gasped and the women all turned toward her at once.

"Are you all right, dear?" Lorinda asked.

A couple of dark spots danced in front of her eyes for a moment before Olivia took a deep breath and nodded.

Julia leaned toward her. "I'm sorry. We forgot you don't know about all the different factions."

"Factions. Is that what we're calling them?" Olivia mumbled.

"For this first reception it will be pack only, and the team will be providing security," Peggy answered.

"Team?" Olivia asked.

"You know Devin, Jack, and Connor. Sheila's husband, Charlie, and Giz are also on the team," Julia answered. "They work for the supernatural Tribunal to help keep the peace and make sure humans don't find out about the supernatural. Except when glowing bellies surprise you."

Alex stuck out her tongue at Julia. "Not funny."

"Back on task, ladies," Lorinda intervened. "Dr.

Jennings, normally for this type of event, Sullivan will introduce Callahan and Maeve to the pack. Do you think there's anything we need to worry about concerning this?"

"Please call me Olivia. I think Sullivan will be fine handling the intro. Callahan will expect to be put in the spotlight, but I'm not sure Maeve will want to share it with him."

"We've dealt with shy brides before," Lorinda said.

It was far more than the case of a shy bride, but Olivia wasn't going to bring it up here. If she had her way, there would be no wedding. Maeve didn't strike her as being ready for a marriage. But first impressions could be deceiving.

"We can work to make her feel more comfortable," Lorinda continued. "What else are we forgetting?"

The women each went around the table and listed some more items while Peggy made note of them on her computer.

"I don't know why I can't supervise the reception," Alex said.

Lorinda patted Alex's hand. "Because Peggy is handling it, dear. Your little one can't be trusted to not make himself known right now."

Alex rested her hand on her baby bump. "It's not like a bunch of wolves would be surprised. They're *wolves*."

Peggy laughed. "You know my dear brother is not going to let you anywhere near that party. He is going to protect you and the peanut you have growing inside you."

Julia nodded. "I'm meeting with Sullivan today, and Jack insists he has to go with me."

Alex sat up straighter. "Why are you meeting with Sullivan? Did you find a way to get him out of the contract?"

"I'm working with Sullivan on some pack business, Alex."

"Uh-ohh, she's using her enigmatic lawyer-speak," Alex countered.

Julia smiled. "Yep, and I know not knowing what's going on is killing you, but there is such a thing as attorney-client privilege."

"Fine, but you better tell us everything you can when it isn't privileged information," Alex pouted.

"Why is everyone so concerned about our safety?" Olivia asked.

The women chuckled at her question until Alex spoke up. "Because they're overprotective cavemen."

Peggy wagged her finger. "You all chose to pair up with the cavemen. Sure, Devin, Charlie, and Jack can be a little bit over-the-top when it comes to protecting you three, but you signed up for it."

"Connor too," Olivia mumbled.

She realized her comment was louder than she intended when all eyes focused on her again.

Alex's expression seemed a little too smug. "Is Connor being protective?"

"He keeps insisting I shouldn't help any more with this negotiation, but I can't—I *won't*—let this go until I know Maeve has a say in her future. I'm not sure why he's so concerned. It seems a bit excessive to me...unless I don't know the full story."

Awkward silence.

"You're not going to tell me what's going on, are you?" Olivia asked no one in particular.

"There's nothing to tell," Alex said, her eyes widening to almost comic proportions.

Olivia could feel her mouth quirk up into a grin before she could stop herself. "You're a horrible liar, Alex."

Alex gaped at her. "I can't believe you said that to me."

"You're not my patient anymore, Alex. I don't have to pull any punches."

"You used to pull your punches?" Julia said. "I seem to remember several punches during my sessions when you didn't hold back."

"We're in trouble now," Alex said.

Peggy and Sheila laughed.

Peggy patted her hand. "We like you, Olivia."

"Indeed," Lorinda said. "Welcome to the team."

Olivia looked around the table at the group of strong, capable women who were welcoming her into the fold. She was excited, humbled, and honored to be accepted. She also got the impression she would never be bored with these women. They might not fit in her normal, controlled world, but that was more than okay.

A rack of party dresses and gowns rolled past Olivia as the room transformed into a makeshift boutique.

Olivia was impressed because the designer had come to Sullivan's lodge for Maeve's fittings. Since the welcome reception was tonight, the boutique owner would make any minor alterations on-site. Apparently Lorinda could be very persuasive with her business associates. And when you only had two days to prepare for an event, drastic measures were called for.

Olivia had switched her afternoon appointments around so she could spend some time with Maeve. And, as luck would have it, this was the first time Maeve was not being trailed by Callahan or by his bodyguards. But then they couldn't exactly be in the room while she tried on clothes.

The designer, who had introduced herself as Janine, selected several gowns for Maeve to try on. "You are going to be a joy to dress."

Maeve blushed as she stepped behind the changing screen with the first gown. And after she'd modeled several more, Olivia agreed with Janine. Maeve looked great in all of them. But the one she wore now was the winner.

Maeve stood in front of a mirror on a small, raised circular dais that had been brought in for the fittings as well.

The long, emerald green gown hugged her petite figure perfectly and made her hazel eyes appear iridescent green.

Janine clapped her hands together. "This is the one. Would you wait right there for a few moments while I get my sewing kit and mark the necessary alterations?"

Maeve agreed and Janine bustled out of the room.

Maeve ran her hands down her sides. They appeared to be trembling.

"How are you doing with all this?"

Maeve's hands froze. "I'm fine," she answered immediately.

Olivia didn't need her training to know she was lying. "Really? I'm feeling overwhelmed myself, and this party isn't being thrown in my honor."

Maeve stared at her in the mirror as if gauging how much to say. "It is a bit overwhelming, but it will be worth it in the end."

Interesting word choice. The end of what? "Do you think you would like to move here?"

Maeve nodded. "I'm marrying Sullivan. He'll expect me to live here with him."

"You've already decided to marry Sullivan?"

"Of course. Sullivan will make a good husband, and our marriage will help unite the packs."

Her answer sounded rehearsed, and Olivia didn't buy it. "What do *you* want to do, Maeve?"

She frowned. "I don't understand."

"Throw your father, and Sullivan, and the pack out of the equation. What would you like to do, or be, or visit?"

Maeve shook her head. "I can't throw them out of the equation."

"Humor me."

She bit her lip for a moment before responding. "I would want to do something with kids. Teach."

"It's a wonderful occupation. Do you want to get a degree in education?"

Maeve shrugged. "I'll be busy enough when I have my own children. I don't think the alpha will want me anywhere but here."

Olivia kept her face neutral. "I can't speak for Sullivan, but I think you should discuss the idea of teaching with him."

Maeve's eyes widened. "No! I shouldn't have brought it up. It's a silly notion."

Olivia moved closer and rested her hand on Maeve's arm. "I don't think it's a silly notion at all. You have the right to do what you want with your life. Whether or not it includes marrying Sullivan. A marriage is a partnership. Right from the beginning you need to talk to your husband and let him know what you're looking for in your life and in the relationship."

An emotion—confusion, or maybe a little bit of pain—flashed across Maeve's face before she glanced away.

Before Olivia could ask her what was wrong, Janine returned carrying a plastic box. "Give me a moment to pin the bottom and we'll be done."

A few minutes later the boutique owner finished the pinning and unzipped the gown. "Let's get this off you, and we'll pick out Olivia's gown next."

"Oh, no. I don't need a dress."

Maeve's eyes widened. "You're not wearing what you have on to tonight's reception."

Olivia ran her hands down her outfit. She had on a gray jacket and black skirt. "What's wrong with it?"

"Nothing if you're going to the office. But tonight is black tie. And Sullivan already told me you're attending."

"But only to help you if you need something," Olivia said.

"And you would be helping me greatly by choosing a gown for tonight," Maeve said with a small grin.

So Maeve did have some backbone. Hopefully Olivia could get her to use it with Sullivan and, eventually, her father. "Fine."

Three failed gowns later, she stood on the raised dais looking at herself in the mirror. The midnight blue gown was simple but tailored. Sleeveless, with a high collar in the front and a V opening down the back, it wasn't something Olivia would normally wear since she didn't attend formal events. Her closet was full of her doctor clothes, and yoga pants and soft shirts for when she was home by herself.

Maeve nodded. "This is the one. It's beautiful on you."

The seamstress checked her over as well. "And it doesn't need to be altered. We lucked out."

"Good. It will give you more time to work on Maeve's gown, then," Olivia said.

Janine hurried out the door to finish the green gown's alterations.

Maeve gave Olivia a side-eye glance. "Connor will like your gown."

"Connor?" Olivia blurted.

"Did I get his name wrong?" Maeve said. "I've met a number of people since I got here, so I may have his name wrong. He's the one who was in the room when I met Sullivan for the first time."

"You got his name right. But why would you bring him up?"

"Because of the way he looks at you."

"He's normally irritated when he's looking at me."

Maeve laughed and then slapped her hand over her mouth as if it was a bad thing. Olivia was taken aback by how carefree she seemed, even in the split second she let herself go.

"He watches you like a hawk, or, more accurately, the way a wolf watches his mate."

Olivia shook her head. "No. No mating going on here. We actually fight more than we get along."

"If you say so."

Her heart liked what Maeve hinted at, but her head argued that Connor had repeatedly made it clear he was not into relationships. She stepped down from the dais and went behind the changing screen.

"I'll be right back," Maeve called out, and Olivia heard the door close.

She reached behind her and pulled on the zipper, which moved only an inch before refusing to budge. Darn it. Olivia tried to pull the zipper up and then down again, but it wouldn't work. The longer she tried, the more her arms ached from reaching behind her.

The door opened and she came out from behind the screen, still wrestling with the zipper.

"Maeve, I need your help."

"It's not Maeve," a deep, familiar voice answered.

Connor stood in the doorway. His eyes flared as he took her in, and heat pooled in her belly. Attraction outweighed common sense, but everyone needed to have someone look at them in just that way.

"What kind of help do you need?" he asked.

Holy Fates, he was being tested. There was no other explanation for why he had walked into this room and found her in that gown. There was nothing especially provocative about it, but the same couldn't be said for her. The deep blue next to her pale skin made him want to howl. Barbaric to a certain degree, but she brought it out in him and his wolf.

Why did he find her so damn sexy? She still had her hair pulled into a tight little bun with her glasses perched on her nose, but she was becoming an obsession with him. One everyone else noticed before he did. He had come to apologize for his behavior the other night, but now she had scrambled his brain. Again.

"What did you say?" she asked.

What the hell had he just said to her? How could he forget what had just come out of his mouth less than thirty seconds ago? He needed serious help. Wait...*help...but not him, her*... "I said, what kind of help do you need?"

Her cheeks flushed a light pink. "Nothing. I'm fine. Maeve should return shortly."

"Actually, I saw Maeve in the hall. She left with one of her bodyguards. Her father wanted to speak with her."

She blew out a breath. "Okay, the zipper is stuck, and I'm afraid I'm going to tear the fabric."

"I can handle a zipper."

Her eyes narrowed. "I'm sure you can."

He smiled. "Turn around."

She did. And he lost his train of thought again. The gown dipped to the middle of her back, and she had the cutest little mole between her shoulder blades.

"Connor?"

"Sorry." He gently tugged on the zipper. Nothing. He leaned closer to get a better view and caught her scent. Damn. Recently he'd made it a point to stay away from her and keep his damn wolf nose to himself.

She smelled like lavender.

Connor gripped the zipper and pulled it down, finally freeing the caught material, and she turned to face him again.

"Thank you."

He cleared his throat. "Are you wearing that to the reception tonight?"

"Yes. Maeve insisted that it was inappropriate for me to wear the business suit I had on earlier."

"Well, you look amazing."

Her pink cheeks darkened. "Was there a reason why you came in here? Something you want?"

Oh Fates, *something I want*? They were truly testing him today. "I, ah, came to apologize for what I said to you the other day."

"I'm sorry too. In fact it's my fault. I started the whole thing."

He couldn't let her take the full blame. "And I finished it."

Her face softened. "You did. Do you think we can stop fighting long enough to help Sullivan and Maeve?"

"I think it can be arranged. But you need to promise to be careful."

Thinking she would balk at his request, she surprised him when she held up her hand instead, palm out. "I promise."

Connor couldn't stop his grin. "You're not being sworn in for something."

"Right. Will you be at the reception tonight?"

"The whole team will be there as security."

"Do you think something might go wrong?" she asked.

"We're being cautious. I don't trust Callahan, and tonight several of his clan will be in attendance."

She pursed her lips. "Well, then you need to promise to be careful as well."

He held up his hand. "I promise."

Up went that eyebrow. "I'll see you later."

Connor walked out of the room and shut the door behind him before he could yank her into his arms. Instead he stationed himself outside the door to stand sentry until she'd finished changing.

Denial was no longer an option. He was in trouble when it came to this woman. The question was, should he follow Giz's advice and go for it? She screamed long-term commitment. And he didn't want to lead her on.

Did he want a relationship? Or maybe the better question was, did he think he could handle a relationship? His once-upon-a-time antisocial brother had found happiness with Julia.

Was it too far out of the realm of possibility to think he could find it too?

Why do we let fear control us so completely?

CHAPTER 19

Olivia watched from the side of the room while the guests mingled. A string quartet played softly, and the bars in opposite corners were busy serving drinks, but the double doors leading to the main meeting area were still closed. The group gathered in an anteroom, waiting to be invited into the main space for food and introductions to the visiting pack.

Once Callahan and Maeve arrived, Olivia would be Maeve's support system for the evening, but for now she checked out the pack members who entered the room. At first glance it appeared as if people were casually talking to each other, but Olivia was an expert at nonverbal communication. This room was full of uptight werewolves. And if she wasn't mistaken, the packs had congregated on opposite sides of the room.

She watched Peggy bustle around the room, making sure everything ran smoothly. Alex's husband, Devin, had introduced Olivia to the rest of the team, Charlie and Giz, whose interesting name Olivia would get to the bottom of at a later date. In the meantime, Charlie and Devin were constantly scanning the crowd like federal agents. She didn't see Giz anywhere, but Devin had mentioned he would be monitoring things using his tech gadgets.

Before she could ask anyone where the twins were, they walked into the room side by side. She still thought they could be models for some rugged outerwear company. But tonight... Tonight they wore tuxedos. She didn't want to stare, especially at Connor, whose ego was inflated enough on a regular day. But he looked amazing. His dark hair curled at the collar of his tuxedo coat and his green eyes stood out against his black jacket.

She and Connor might have made up earlier, but she still needed to tread carefully with him. She was normally calm and rational, but ever since she met the man, she had repeatedly lost control of her common sense and a few other things. And she was not one to lose control.

Although hadn't she admonished herself after her argument with Connor the other night that she needed to let go of the reins?

Jack and Connor walked over to the double doors and opened them, inviting everyone to enter the main space. When the crowd followed them into the room, it was time for Olivia to go to work. She wound her way through the people until she stood at the side door leading to where Maeve would wait until she was introduced to the pack.

Olivia nodded to Phillip, one of Sullivan's guards posted in front of the door. After a moment he opened the door and let her inside. Maeve stood by herself in the far corner of the room. She had on her new gown, but, unlike earlier today, she hugged her stomach, as if folding in on herself. Had something happened? Or was this her reaction to her imminent introduction to the pack?

Olivia walked over to her slowly, not wanting to spook her. "Hello, Maeve. The green is a lovely color on you."

Maeve smiled, but it didn't reach her eyes. "Thank you."

"Is there something I can get you? Some water, or something to eat?"

Maeve shook her head. "No I don't think I could eat anything right now."

"Are you worried about tonight? I'll be right beside you if you need anything, and Sullivan won't be far away either."

Maeve recoiled a little at Sullivan's name.

Olivia took a step closer and reached out her hand. "Maeve, what's wrong? Has something happened?"

Maeve jerked away. "No. Everything's fine."

Red clouded Olivia's vision for a moment, and she took a breath, tamping down her own emotions, which were not important right now. This was about Maeve. Olivia scanned her quickly, but didn't see any bruises on her arms or shoulders. "Did someone hurt you, Maeve?"

Terror suffused the girl's face before she pasted a fake smile on top of it. "Of course not. Everything's fine. I'm just a little nervous right now. I don't want to say or do the wrong thing tonight."

Olivia moderated her tone, hoping it would help soothe the frantic young woman. "You won't say or do anything wrong. Besides, I'm not leaving your side, so I'll be ready to help if you wish it."

Olivia had to figure out a way to get Maeve to open up to her. Not an easy task since it meant Maeve needed to trust her, and how could she trust a virtual stranger when she couldn't trust those closest to her?

Phillip stuck his head into the room. "It's time."

Maeve straightened her hunched shoulders and

walked toward him as if she were on her way to the guillotine. She paused for a moment and glanced back at Olivia.

Olivia walked up to her side. "I'll be right beside you."

They walked into the hallway where Callahan waited, obviously impatient. He looked Maeve up and down, then leaned over and murmured something in her ear. She blanched before answering him with a sharp nod.

Olivia managed to keep her expression neutral even though she would dearly love to tell the East Coast alpha to go to hell. But if she indulged her fantasy, he would keep her away from Maeve, and she wouldn't be able to help her.

They walked into the main reception space, and the crowd quieted at their arrival. Olivia caught sight of Connor across the room watching the crowd intently. Sullivan joined them with a friendly smile that he made a point of directing to Maeve. She responded with the same pasted-on smile she'd given Olivia earlier. Sullivan hesitated for a moment, and Olivia held her breath, afraid he might ask Maeve what was wrong.

"It's good to see you, Maeve. You look lovely tonight."

She didn't say anything for a moment, and Olivia could see and feel Callahan tense beside them.

"Thank you," Maeve responded. "You...look nice dressed up too."

He shrugged. "I don't have to pull out a tuxedo very often, so I worry that I might look ridiculous in it."

"You don't. You look like a spy."

Sullivan's head fell back as he laughed. "I'll take that as a compliment. Are you ready to be introduced?"

"Of course she is," Callahan interrupted.

Sullivan stared at the alpha for a moment. "I was talking to Maeve."

Callahan's back straightened and his eyes narrowed.

Maeve stepped closer to Sullivan and placed her hand on his arm. "I'm ready."

Sullivan held Callahan's stare for a drawn-out moment before turning to Maeve. "Okay. Here we go." Sullivan turned to the crowd, who had been watching the interplay with fascination. "Good evening. I'm glad you were all able to come to our reception. Tonight we have special guests. I would like to take a moment to introduce Alpha Callahan and his lovely daughter, Maeve."

A smattering of anemic applause had Olivia's warning bells going off. This was not going to be an easy evening.

Sullivan looked around the room before continuing. "There are several other East Coast pack members in attendance as well. If you haven't had a chance to introduce yourselves yet, please do so over the course of the evening. As the alpha I welcome you, as does the rest of the West Coast pack."

The more time Olivia spent with Sullivan, the more impressed she was. He had gently reminded his pack about their obligations as hosts while also introducing Callahan and Maeve.

After a couple of silent moments, people started talking again, and introductions were made while the crowd mingled. When Callahan split away from them to talk to his advisors, Maeve visibly relaxed. Sullivan frowned slightly as he caught Olivia's eye. Just as quickly, he schooled his features and continued introducing Maeve to his pack members.

Olivia stayed slightly to the side and observed the couple while they talked to the guests. There was no reason to complicate things by being part of the conversation. This was about Maeve.

But every few minutes she felt as if someone watched her and would glance around as casually as she could. At one point she caught Connor staring at her from his spot across the room. She nodded slightly before returning her attention to Sullivan and Maeve, who were on the move again, toward a new group of people.

One of Sullivan's advisors stopped him for a moment, and he suggested that Maeve and Olivia continue to the buffet table.

Maeve stiffened beside her when they walked past two women.

"What's wrong?" Olivia asked.

"Nothing."

Olivia glanced behind them and saw both women smirking at them. "Did they say something?"

"Just giving their opinion of who Sullivan should marry, and it isn't me."

"I'm sorry you had to hear it."

"They're not," Maeve said. "They knew I could hear them. Wolves have great hearing."

"Doesn't make them any less petty." Olivia gestured to the table. "Let's get some food. You have to be hungry by now."

They stepped up to the table and Olivia handed Maeve a plate before she could refuse. She added a few appetizers to her own plate and pointed out items to Maeve, who picked them up and put them on her plate. Olivia wasn't sure if she did it because she was hungry or to appease her. Either way, she hoped to get a few bites of food into the skittish young woman.

A low growl sounded somewhere nearby, and the

hairs stood up on Olivia's bare arms. She set down her plate as she turned to see where it had originated.

The crowd grew silent as they watched several East Coast and West Coast guards face off.

Sullivan muscled his way into the middle of the group. "What is going on?"

One of Sullivan's guards spoke up. "They're saying you shouldn't get to sniff around Callahan's daughter. That the West Coast pack needs to stick to their own."

Olivia looked around and saw Jack, Connor, and the rest of the team moved toward the angry men in the middle of the room. However, Callahan stood over to the side, away from the impending trouble.

Sullivan scowled. "No one has the right to sniff around anyone. That behavior is barbaric and is not tolerated in this pack. All women and men have the right to choose who they want to be with."

A harsh laugh erupted from one of Callahan's guards. "Pretty hypocritical, since there's a contract forcing her to marry you."

Angry gasps and growls filled the air.

Sullivan held up his hands. "I do not intend to force Maeve to marry me."

"You can't have her!" someone yelled.

"We don't want her tainting our pack anyway!" someone else growled.

The plate Maeve held hit the ground and shattered. The sound catalyzed the opposing groups of guards, and they lunged at each other.

Olivia shoved Maeve behind her as they backed away from the melee. They ducked out of the way as two men grappled with each other and landed on the buffet table, knocking dishes and food off to shatter and spray across the floor.

Olivia grabbed Maeve's hand and pulled her through the side door into the hall while more growls and shouts erupted from behind them. It was time to get Maeve to safety.

Olivia tripped over her gown, then yanked up the skirt, kicked off her heels, and ran down the hall with Maeve in tow. She shoved open the door to a small sitting room, then closed and locked the door.

Maeve sat on the couch hugging herself. "I'm sorry. I didn't mean to."

Olivia sat next to her and put her arm around her shoulders. "Good heavens, *you* didn't do anything, Maeve. There's nothing to apologize for."

"I'm going to be in trouble."

Why in the world she thought she was going to be in trouble for what happened in there was anyone's guess. "Everything will be fine as soon as people calm down."

They both jumped when a loud bang sounded against the door. "I know you're in there, Maeve," a man shouted. "You're mine!"

They both stood and Olivia looked around for another exit. The only other door led to a small closet. "Get in here, Maeve."

She shook her head. "You can't hide from a wolf. They'll always find you."

Maeve's statement felt like a needle piercing Olivia's heart. The sensation of being trapped reminded her of her childhood. She tried to suck air into her lungs, but it felt like she was breathing underwater.

No! She would *not* do this now. They needed to find something to protect themselves.

The door rattled again, and a moment later it burst open and slammed against the wall. Phillip stood in the doorway. Olivia pushed Maeve behind her. She had to defuse the situation somehow. She could handle this. She could...

Hair spouted on his face and hands. Olivia's heart

tried to escape her chest at the sight of his glowing eyes. He opened his mouth and fangs appeared.

Olivia froze.

Monster. The monsters were back. They were here to hurt her. To take her away from her home. *Momma! Momma!*

Connor ran down the hall after the guard who had gotten away when the fighting broke out. Where had Olivia and Maeve run off to? Were they safe?

When he heard pounding followed by the sound of splintering wood, he raced down the hall and into the room with the gaping hole where the door used to be. Olivia and Maeve were across the room, but he barely spared them a glance before he tackled the transitioning guard, slamming him on the floor face-first and pulling his arms behind him.

The man howled and tried to bite him, but Connor snapped on the magic-dampening handcuffs the team always carried and the wolf collapsed. Instead of turning to human, he remained in his half-turned wolf state, which surprised Connor, but he didn't have time to think about it now.

He stood up and saw Maeve's eyes were glowing, and she had taken a protective stance in front of Olivia, who stood as still as a statue.

"I won't hurt you," Connor said, putting his hands in the air, palms out.

A moment later, Sullivan ran into the room, followed by Jack, and Maeve flinched at their appearance.

Sullivan stopped and put his hands up, mirroring Connor's stance. "It's okay, Maeve. We're here to help."

She blinked before her eyes returned to normal. "I'm okay."

"What's wrong with Olivia?" Connor asked.

"I think she's in shock."

"Did he hurt her?" Sullivan asked.

"No. She was protecting me, but when he ran into the room and started to change, she froze."

"I'll take care of her," Connor said, yanking the wolf to his feet and handing him off to his brother so he wouldn't beat the asshole himself. "Get him out of here."

Jack hauled the attacker out of the room.

"Has the fighting stopped?" Maeve asked.

"Yes, everything is under control...for now," Sullivan answered.

Connor walked slowly toward Olivia, not caring about anything else right now but making sure she was okay. She stood stiff and unmoving.

"Will she be okay?" Maeve asked.

"I'll make sure of it," Connor said. "Why don't you guys leave us alone for a few minutes?"

Sullivan led Maeve toward the door. "Let me know if you need me to have a healer come check on her."

Connor nodded as he took a step closer to Olivia, and Sullivan closed the door behind them...or tried to, but the door hung crookedly from one hinge.

He reached for Olivia, but she cowered away from him.

"Momma!"

"It's okay, baby. It's Connor. Everything is going to be okay now."

She let out a whimper, and his heart seized at the sound. This was more than being startled. She was petrified, and her eyes were unfocused, as if she was not conscious of her surroundings. She was trapped in some sort of nightmare.

He finally got close enough to rest his hands on her shoulders as she mumbled to herself about the monsters. Should he hold her? How in the hell did he bring her back?

"Olivia," he said, shaking her gently. She stood silently, so he shook her a little harder. "Olivia!"

Finally she blinked, her eyes coming into focus. "Connor?"

"Yeah, it's me. Take a deep breath."

She sucked in a breath and blew it out again.

"That's it, baby. Do it again. Slowly."

Olivia took a deep breath. Connor could feel small tremors run down her arms. What was wrong with her? Olivia was tough, and resilient, and somehow that damn wolf man had managed to terrorize her without laying a hand on her.

He rubbed his hands along her cold arms, and she trembled harder. "I'm going to hold you for a couple minutes, okay? We need to warm you up."

She nodded, and her easy acceptance scared him more than anything else had. He pulled her slowly to him and wrapped his arms around her. She rested her cheek against the middle of his chest and he was sure she could feel his heart pounding. Hell, he could feel it in his throat.

After a couple minutes her tremors subsided and her breathing slowed to normal, but he continued to rub his hand up and down her back in a soothing gesture. He wanted to ask her what was wrong, but he didn't want to pressure her. Having her in his arms just felt right. A perfect fit and he didn't want to let her go.

"Go ahead, say it," she mumbled into his chest.

"Say what?"

"That you told me so. That you warned me I could get hurt and I ignored you. That I insisted I would be fine, but I was wrong. The first sign of trouble, and I fell apart. I couldn't even protect Maeve."

"You did protect Maeve. You got her out of the room so you two weren't caught in the fighting. Maeve said you stood in front of her to protect her, too."

"Until I froze."

"A man broke into the room who wanted to hurt you and Maeve."

"I—"

Connor moved her away from his chest so he could see her face. "Olivia. Cut yourself some slack. It was a scary situation. You didn't expect the guy to sprout hair and fangs."

Her eyes started to glaze over.

"Olivia, do not go away again. Tell me what's wrong."

"I can't. I should go make sure Maeve is okay," she said as she backed away from him.

He immediately missed her warmth, but as much as he wanted to pull her against him again, this time he was pretty sure she would protest.

"Maeve is fine. Sullivan will make sure of it."

Olivia shook her head. "She has to be terrified."

"Actually, when we got here, she was protecting you. Stood in front of you, ready to challenge me."

Her eyes widened. "Well. Good for her."

Connor smiled. Leave it to Olivia to be thinking about others instead of worrying about herself. "She must think very highly of you to risk doing something like that. She seems skittish to me."

"She is. Something or someone terrifies her. I think it stems from the way her father treats her."

"And it debilitates her."

"Yes. As you just witnessed, fear can bring someone to their knees."

"Please tell me what's wrong, Olivia. I want to help you."

She sighed. "I don't know if there is any help for me. When I was five, my mother and I were in a car accident. We were driving along a winding road and the car plowed over the side of a cliff."

Connor's gut twisted. "I'm so sorry."

"I remember the crunch of metal, and flipping through the air before landing hard on the ground outside the car." She closed her eyes. "I screamed for my momma, but she didn't come for me."

Connor fisted his hands to keep from cupping her face.

She opened her eyes, and they were filled with pain. "My mother died in the accident."

He did reach for her then, holding her small hand in his much bigger one. "Were you hurt?" He cringed at his stupid question. Of course she was hurt. She lost her mother.

Olivia understood what he'd meant to ask. "I wasn't injured physically."

"How long did it take for rescuers to find you?"

"They didn't find me. I was missing for two days before they found me by a ranger station. The station was twenty miles from where the car went off the cliff."

Connor gripped her hand tighter. "Someone must have brought you there."

"That's what the ranger and the authorities decided. How else would I have gotten there on my own? And survived without food and water? But I don't remember much of those days other than darkness and terror, and being surrounded by woods and monsters."

"You mentioned monsters earlier. What do you mean?"

"If I try to think about that time, I see flashes of fur, teeth, and glowing eyes. I've always believed my terror manifested itself into a living, breathing monster, and decades later I still can't escape those flashes."

"And today you saw those fears come to life and kick the door in." He let out a hard breath. "I'm sorry you lost your mother and for whatever happened to you in those woods. And I'm sorry you were dragged into this. I knew you shouldn't get more involved."

Olivia gazed at him for a moment. "I had no idea my fears would manifest here. But phobias often sneak up to paralyze you emotionally and physically. I know from firsthand experience."

Connor's admiration grew. "Jack told me you're an expert in phobias and grief counseling. You became a therapist to help people."

"Yes. I didn't want my patients to spend their entire lives living in fear the way I have. You asked me why I'm so controlled, Connor. I've experienced what it's like to not have control. To let the monsters almost get you. It's better to not risk the unknown. Control is comfort."

Holy Fates, how was he supposed to argue with that? He couldn't. Her safety was his only concern at this point.

"Then let's take you away from here and return you to your comfort zone."

Olivia's eyes widened at his acquiescence. Had she thought he would disagree with her?

She hesitated before replying. "As much as I want to, I can't leave now. We have to protect Maeve and stop the packs from destroying each other."

"It isn't your responsibility, Olivia. You don't have to do this."

"I'm not being totally altruistic. I need to get over this phobia. I'm sick of letting it control me."

He reached for her face and rested his palm against her cheek, brushing away a tendril of hair dangling from her normally tidy, ever-present bun. Both eyebrows rose above her glasses this time.

What was he going to do with her?

His wolf wanted him to hold her, to kiss her. But she was emotionally vulnerable right now, and he refused to take advantage of this situation...or her.

Olivia backed up a step, and even though he knew it was good she had moved away from him, he didn't like having much space between them. He captured the loose tendril of her hair that had fallen from her bun between his fingers, wondering why he'd never noticed her hair had red in it. She normally had it skinned back so tightly it appeared dark brown. But there were definitely auburn highlights. She continued to surprise him.

"Then that's what you should do. Stay and help."

He let go of her hair and dropped his hand away instead of dragging her out of there and hustling her across town to her apartment and her orderly life. To protect her and to never let her out of his sight.

But wouldn't that be nothing more than exchanging one form of control for another?

You can't make someone stand up for themselves.
If you try, you're part of the problem.

CHAPTER 20

Déjà vu settled over Olivia when she entered the small sitting room where she and Maeve had begun the evening. Maeve had changed into a pair of yoga pants and a T-shirt and sat with her legs tucked up on the couch and her arms wrapped around them.

She scrambled to her feet when she saw Olivia. "Are you okay?"

Olivia walked over to her. "I am. I'm sorry if I scared you."

Maeve shrugged. "You didn't scare me. I was worried about you."

"Connor said you protected me." Olivia sat down and beckoned for Maeve to join her.

Maeve sat down. "How could I not? You have been trying to protect me since we met. You pulled me away from the fighting and tried to help me escape without worrying about yourself. I've never had anyone do something like that for me before."

Olivia reached over and squeezed her hand. "I'm sorry to hear it. Everyone deserves to have a champion."

"Like Connor is for you. He insisted on taking care of you, practically kicked us out of the room. He told Sullivan what he was doing instead of asking permission."

Her heart picked up speed at Maeve's declaration, but she needed to stay on task.

"I take it your pack doesn't question the alpha."

Maeve's eyes widened. "No. There is no *discussing* with my father. There is just obedience."

"Where's your father now?"

"He and Sullivan are talking to the guards who got into the fight. Father tried to blame the West Coast pack for starting it, but Sullivan isn't buying it."

"And the guard who attacked us?" Olivia asked.

Maeve frowned. "Phillip was placed under arrest, but it wasn't his fault."

Olivia leaned forward. "What do you mean?"

Maeve stared at the floor. "Nothing. There's so much anger between our packs that we can't expect everything to be healed by a reception."

"And you think a wedding will heal relations?" Olivia asked.

"Yes," but she still wouldn't meet Olivia's eyes.

Did she dare push her? "Or are you saying what your father wants you to say?"

Maeve pulled her hand away from Olivia. "No. I think our two clans will benefit from the union."

"Maeve—"

"Don't!" Maeve stood and jerked on the bottom of her shirt when it rode up slightly. "They're *my* words. Mine."

Olivia wanted to kick herself for pushing too hard. She stood as well. "I'm sorry. This has been a stressful night for all of us. I didn't mean to interrogate you."

Maeve looked down at the floor again.

"I just want to help you, Maeve. And I'm here for you. Remember that.

Connor studied the damage to the reception hall. Tables were overturned, and broken dishes and food littered the floor. He walked over to Charlie and Devin. "What did I miss?"

"Sullivan and Callahan reprimanded all the guards," Devin said. "The ones who aren't locked up are supposed to report here to clean up this mess."

"Is Peggy okay?"

Devin smirked. "Elf, remember? My sister is not scared off by rumbling werewolves. She actually knocked two of the guards' heads together to stop them from toppling the bar. Right now she's helping the caterers in the kitchen, and you can count on her being here in time to supervise the cleanup."

"Where's the guard who attacked Olivia and Maeve?"

"He's under arrest."

"I want to see him," Connor said.

Devin shook his head. "Not a good idea right now."

"Why not?" Connor pushed.

"Because we've had enough violence tonight. We don't need you attacking him."

"I still want to see him."

"A healer is checking him over," Charlie said. "Jack is watching him. Something isn't right. He hadn't turned back fully to human when Jack took him away."

Connor frowned. "That doesn't make sense. We normally can't hold mid-transition for so long. It's too painful."

Devin nodded. "Which is why Jack is staying close to him and we've called in a healer. How's Dr. Jennings doing?"

"Shaken up. But she's doing better. She's checking on Maeve right now."

"I want someone watching Maeve and Dr. Jennings at all times while they're here," Devin said.

Connor had already come to the same conclusion. "From now on I'm not letting Olivia out of my sight. And since she's here to spend time with Maeve, I can watch over both of them."

Devin's eyes narrowed at Connor. "Charlie and I will go interrogate the werewolf. You go stand guard with the women, and I'll have Jack guard Sullivan."

Connor returned to the side room and found Olivia sitting alone on the couch looking distracted. Was she lost in the past again?

"Olivia?"

She looked up at him, and he breathed a sigh of relief to see her expression was one of frustration rather than fear.

"Where's Maeve?"

"Her father came and got her. He's sending her back to the house where they've been staying. Some secret location Callahan hasn't told anyone about. Although after tonight, I don't think his secrecy is too over-the-top."

"How are you doing?" Connor asked.

"I'm okay, even though I just blew it with Maeve."

"What happened?"

Olivia got up and paced around the couch, her bare feet peeking out from underneath the blue gown she still wore.

"I pushed her too hard. I want to help her, but she's not ready to stand up to her father."

"You're doing the best you can."

When she spun toward him and caught her feet in the gown, his hands wrapped around her shoulders to stop her from toppling to the floor.

"You okay?"

"Stupid dress. Thanks."

A throat cleared from behind him and Connor turned. Jack stood in the doorway. This was the second time he hadn't sensed his approach.

"Why aren't you guarding Sully?" Connor asked.

"Charlie's watching him right now. Devin called me in so I could participate in the interrogation of the guard. His name is Phillip Carrington, and he's one of Sullivan's personal guards."

"Is he still partially transitioned?"

"No," Jack said. "He's back to human. The healer can't figure out what, if anything, is wrong with him."

"How did the interrogation go?" Connor asked.

Jack frowned. "Not good so far. He keeps saying he wasn't in control, which we know is a crock. Devin is going to talk to him again in a few minutes, but I don't know if it will do any good. And I'm not getting a good enough read off him to know if he's lying."

"Let me talk to him," Olivia said.

Connor stepped toward her. "I don't want you anywhere near him."

She opened her mouth as if to argue with him and then stopped. Stared into his eyes for a few seconds like she was reading his damn soul.

"What if I just watch the interrogation? Is there a way for me to do that?"

"Yes," Jack said.

"No," Connor answered at the same time.

Up went her eyebrow. Connor wanted to kiss that eyebrow into submission. But he didn't see it happening anytime soon.

He kept his gaze on her even though he talked to Jack through their twinspeak. *I don't want her in the same room with him.*

She won't be, Jack replied. *They have an interrogation room set up. Giz has monitors outside the room recording the interrogation.*

Olivia frowned. "You two are being rude, talking to each other when I'm standing right here."

Connor grinned. Of course she'd figured out what they were doing. She was amazingly good at reading people. Which meant it made sense for her to listen in on the interrogation. "We were just talking about how stubborn you are."

Jack held up his hands. "That's not how I remember the conversation."

Connor glared at Jack. "You just threw your only brother under the bus."

"Only because you did it first. I'm not taking flak for you."

"Fine. We were talking about a way you could watch the interrogation without having to be anywhere near the guard."

"Based on the scowly face you have going on right now, there is a way to do it. But even though you're worried about me, you will let me do it to help the pack."

Jack tried to cover up his laugh with a cough, but it was a lame attempt at best.

Connor blew out a hard breath and faced her. "I don't even need to talk now. You can carry on the argument for the both of us."

She beamed, and his heart stammered. "What a great idea. We'll finish our arguments much faster and more amicably."

Jack laughed out loud this time, not even trying to hide it. "Okay. As much as I'm loving whatever this is between the two of you, we should probably get to the interrogation room before Devin starts again."

Olivia sat next to Giz while he watched the monitor on the table. She wasn't ready to look at the man, Phillip, yet, even if it was through a monitor. So she watched Giz instead. He was lean, with dark hair on the shaggy side and pale blue eyes. He also was very tuned in to the monitors and other gadgets littering the table in front of him.

She was surprised when he glanced up at her and smiled. "You doing okay now?"

"Yes. Thanks."

"This world can be kinda hard to handle. Especially when you get thrown into the middle of it."

She nodded. "After tonight, I can't deny I'm in over my head."

Giz's expression softened. "We're all in over our heads at one point or another. Which is when you reach out to your family and friends."

"I don't have a family. And I can't very well tell my friends what's happening." Olivia wasn't sure why she was sharing so much with him. Maybe she was still in shock from earlier, or maybe it was as simple as sensing he was genuinely willing to listen to her.

"You have Alex, and Julia, and I think you've won over some other people on the team as well." He looked pointedly at the corner of the room.

Devin, Jack, and Connor stood there talking. From snippets of their conversation she caught earlier, they were discussing the best way to interrogate the guard again. Even though they were trained at this, it would have been nice to be part of the conversation. But she wasn't going to shove her way in. She had already fought and won the battle to watch the interrogation. She wasn't going to push her luck.

Olivia turned back to Giz. "For such an insightful man, you sure have a silly nickname."

Giz chuckled. "My name is Tim Kelly. Giz is short for Gizmo. It was my call sign when I was a SEAL."

She blinked at him, at a loss of what to say, and he chuckled louder this time.

"I get that reaction a lot. People don't expect someone like me to be a SEAL. It's where I met Charlie. Now, he's what you would expect a SEAL to look like, right? I was the tech guy on the team. Kept an eye on everyone's six. While they did the ass-kicking and the name-taking."

Olivia straightened. "Which doesn't make your job any less important. So don't downplay your accomplishments."

His eyes widened. "Yes, ma'am."

"And while Charlie is good-looking, and he well knows it, you're no slouch yourself, Tim."

Giz's eyes twinkled. "I could fall in love with you if you weren't already taken."

What is he talking about?

Connor appeared at the table, and she jumped slightly since she hadn't heard him coming. Jack and Devin joined them a moment later.

"What are you two laughing about over here?" Connor asked.

Giz winked at her. "The good doctor has been setting me straight. From now on I'm going to speak my mind."

Connor crossed his arms. "I was already on the receiving end of you speaking your mind the other night. I don't know if we need to encourage him to keep it up."

Olivia shrugged. "Tim is an important part of this

team and his opinion is as valuable as the opinions of some of you who voice them a lot."

Devin and Jack elbowed each other while Connor scowled.

"Are we ready to interrogate Phillip again?" Connor asked as if to change the subject.

"May I offer a suggestion?" Olivia asked.

"Of course," Devin replied.

"I had originally wanted to interrogate him myself." Connor growled. "Olivia—"

She held up her hand to stop him. "I'm not asking to be in the room, but I have an idea for the next best thing. I'd like to be able to offer suggestions while the interrogation is going on. Can Connor or Jack lead the discussion and the other stay out here with me? I can make suggestions and you can use your twinspeak to relay them."

Devin blinked. "That's a really good idea."

"I'll go in," Connor said.

"Are you going to behave yourself?" Devin asked.

"Don't I always?"

"I'm thinking Jack should go in instead," Devin countered.

"If he's lying, I think the person who's the most motivated to find out the truth should go in the room with him," Jack said. "And that's Connor."

Devin looked back and forth between the twins and finally sighed. "Fine. But don't make me regret my decision, Connor."

Connor and Devin walked toward the door to the interrogation room, and Olivia knew it was time to finally face the monitor. She took a breath and turned toward it.

Phillip sat with his arms resting on a table and his gaze locked on the tabletop, as if something fascinating was there besides the worn, pockmarked wood. He didn't look like the monster from earlier. He looked dejected, defeated.

Her heart sped up a bit, and it wasn't due to being afraid of him now, but rather what happened earlier. Why was fear so locked in the past? Most thought people were paralyzed by fear of the unknown. In Olivia's experience it was not so simple. Instead, people were afraid that the horrible and depressing things they had experienced would happen again. If you live your life waiting for pain and despair to manifest itself, it's no wonder you don't put yourself out there. Don't risk looking up from the pockmarked wood tabletop.

Up went her heart rate again as she watched the door open and Connor walk into the room.

Psychology encompasses the mental, physical, emotional, and now...magical?

CHAPTER 21

When Connor entered the room, he immediately had to tell his wolf to calm the hell down. He pawed at Connor's chest to be released, and, as much as Connor wanted to show Phillip what it felt like to be at the mercy of fear and intimidation, he wasn't going to do it by beating him. And since Devin stood just inside the door of the room, he wouldn't let Connor get away with much.

It took a moment for the man to even raise his eyes. When he did, his expression took Connor off guard. He had been expecting anger or satisfaction or some sick emotion. What he didn't expect was confusion and remorse.

"Are you ready to talk now?" Connor asked.

"I don't know what else you want me to say."

"Why did you try to attack Maeve tonight?"

"I don't know."

Connor took a step closer. "Were you working on your own or with someone else?"

"I'm not working with anyone."

"What was your plan once you caught up with Maeve?"

"I didn't have a plan."

"Were you going to hurt her? Kill her?" Connor pushed.

"No!"

"Then why did you break down the door to get to her?"

Phillip slammed his cuffed hands onto the table. "I don't know! I don't even remember how I got into the room."

Connor, hold up for a minute. Jack spoke to him.

Connor took a breath and watched the man in front of him.

Ask him what he remembers of the evening. Does he remember guarding Maeve?

Connor gritted his teeth before responding. *Fine.*

And Olivia said to dial down the animosity. It's not helping right now. Sit down across from him.

Connor took three deep breaths before sitting down. "Okay, let's go back to the beginning. What can you remember from tonight?"

"It was the pack reception."

"And you were on duty?"

"Yes. I was assigned to guard Maeve before she was introduced to the rest of the pack."

"And did you?"

Phillip nodded. "Yes. I stood outside the room to make sure she was safe."

"And did you let anyone else in the room?"

"The alpha told me to allow the human woman, Olivia, in the room."

"Do you remember anything else?"

"I received notice from the alpha when it was time, and I escorted the women to Alpha Callahan. He took them inside."

"And then?" Connor pushed.

"I was in the room with everyone else...and then things got blurry. I remember shouting and growls." He opened his hands and dropped them to the table. "Then nothing."

Jack interrupted him. *Ask him if he can remember what he was feeling.*

Are you kidding me? Connor growled through his twinspeak.

Olivia says to do it.

"Can you remember what were you feeling when you were in the room?"

Phillip stared at him for a moment before answering. "I don't know what you mean."

"Did something or someone upset you?"

He closed his eyes for a moment before opening them again. "I was fine until we got to the main area, and then I got anxious. I don't know if I could feel the anger between the two packs or what, but my wolf started pacing."

Ask him about his wolf. Was his wolf upset?

"Why was your wolf pacing?"

"I...he wanted me to protect Maeve. They were yelling about her, and he didn't like it."

"So you let your wolf take over?"

"No. No...I don't know." His hands shook, making his cuffs scrape across the wood table. "I would never hurt a female. Never. I don't know what happened."

"You started to turn, do you remember doing that?"

He frowned. "I remember the pain and my bones fighting to change."

"What were you feeling then?"

"I remember fear and wanting to protect what's mine."

"Except she's not yours," Connor pushed.

"I know that! I'm telling you, I don't understand what happened. It was like I wasn't in control."

Connor leaned toward him. "Why should I believe you?"

Phillip blew out a harsh breath. "You shouldn't. I wouldn't if I were you. But that doesn't make it any less true."

Connor stood, and he and Devin walked out, shutting the door and going over to talk to Giz, Jack, and Olivia at the monitors. Sullivan and Charlie had joined the group.

"Did you see everything?" Connor asked his alpha.

"Yes. What do you think, Olivia?"

"I don't think he's lying. He doesn't remember."

"Connor?"

"I agree."

Sullivan rubbed his jaw. "So where do we go from here?"

"We need to figure out why he did what he did," Olivia answered. "Has he shown emotional or psychological issues in the past?"

"No," Sullivan said. "I actually brought him on as one of my personal guards after my father died."

"Are werewolves susceptible to drugs?" she asked.

"Not to the extent that humans are. It would take a pretty high dose to cause a wolf to lose himself to a drug," Jack answered.

Connor watched her. He could actually see her brain working, sorting through the different angles. She was amazing.

"Did the healer find anything when he examined him?" Olivia asked.

Devin shook his head. "No, the pack healer was baffled. He couldn't find anything physically wrong with him."

Sullivan looked down at the monitor. "We need to

find out if this attack was connected to the attempt on my life."

"Someone tried to kill you?" Olivia gasped. "Did you catch them? Do they not remember what happened either?"

"A coward with a gun, and we didn't catch him," Sullivan said.

Olivia straightened her glasses. "So it's even more important for us to find out why the guard lashed out. If the cause isn't physical, or emotional, or psychological, then what does that leave?" she asked.

"In our world, quite a bit," Connor said. "I think we need to bring in a healer to investigate the other possibilities."

Olivia hadn't known what to expect when they called in a faerie healer, but it definitely wasn't Darcinda. The woman in front of her had on purple combat boots, black pants, and a T-shirt that said *Faeries Rock Around the Clock*. She had long hair, with fluorescent pink streaks surrounding her face. A face to put a runway model to shame.

Why were all these supernatural women so beautiful? With Maeve, she was beautiful but unsure of her own self-worth, but it certainly wasn't the case with the newest arrival.

They were meeting with Darcinda in the small sitting room. Charlie and Giz—Tim—were watching Phillip. Which left her, Connor, Jack, Devin, and Sullivan meeting with the surprising woman.

"Darcinda, thanks for coming on such short notice," Devin said.

She shrugged. "That's the life of a healer. But I'm happy to be here. I love spending time with wolves."

She winked at Jack and Connor. "Hiya, twins."

Connor laughed. "Darcinda, always a pleasure. Let me make some introductions. This is our alpha, Sullivan Ross."

"I've been hearing rumblings about you, Alpha."

"Are they good or bad rumblings?" Sullivan asked.

"Since your father was an awful leader, I think rumblings means you're shaking things up a bit, which is a good thing."

Olivia glanced at Sullivan to see his reaction.

After a moment he smiled. "You're refreshingly honest."

Darcinda smiled back. "Yes, I am. It's good you recognize it right from the start."

Connor spoke up again. "And this is Dr. Olivia Jennings. She's helping the pack right now."

Darcinda's eyes widened. "A human doctor. I'm intrigued."

"I'm a psychiatrist."

"Even better." Darcinda rubbed her hands together. "Who's going to fill me in on what's going on?"

Devin took the lead and did most of the talking while Sullivan and the others interjected comments. Olivia sat quietly and observed the discussion. Darcinda was smart and insightful and incredibly honest.

When she had been brought up to speed with everything, Olivia expected her to ask to see the patient. Instead, she turned to Olivia. "You've been quiet throughout this discussion, Dr. Jennings. I'm curious about your take on what's going on."

"I'm new to this world."

"Doesn't make your opinion less relevant."

Olivia liked this forthright woman. "I think if he isn't suffering from some sort of psychological issue that has erased his actions from his conscious mind, then he's being compelled."

"Interesting word choice. It could be something magical."

"You don't think we're dealing with a siren again, do you?" Devin asked.

Siren? Again? Olivia needed some sort of supernatural encyclopedia to keep up with all this.

"The odds are slim it's a siren. Plus, what you described to me is different from what we've encountered in the past. Let me examine him first to see what I uncover. But it might take me a while to come to any conclusions."

Sullivan nodded. "Jack, would you take Darcinda to see Phillip?"

After they left, Sullivan turned to Olivia. "I had Sharon prepare a room for you in the lodge."

"That's not necessary," Olivia said.

Connor appeared beside her. "Olivia, it's after midnight. You heard Darcinda. She's going to be a while. And you're going to want to hear what she has to say later, right?"

She couldn't argue with him when he was being logical. "Fine."

"Come on, I'll take you to the lodge."

She sighed. "It's the building next door, Connor. I'll—" She stopped when his eyes took on that familiar, stubborn glint. "Fine."

As soon as they stepped outside, Olivia realized she was still barefoot. She had kicked her shoes off earlier in her rush to protect Maeve and had never put them back on. She didn't even know where they were at this point. And they had a large circular stone driveway to cross to get to the lodge.

"This won't do," Connor said as he scooped her up in her arms.

"Hey!" Olivia sputtered as she clutched his shoulders for balance.

"I'm not letting your stubbornness damage your feet."

His green eyes danced, and this close she could see bits of blue in them as well. Her stomach warmed as she got a whiff of him. He smelled like the outdoors with a touch of citrus. Not good. Connor strode across the driveway and up onto the front porch of the lodge. Somehow he opened the door with her still in his arms and carried her into the foyer.

A massive log staircase greeted them, and she wiggled for him to put her down. "You are not carrying me up that staircase, Connor Dawson."

He grinned. "You used my full name. Am I supposed to be intimidated?"

"I'm not a damsel in distress. You can put me down now." Flashes of the staircase scene in *Gone with the Wind* had her nerves jumping.

He gazed at her for a moment with those ridiculous green eyes and finally set her down. "Suit yourself."

They walked up the stairs to a long hallway. Three doors down, a door stood open, and Connor walked with her to the room.

She stopped outside the door and turned to him. "Thank you for making sure I got here safely. I can take it from here."

He looked down at her, and her breath stopped as if stuck in her chest.

Then he backed up a step. "'Night, Olivia."

She shut the door and leaned against it, willing her chest to stop holding her breath hostage. It was time to admit she had feelings for the infuriatingly stubborn man. Olivia sucked in a breath before she made herself light-headed.

A slight rustling sound had her leaning her ear against the door to listen. She cracked the door open an inch and found Connor propped against the wall with his arms crossed.

"Why are you still here?" she asked.

"Oh, I'm not going anywhere," he answered like it was the most natural thing in the world for him to be standing outside her bedroom door.

She opened the door wider. "Excuse me?"

"There is no way I'm going to leave you unguarded right now. Not after what happened tonight."

"So you're just going to stand out here?"

"Yes. Get some sleep, Olivia. You have to be exhausted."

And so did he. Now what? Before she could talk herself out of it, she opened her door wider. "Come in."

His eyes widened.

"You are not standing outside my door all night. And since I know you won't leave, you can guard me from inside, can't you?"

"Absolutely."

He walked into the room and closed the door, locking it. The room seemed to shrink, and she was having trouble breathing again. *Enough!*

She looked around. A large bed sat in the center of the room where Sharon had laid the suit Olivia wore earlier, along with what appeared to be pajamas. An open door on the right wall led into a bathroom. There was also a chair in the corner of the bedroom next to the window.

Olivia hung her suit in the closet for something to do to calm her nerves and then turned to Connor.

He walked over to the window and peered outside. "I'll stay on the chair tonight. Why don't you use the bathroom first and get cleaned up?"

She nodded, both relieved and yet irritated by his announcement. She snatched up the pajamas and marched toward the bathroom.

"Olivia."

She stopped and turned to look at him.

"Let me get your zipper."

She sighed, and he made quick work of unzipping her dress. She held her breath so she wouldn't make a fool of herself.

"Thank you," she said, without turning back to him, then disappeared into the bathroom and shut the door.

Fortunately, Sharon had left out toiletries for her, and she brushed her teeth and washed her face before looking at herself in the mirror. Should she take a shower? Connor was in the next room, and the idea of him being so close while she showered set off all sorts of conflicting emotions.

But her body was so tense from the attack earlier, she knew she'd never relax unless she did. Decision made, she turned the shower on and undressed. After testing the water temp with her hand first, she walked into the massive shower stall, planning to be quick and not worry about her hair tonight.

And she would not think about the man in the next room.

Dreams aren't all about puppy dogs and lollipops.

CHAPTER 22

Connor was in trouble. He had been a stubborn ass up until now, rejecting the idea of a relationship with Olivia. But when he ran into the room tonight and stopped the wolf from doing the Fates only knew what to Olivia, his damn heart decided it was time to be in charge, kicking his brain out of the alpha position.

And when his brain tried to fight back, it lost the battle when Connor held her trembling in his arms, and again when he scooped her up in the courtyard. Now she had invited him into her room. And both man and wolf wanted to howl at the moon.

But now was not the time to say anything. She was tired and vulnerable, and he would not take advantage of her. Instead he tortured himself by unzipping her dress and then shooing her into the bathroom. He sensed his brother before a light knock on the door told him he was there. He opened the door and Jack handed him his go bag.

"Thanks. Is Darcinda finished with her examination already?"

"No. The rest of the team is taking shifts watching over her while she works with him. I think she's amused by it."

Connor shook his head. "I have a feeling Darcinda can handle herself just fine."

Jack chuckled. "I think you're right. How's Olivia doing?"

"Better. She's in the shower now."

Jack hesitated for a moment and Connor continued, "Don't worry, I'm not going to take advantage of her. I'm a wolf, not a pig."

Jack rested his hand on Connor's shoulder. "I know you wouldn't do that. I know what kind of man you are, brother. You are the one who doubts yourself. Get some sleep, and I'll see you in the morning."

Connor gaped at his retreating brother for a few moments before shutting the door. Was his brother right? Was Connor the only one who thought he was inadequate? Well, not the *only* one. His father and some of the pack felt the same way.

He set his bag on the bed and unzipped it.

The bathroom door opened and Olivia stood in the opening. She still had her glasses on and her hair in a bun. But she wore size huge pajamas, and had rolled the arms and legs up so she could walk across the floor without tripping.

She looked adorable.

She noticed his bag on the bed before coming into the bedroom. "Where did you get the bag?"

"It's my go bag. I always have one packed in my SUV in case I get called on a case. Jack brought it to me."

"Go bag is a military term, isn't it?"

"Yeah. Got it from Charlie and Giz."

"They were SEALs. Tim was telling me about it."

Tim? Why was he not surprised to learn she was on

a first-name basis with Giz? She could talk anyone into anything. It was her superpower.

She tilted her head. "Why are you frowning at me?"

He would not be enlightening her about his thoughts at the moment. "You're not going to sleep with your hair up all night, are you?"

She reached up and touched the bun. "I left it up so my hair wouldn't get wet in the shower."

"Looks uncomfortable."

She gazed up at him for a moment, and he wanted to reach up and rest his palm against her cheek. A cheek that was still pink from her shower.

But now was not the time.

"Turn around."

Apparently he had decided to continue torturing himself.

She turned slowly, and he lifted his hands to her hair and gently pulled out the first pin. He set the pin on the dresser.

His hand shook a little bit, and he was glad she faced away from him. He pulled out the second pin.

And the next, carefully putting the bobby pins on the dresser so they'd be handy when she put up her hair again in the morning.

And they continued in silence, the only sounds the slight click of the pins as he set each one on the dresser.

His wolf liked being close enough to feel the warmth radiating off her from her shower, but her normal lavender scent had been replaced by something fruity—apricots, maybe?

He pulled the last pin out of her hair and it unfurled. Connor couldn't stop himself from fanning it out and running his fingers through the silky strands once, and then a second time.

Holy hell, it wasn't just slightly auburn as he had thought. It blazed with red-hot highlights.

Olivia stepped away and he dropped his hands before he reached for her. "Why don't you get settled while I take my turn in the bathroom?"

She padded over to the bed and pulled down the covers. Connor picked up his bag and hurried into the bathroom, shutting the door before he could see her crawl into bed.

He got ready for bed quickly, shedding the tuxedo and pulling on a T-shirt and sweatpants. More clothes than he normally wore to bed, but he wasn't about to walk around in his boxers while Olivia lay in the bed across the room from him.

He opened the door and set his bag out of the way. Olivia lay in the bed with the covers up to her chin. Her glasses were next to her on the bedside stand and her hair tucked to the side. She blinked up at him, and he got a good look at her eyes for the first time. He knew they were blue, but now he could see they were so much more. They actually shimmered in the low light of the bedside lamp.

"Good night, Olivia."

"'Night, Connor."

He turned off the bathroom light and walked over to the chair. She had left a pillow and a blanket on the ottoman for him, and he settled in, putting his legs up on the ottoman. He had slept in much worse places over the years, and he'd survive a night on a semi-comfortable chair.

Even with Olivia in the room.

She turned off the light and the room plunged into darkness. Connor relaxed in the chair, his eyes adjusting immediately to the dark. A benefit of his wolf. Or in this case more like a curse. He could see Olivia lying in the bed, alone. He wanted her in his arms.

Olivia rustled around for a couple minutes before

settling on her side, her even breathing telling him she had finally gone to sleep.

He didn't think he would be so lucky. His brain was in overdrive. They had to figure out Callahan's agenda, plus who tried to kill Sully, and why Phillip had lost his shit and tried to take Maeve. And if that wasn't enough, the beautiful, brilliant, engaging, stubborn woman sleeping in the bed across from him had taken up residence in his heart.

He wasn't sure how long he napped in the chair before Olivia began moving around in the bed. She tossed to one side and then turned to the other before he heard her whimper. Connor was up and by her side in the pulse of a heartbeat.

Her face scrunched up as if she was in pain, and she whimpered again. Did he dare touch her? Or would it make things worse?

She cried out softly, and he turned on the bedside lamp and knelt down next to her.

"Olivia. Baby. Wake up."

She fought with the blankets like they were pinning her down, and he pulled them off her.

"Olivia!"

She jerked upright and clutched at the collar of her pajamas like they were choking her.

"It's okay. Olivia. You're okay. It's Connor."

She scrambled up the bed and pushed with her feet, slamming her back against the headrest, kicking pillows out of the way to escape him.

He held up his hands, palms out in front of him, to show he wasn't going to hurt her, anger surging through him for being helpless to stop the terror.

"Connor?"

"Yeah, it's Connor. You're safe, baby."

She let out a shuddering breath.

"Take a deep breath. You're safe." He gave her space

even though he wanted to pull her into his arms and never let her go. "What can I do? Do you want a glass of water?"

Instead of answering him, she squinted at the nightstand.

He reached for her glasses and held them out to her. "Here. Do you want your glasses?"

She put them on and glanced around the room, as if trying to get her bearings. "Sullivan's house," she rasped out softly.

"Yes. We're at his lodge. Let me get you a glass of water." He got a glass from the dresser and filled it halfway with water from the bathroom tap before returning.

Olivia had rearranged the pillows so she could prop herself up against the headboard. He handed her the glass, and she thanked him before taking a few cautious sips and then handing it back. He set it on the nightstand.

"Better?" he asked, trying to keep his own voice calm.

"Yes. Sorry about that."

"There's nothing to apologize for."

She looked away from him. *Damn it!*

"There's nothing to be embarrassed about either," he said, a bit too roughly.

Olivia's gaze locked on his, and he actually saw just a hint of a smile appear. "Yes, sir."

He gestured to the bed. "May I sit?" She nodded, and he sat down. "Do you want to talk about it?"

"After what happened earlier, I'm not surprised I had a night terror."

Connor clenched his fists. "The monsters."

Olivia pulled her beautiful hair away from her face and tucked it to the side. "Yes. The dream is usually the same. I'm lost in the woods, and they're after me.

I'm running, and the trees are snagging on my clothes and scratching me. It's dark, and I can't see them, but I know they're close, and they take hold of my shirt and pull it, choking me."

Connor reached out and took her hand when he couldn't fight the need to touch her any longer. "I'm sorry. I've heard people talk about night terrors before, but I didn't know they were this vivid."

"It's okay. Most people don't know how awful they are unless they've experienced them firsthand. I work with a lot of vets who experience terrors as part of their PTSD."

He squeezed her hand. "You are amazing."

"Not so amazing that I can break through my own issues and let the past go."

He hesitated before asking his next question. "Have you talked to someone about them?"

"Yes, I've seen several different specialists, but no one's ever been able to determine what the monsters represent. Dreams are often full of symbolism. People, places, and things aren't necessarily what they appear to be in our dreams."

"So the monsters aren't real. They're your fear."

"That's what I've always thought," Olivia said, then frowned.

"Why do I think there's a but coming?"

"Because tonight I saw the monster for the first time. It was a wolf. Which means either the monster took on that form because of what happened to me tonight, or..." She hesitated, as if she couldn't say the words.

Connor's heart pounded like a bass drum. "Or you were taken by a wolf as a child."

Olivia trembled as she nodded. "A wolf with glowing eyes."

Connor held both Olivia's hands. He didn't remember when he grasped the other one, but he had to do something for her. This feeling of helplessness was chewing a hole in his gut.

"What can I do for you? How can I make this better?"

She shrugged, still trembling. "There isn't much you can do to make it better. I usually take a shower after the terrors to warm me up, but I'm so tired I don't have the energy to do it right now."

"Why don't you lie down and I'll cover you up?"

She lay down, and he pulled the blankets up to her neck, and then brought over the blanket he'd been using and laid it on top as well. "Better?"

She nodded, even though he could still see her trembling. He took off her glasses and set them on the nightstand.

"Don't turn off the light," she blurted.

His gut clenched. "I won't."

He sat on the bed with his hands on both sides of her, holding the blankets down, willing some more heat to warm her up.

"Olivia. Will you let me hold you? Would it help?"

Her eyes filled with tears, and he wanted to kick his own ass for the suggestion. She had to think he was an opportunistic pig. "I'm sorry, I wasn't trying to hit on you. I just—"

"Connor," Olivia said, interrupting him. "Stop. I know you're trying to help me."

She pulled up the cover and scooted over. "I could use a giant heating pad right now."

He hoped he smiled reassuringly, even though he felt like swallowing his tongue. To have her trust him like this was priceless. He climbed in the bed and pulled her against his side, wrapping his arm around her shoulders. She snuggled against him and rested her head on his chest. He tucked the covers around the both of them.

And it was perfect.

Connor couldn't remember the last time he simply held a woman. A woman who trusted him enough to tell him about her past. A woman who wasn't afraid to put him in his place. A woman who had used her painful past as a catalyst to help others.

And Connor wouldn't rest until he helped her free herself from her monsters, wolf or no.

Friends often make the best counselors.

CHAPTER 23

Olivia was so relaxed she didn't want to move. Warmth radiated against her right side, and she snuggled deeper into the blankets. Except instead of softness, she encountered a warm chest, and...an arm wrapped around her?

Oh...yeah.

She opened her eyes slowly and found Connor watching her. His mouth lit up in a grin, making her already-toasty body threaten to combust.

"Morning," she said, cursing her raspy voice.

"Good morning. I'm glad you were able to get some sleep last night."

Her face heated. "I'm sorry I used you as a mattress. You probably didn't get any sleep at all."

"I got some sleep. Are you feeling better?"

"Yes. Thanks for listening last night."

His gaze narrowed on her. "I get the impression you help everyone else and don't have anyone who listens to you."

She glanced down at his chest to avoid his probing look. Bad mistake. Even though he wore a T-shirt, it clung to his chest and abs, leaving nothing to the imagination. Her hand rested on his abs. She would not rub her hand across his stomach. She would not rub her hand across his—

"Hey." Fingers touched her chin and tilted her face up so she gazed into his green eyes again. Damn those blue speckles she could see when she was this close.

"I'm sorry," he said. "I shouldn't push you. It's none of my business who you have in your life or not."

"It's okay. You're right. I don't have a lot of close friends, and I do take the weight of the world on my shoulders." And yet her head rested on his shoulder, and she liked it. A lot. Maybe too much.

Before he could respond, Connor's eyes went slightly unfocused for a few moments.

"Is it Jack?" she asked.

"How do you always know when we're talking?"

"It's the expression you get on your face. What did he say?"

"Darcinda is going to talk to the group over breakfast. Are you ready to get up?"

Not really, if she was honest, but she had spewed enough honesty over this man the past couple days.

He tossed off the covers. "You want to go first?"

"No. Go ahead."

He climbed out of bed, and she watched him pick up his bag and saunter into the bathroom. She took a deep breath and pushed herself out of bed, getting her suit from yesterday out of the closet. She dressed quickly and pulled her phone out of her jacket pocket.

She had a text from Alex wanting to hear all about the reception brouhaha, since Devin hadn't been home and wasn't telling her *anything*. Olivia smiled and shook her head. Alex was a sweetie, but she also was incurably nosy.

The next several texts were from Elena. From the escalating tone in each, her friend was worried about her. She had even threatened her in Spanish. Or at least Olivia thought it was a threat, since she'd just begun learning Spanish with her friend's help.

Elena was the only person she could lean on, and she hadn't totally opened up to her in the past. She wasn't sure what it meant in terms of violating the friendship code, but she needed to do a better job of letting her in, even if she couldn't tell her about the supernatural.

She dialed Elena's number.

"Where have you been?" Elena asked before Olivia could get a word out.

"I'm fine, Elena. And I'm sorry, I didn't even check my messages yesterday. I'm working on a project, and I let the time get away from me."

Elena sighed. "You have to stop working so much."

"I know. Why don't I call you in a few days and we can see about getting together. Is everything okay with you?"

Elena spent a couple minutes telling her about her new business class. She was close to finishing her business management degree.

The bathroom door opened. "Are you ready to go down for breakfast?" Connor asked.

She held up her hand.

"Oh, sorry," he said.

"Who was *that*?" Elena had ears like a bat. Or a wolf?

Olivia cringed. "Nobody."

"Nobody sounds *sexy*. Is he your project?"

Olivia looked over at Connor, who grinned. Could he hear what Elena was saying?

"Elena. I can't talk right now. I have things to do."

"I hope that's code for getting busy."

Connor chuckled.

"I'll call you in a few days. Bye." She disconnected and put her phone in her pocket before turning to him. "You heard the entire conversation, didn't you?"

"I did." He tapped his ear. "Wolf hearing."

"But you didn't hear me talking to her when you came out of the bathroom?" Olivia asked.

"Sorry. I was thinking about something else. Your friend sounds interesting."

"My friend is the assistant manager who had the bouncers throw you out the other night."

His eyes widened. "Ah. No wonder they took your side right away. You had an unfair advantage."

"Not really. I've never thrown a drink in someone's face."

"Then why did you do it?" he pressed.

Olivia shrugged. "You bring out the devil in me."

Again with the quirky grin. "I'll take that as a compliment."

She laughed. "You're impossible. Let me brush my teeth and put my hair up and we can go downstairs."

He studied her for a drawn-out moment. "Do you need help with your hair?"

She gulped. Actually gulped before answering him. "I'm good." She snatched the pins off the dresser and darted into the bathroom, closing the door before checking herself in the mirror.

Her face was flushed. He had to bring up taking down her hair last night. Was it pathetic to have found it incredibly sexy? Something about him touching her hair was magical. Yep, he brought out the devil in her, but if Elena was here, she'd say it was a good thing.

Maybe Elena was right. Once they got through all this mess, could she convince Connor to give her a chance, and help him learn that "relationship" wasn't a four-letter word?

They entered the dining room and joined a growing crowd. Sullivan sat at the head of the table with the rest of the team—Devin, Charlie, Giz, and Jack—on either side. They were all enjoying breakfast, especially Giz, who was eating a huge stack of pancakes.

Connor led her over to the sideboard where she heaped her plate with eggs and potatoes. Olivia was starving since last night's reception deteriorated into mayhem before anyone had a chance to eat.

As soon as they sat down, Sullivan said, "Olivia, I'm so sorry about all of this, and even more sorry if this situation is impacting your work."

She was relieved he kept his apology vague and didn't directly mention her breakdown last night. "I'm okay with work. I already rescheduled my Friday appointments even before the reception occurred, in case I needed to be here."

"Can you stay a bit today, then? Callahan and Maeve will be coming here to discuss the contract."

"Of course." She wanted to see how Maeve was doing after last night.

"Do you think he wants to nullify the contract after what happened last night?" Devin asked.

"I don't think so. Knowing Callahan, he's going to use the incident to his advantage somehow. Or at least he'll try. In the meantime, I'd like the team to interview the guards who were involved in the fight. Mine *and* Callahan's. I don't know if the fight last night was a result of hotheads, or if it was a diversion so Phillip would be able to kidnap Maeve."

"Agreed," Devin said. "We'll interview them and

have Giz record the sessions, so if we flag anyone as acting suspicious, we can have you look at it again."

Silence descended while everyone ate. Darcinda came in a few minutes later and sat down at the end of the table.

"What did you find?" Sullivan asked.

"Not much, unfortunately. I didn't find anything physically wrong with him. He's perfectly healthy and, other than the general confusion and frustration he's feeling about what happened, he doesn't appear to be affected mentally, either."

"So we don't have anything to go on," Devin said.

"I didn't say that either. While I would say he's fit, his wolf isn't."

"What do you mean?" Olivia asked.

"I think someone attacked his wolf. And in doing so, threw off the balance between the two halves."

"How could that even happen?" Connor asked.

"I don't know for sure yet. Unfortunately, his wolf has retreated and isn't willing to talk to us right now."

Jack frowned. "He hasn't lost his wolf, has he?"

Darcinda's expression softened. "No. His wolf is still there, it just seems to be blocking attempts to communicate."

"Do you want me to talk to him?" Jack asked.

"It might help."

Jack stood. "I'll go talk to him now. Do you know if he's eaten yet?"

Darcinda shook her head. "He refused food a while ago, but if you take him something, it might tempt him to eat."

Jack loaded up a plate and left the room.

Olivia watched him leave, trying to figure out what she had just missed.

Connor set his fork down. "I see those wheels turning, Olivia. Ask your questions."

"Why is Jack going to talk to him?"

"Because Jack lost his wolf a couple months ago. Maybe he can help Phillip by talking to him."

"But he's okay now?" Olivia asked.

"Yes. His wolf is back, and he's with Julia now, so he's good. Better than he was before, actually, and that's partly because of you."

"I didn't do anything," she answered quickly.

Connor reached over and put his hand on hers. "Don't sell yourself short. You helped Julia, and she was able to open her heart to Jack."

Olivia stared at her plate. Why did she always deflect compliments when it came to her work? She was a damn fine psychiatrist, and while the heavy lifting was done by her patients, she hoped her influence helped them. If not, then she should find another occupation.

"Thank you."

She glanced up when she realized the rest of the room had gotten quiet. Darcinda was over loading up her own plate. The men at the end of the table were watching the two of them with a variety of amused expressions. Connor lifted his hand from hers and scowled at them. "Don't you have anything better to do?"

Sullivan stood. "I'm going to look over the contract again before Callahan gets here."

"We'll go get set up for the interviews," Devin said as he and Charlie left the room.

Giz sat at the table, poured more syrup on his pancakes, and started eating again...until he must have felt Connor's glare. "What?"

"Aren't you going to help them interview the guards?"

"I already have everything set up with the monitors. Charlie can handle things until I get there. Are you going to eat your bacon?"

"I'm a wolf. What do you think?"

Darcinda returned from the sideboard with her food. When she placed a couple of pieces of bacon on Giz's plate, he smiled at her. She sat down next to Olivia and pinned her with a stare. "So you're the counselor who helped Alex and Julia. They've mentioned you before, but I didn't make the connection."

"Yes. I'm sorry to say they haven't mentioned you to me yet."

Darcinda popped a strawberry into her mouth and shrugged. "I don't know how they could have. I'm a faerie healer, and most of the stuff I do wouldn't have been something they could talk about in front of humans. But now that Alex and Devin's baby decided to say 'hi' to you, the secret is out of the supernatural bag."

Olivia chuckled. "To say it was a shock when her stomach glowed is an understatement."

Darcinda laughed. "I can imagine. I have a feeling this baby is going to show all of us a new trick or two."

They ate in silence for a while, simply enjoying the food.

"I better go help Charlie." Giz popped the last of the bacon in his mouth before leaving.

A few minutes later Connor finished his coffee and leaned back in his chair.

"Go help if you want to," Olivia said. "I'll be safe in the dining room. I promise."

"I'll protect her," Darcinda said.

Olivia peeked at Connor to see if he was going to protest, but he just nodded and left the room.

Olivia watched him leave, waiting for him to turn around and decide not to leave her, but he kept on going. "He doesn't usually agree with me so easily."

Darcinda raised her eyebrows. "I'm not one to be messed with."

"Apparently."

"And he's also not emotionally attached to me."

Olivia's breath caught. "What? No. We're just working together."

Darcinda set down her silverware. "You might be working together, but that doesn't mean there aren't feelings involved. Do you know how many relationships start in the workplace?"

Before Olivia could respond, Darcinda continued. "I've said all along the twins are scrumptious. And when Jack fell for Julia, I thought maybe I should approach Connor."

Olivia shifted in her seat. To hear this beautiful woman say she was attracted to Connor made her stomach bottom out. "Why didn't you?"

"Because when he looks at me, he uses the typical cocky-Connor look he gives most women. And before you ask, he is definitely not looking at you that way." Darcinda stood. "I'm going to go see how Jack is doing with Phillip. Do you think you're safe in here by yourself?"

"I've got a butter knife at my side. I should be fine."

"I thought as much. When this is all done, I would love to spend some more time with you. I suspect there's some feistiness under that professional demeanor of yours."

"I'd love to spend time with you as well."

Darcinda left the room and Olivia took a sip of tea while she reflected on their conversation. Connor did hide himself away behind cocky grins and winks, but she had learned there was a great deal more under the player surface, especially last night.

When she heard raised voices outside the door, Olivia walked over and cracked the door open, to see Connor facing off with Sullivan's advisor Jonathan in the hall.

"Why was I not advised that your team is interrogating my guards?" Jonathan demanded.

"I don't know. Sullivan assigned us to interview all the guards involved in the fight last night. Take it up with him."

"We don't want your team here."

Connor shrugged. "You've made it abundantly clear. Again, not my problem."

"And if I had my way, you wouldn't be part of this clan."

Olivia stifled her gasp. Who *was* this guy?

"Me being part of the clan is more your fault than mine, wouldn't you say?"

Jonathan scowled. "I will be petitioning for your removal."

"Do whatever you want," Connor said in a tight voice.

Olivia gripped the doorknob. The urge to open the door and give this jerk a piece of her mind was imminent until she saw Jack walk up to the two men.

Jack stood next to Connor. "You might as well add my name to the petition as well."

"That won't stop me from doing it this time," Jonathan hissed before stalking off down the hall.

"What did he mean by this time?" Connor asked.

"Nothing. He's just ranting, as usual."

"You don't always have to come to my rescue," Connor barked.

Jack gripped his shoulder. "Shut up. It will always be you and me against them. Remember that."

Some of the tension left Connor's face. "You have turned into a real badass, brother. I like it."

Jack laughed. "Good. Since I don't plan on changing back."

Olivia felt like an intruder now as she watched them. There was such a strong bond between those two. But they shouldn't have to fight against the clan like this.

Did Sullivan know what his advisor threatened? She couldn't imagine he'd be okay with it. At all. After a moment, the brothers lapsed into silence, and Olivia realized they were talking to each other through their link.

Jack nodded after a moment and slapped Connor on the shoulder before going down the hall.

"You can come out now, Olivia," Connor said as he turned to face her.

Busted! She opened the door fully. "I'm sorry, I didn't mean to intrude but I heard raised voices—"

"And you hurried toward them instead of away."

"When you say it that way, it sounds—"

"Reckless?"

"Maybe. I'm sorry I intruded. But I couldn't walk away when I heard what Jonathan said to you. Why does he think he can talk to you both that way? What did you do to him?"

Pain flashed in Connor's eyes before he responded. "He's our father. And I guess our sin was being born."

Olivia had heard a lot of horrible things over the years. Her patients' different backgrounds and stories could be gut-wrenching. But she had never experienced the horribleness *with* them before. To watch another person denigrate someone and then to find out it was a father speaking to his sons...

Anger took form in her belly like a living, breathing dragon. But it wasn't going to help the situation if she let the dragon out.

"I don't understand."

He sighed. "Join the club."

She held up her hands. "I'm sorry. If you don't want to talk about this, we don't have to."

"No. It's okay."

She reached for his hand, and he grasped it before

she pulled him into the dining room and sat him down, Olivia making a point of pulling out a chair and facing him.

Connor's eyebrows rose. "This looks like you're setting up a therapy session. Are you talking to me as a psychiatrist or as a friend?"

"A friend." Maybe more, but now wasn't the time to explore it. Connor was hurting, and, from his wary expression, he was having second thoughts about telling her anything. "After you listened to me last night, it's only fair for me to be here for you."

"A therapy session for a therapy session?"

She shrugged. "If you like."

He nodded, but then didn't say anything, so she decided to help jump-start the conversation.

"When I met with Sullivan, he mentioned you and Jack were almost ostracized from the pack for being identical, but he didn't explain why."

"Our pack believes we each receive a wolf from the Fates at birth. A wolf that is an individual, powerful entity. When Jack and I were born, the theory was called into question. We are identical, which means we split from one, as did our wolves."

"And why is it a problem?"

Connor shrugged. "To them it means something went wrong. We are supposed to be one being and one wolf. Now we're 'less than' in their eyes."

Olivia resisted the urge to get up and pace. "That's ridiculous. And your parents believe this as well?"

"My mother blamed herself for our birth, as if we were a curse. She had a hard time accepting us, and she passed away a couple of years ago. As for my father, he sees my birth as a slap in the face."

"Why your birth?"

"Jack was born first. He was named after our father, and all was right with the world until I decided to make my presence known twenty minutes later."

Olivia clenched her fists. "So he ignores his second-born son?"

"Yes. He's threatened to banish me from the clan for as long as I can remember, but then he never carried through with it. Now I understand why. Jack must have threatened to leave as well. Up to now it apparently was enough to dissuade him, but I guess all bets are off at this point."

"I can't imagine Sullivan would agree to let your father banish you."

"He wouldn't, but he doesn't have final say in cases like this. The wolf council hears this sort of petition, and while Sully is the head of it, he can still be outvoted."

"If it comes to that, I'm sure he'll make them see reason. This whole thing is ridiculous."

Connor grinned. "You already mentioned that."

"Because it is! Ridiculous, and closed-minded, and—"

Connor reached for her clenched fists and smoothed them out. "Take a deep breath, Olivia."

She listened to him and took a breath. Apparently the angry dragon she had felt in her belly earlier decided to make her presence known after all.

"I'm sorry," she said. "This is not about me or my emotions."

"Don't be sorry. I like that you're angry for me."

"You do?"

"Yep." His eyes danced. "It's kind of a turn-on, actually."

She laughed. "You are something else, Connor Dawson."

His expression turned serious. "So are you."

He leaned toward her, and she took a deep breath to stop herself from yelling no...yes...she wasn't sure what.

He was going to kiss her, and she was going to let him.

The dining room door opened.

They backed away from each other, heat surging into Olivia's face. She turned to see Sharon standing wide-eyed in the doorway.

"Sorry to interrupt, but Sullivan asked me to find Olivia. Callahan and Maeve have arrived."

Connor squeezed her hands before Olivia got up and followed Sharon. Before she left the room, she glanced over her shoulder at him. Her belly heated at his expression.

It was a this-isn't-over-yet look.

You can guide and support,
but people have to find the strength to stand up for themselves.

CHAPTER 24

Connor walked toward the interrogation area trying to sort through his chaotic thoughts. He had almost kissed her. So damn close! The more time he spent with Olivia, the more he wanted her.

And not for a fun-filled evening or two. Was he ready for a real relationship? Hell, it hadn't been too long ago when he told Jack he would be a fool for letting Julia go. Was he the fool now if he didn't at least try with Olivia?

He walked around the corner to find Giz and Jack watching the monitors while Devin and Charlie interrogated the guards in two separate rooms.

"How's it going?" Connor asked.

"Pretty uneventful," Jack replied. "We haven't uncovered any major plot to kidnap Maeve. So far, it's been the same story."

Connor watched the monitors for a moment as well. "Do we know how they found out about the wedding contract?"

"Not specifically," Giz answered, "but it was bound

to get out on both sides. The minute more than one person knows a secret—"

"It's no longer a secret," Connor finished.

"Giz, can you watch the monitors for a minute on your own?" Jack asked.

"Sure."

He walked out of the room and Connor followed.

"Are you okay? Your emotions have been all over the place since our confrontation with Jonathan."

"Sorry, I didn't know I was projecting." He usually could control his emotions, but then a lot of things had changed in the past few days.

"It's okay. Tried to find you earlier and heard you and Olivia in the dining room." Jack held his hands up. "Don't worry, I didn't eavesdrop. I left once I knew you two were together."

Connor nodded. "Yeah. She overheard Daddy Dearest threatening us. About that. You brushed off what he said, but I want the truth. Did you threaten to leave the pack if he banished me?"

Jack's eyes tightened. "I did. Don't look at me like that, Connor. You would have done the same for me. It wasn't a sacrifice. We left this clan years ago when they wouldn't accept us, and we've done fine without them. If they want to make it official by booting us out, then let them."

Connor's throat tightened. "Thanks."

"You're welcome. Now let's talk about Olivia."

"What about her?"

"When are you going to admit you have feelings for her?" Jack asked.

"When are you going to ask Julia to marry you?"

"Don't try to deflect the question, brother."

"This is not the best time to explore anything with her. Once things have calmed down, we'll see how things go. Okay?"

"I'm holding you to it."

Connor nodded. His brother had officially downed the couples Kool-Aid. In the past Connor thought it would be a little too sickly sweet for him, but after spending time with Olivia, he might be willing to give it a try.

Olivia walked into the conference room where Sullivan and Callahan were sitting across from each other, a stack of papers on the table between them.

Maeve sat at her father's side. As usual when she was in her father's presence, she folded in on herself.

Sullivan stood and pulled out the chair next to him. "Hello, Olivia. Thanks for joining us."

Olivia sat down. Callahan gave her a scowl, but Maeve didn't look up from her study of the tabletop.

Sullivan gestured to the papers. "I see you brought the contract. What do you want to talk about?"

"I want to make sure you're not planning to back out of the agreement."

Sullivan's eyebrows went up. "I'm surprised, after what happened yesterday, to find out your first concern is the contract."

Callahan frowned. "I know you must be disappointed about Maeve's conduct. I have spoken to my daughter, and she will watch who she speaks to and will not encourage anyone else."

Olivia gasped before she could stop herself. *Is this guy serious?* She bit the inside of her cheek to stop the words from erupting. She glanced at Sullivan, who scowled so fiercely she wanted to scoot her chair away from him.

Sullivan leaned forward. "You cannot honestly be blaming Maeve for what happened yesterday."

Callahan opened his mouth, but Sullivan held up his hand to stop him.

"Let me make something clear. I am not disappointed in *her* conduct. But I am more than disappointed in yours. My first priority is your daughter's safety, and it should be your priority as well."

Callahan's face turned an interesting shade of red, and Maeve looked up at Sullivan with wide eyes.

On the one hand, Olivia wanted to cheer out loud. On the other, she wanted to gather Maeve in her arms and tell her she should expect people to stick up for her. Unfortunately, based on her shocked expression, she hadn't experienced it before.

What was even worse, Olivia was pretty sure Callahan's red face was the result of anger and not embarrassment for treating his daughter like chattel.

"I don't need you to tell me how to treat my daughter," Callahan sputtered.

"And I won't let anyone treat any woman, especially my potential future wife, like she is responsible for someone attacking her."

Sullivan turned to Maeve. "The real question is whether or not you want to continue this."

Callahan spoke. "Of course—"

Sullivan growled, cutting off Callahan's response. The sound had the hair on the back of Olivia's neck standing at attention, and she had to lock her knees to keep from running out of the room.

"I am speaking to your daughter. You need to remember you are in my territory and a guest in my home."

A shiver ran down Olivia's spine. While she knew Sullivan was the alpha for his pack, and had watched him lead over the past few days, she had not experienced the true weight of his authority until this moment.

"Since you can't seem to stop speaking for her, then step outside now and give me a moment with her. And before you protest, let me remind you I can and will rescind this contract, regardless of any threats of retaliation."

Callahan glared at Sullivan before turning his glare on Maeve for a moment and then stalking out of the room.

Olivia could tell Maeve was retracting into her shell in response to the tension, but she also noticed that as soon as Sullivan looked at Maeve, his face relaxed. "I'm sorry if I frightened you just now. I'm not upset with you. I just want to be sure you're okay. After last night, I wouldn't blame you if you didn't want to see me anymore."

Maeve shook her head forcefully. "Please don't send me away. I would like to stay with you."

Sullivan stared at her for a moment. "You want to stay here in the clan, or you want to be my mate?"

"Your mate, of course." Although Maeve responded quickly, Olivia wasn't sure it was sincere.

Sullivan nodded. "Let's spend some more time together then, if it's okay with you?"

Maeve blew out a breath before smiling. "Yes. That's good."

They spent a few more minutes talking about nothing in particular. A getting-to-know-you session, awkward at times, but at least the two of them were talking.

When Maeve and Callahan finally left, Sullivan started to pace. Olivia let him walk back and forth for several minutes while he obviously tried to work out his thoughts.

He finally stopped and turned to her. "I'm surprised you haven't told me to stop pacing already."

She shrugged. "Why would I do that? You need to work off your frustration. Makes perfect sense to me."

Sullivan sighed. "I don't know what I'm going to do, Olivia. She needs my help, and I feel a powerful need to protect her. But she's not ready to marry, and even though she's beautiful, I don't feel that way about her. Do I sound crazy to you?"

"Not at all."

"Except it doesn't solve my dilemma. How can I save her if I don't marry her?"

Olivia pushed back her chair and walked over to him. "I face this same type of question all the time with my patients. They tell me what destructive behavior or relationship they're in, and I want to tell them to stop doing what they're doing, or to get away from a particular person, even if they're a family member. I can listen and suggest, but I can't save them. Because they ultimately have to save themselves.

"Maybe we're here to help Maeve find the strength to stand up to her father. Then she won't need you to save her."

Sullivan nodded. "Remind me later, whenever I want to throttle Callahan."

"Only if you do the same for me. I almost dove across the table myself."

He laughed. "I really like you, Dr. Jennings."

"And I like you, Alpha Ross."

"I'm going to go get a report from Devin on how the interrogations have been going. Want me to have someone drive you home?"

Olivia shook her head. "No. I'll stick around for a bit, if it's okay with you." She pulled out her phone. "I'll get caught up on some e-mails. We can strategize later about how to help Maeve."

"Sounds like a plan. Why don't you meet me in my study in an hour?"

Olivia agreed. Next she checked her e-mails to see if there were any emergencies she needed to deal with.

She had an on-call service in the event one of her patients needed her after hours, but thankfully it had been relatively quiet.

Marcie was manning the office this morning completing some paperwork, but Olivia had given her the afternoon off. She started reviewing some e-mails Marcie had sent, responding and clearing up some paperwork and invoicing questions.

A text popped up on her phone from Elena.

Want details on sexy project — soon!

Olivia laughed. She wasn't about to answer her best friend now. For one thing, it would trigger a flurry of texting, and for another, she didn't know what to tell her. She and Connor had almost kissed. The memory of it made her warm and a little gooey on the inside, which scared her.

She had wanted that kiss, but would it lead to anything? Hadn't Connor already told her he wasn't looking for a relationship? But then if Elena were here, she would more than likely say, so what? And then tell Olivia to go for it and figure it out along the way.

Olivia needed to stop second-guessing herself all the time. If she didn't take a chance and veer out of her controlled comfort zone, then she would end up alone.

Being alone wasn't a bad thing. There were many people living healthy, fulfilling lives on their own. She counseled people who would be better off on their own. It was hard to help people realize the worst thing they could do was enter a relationship because they were scared to be alone. Because they thought something was wrong if they weren't married. Because they were convinced someone else could fix what was wrong on the inside.

Those conversations were like the one she had just had with Sullivan about helping Maeve stand up for herself. Relationships were about partnerships, not co-dependencies.

But knowing it didn't make her want to stop trying to find someone. She couldn't remember a time when she wasn't alone. Losing her mother when she was so young and then living with her Aunt Susan. Her aunt might not have said it out loud, but she still let Olivia know in countless small ways that she was considered a burden.

It was time to veer off course. She smiled. To order something new from the menu.

Olivia slipped her phone in her jacket pocket and went to the interrogation area. Maybe she could watch the interrogations and provide some sort of help.

She found Giz and Connor watching the monitors while Devin, Charlie, and Jack were in rooms talking to the guards.

"Did Sullivan stop by?"

"Yeah. We gave him an update. We should be finished pretty soon." Connor stood and gave her his seat. Olivia sat down and watched the sessions, rotating among the different monitors. Their responses started to bother her for some reason.

"What's going on in that head of yours, Olivia?"

She glanced up, surprised Connor had picked up on her agitation. "I'm not sure yet. Tim, have you recorded all the sessions so far?"

"Yep."

"Is there any way I can watch them?"

He gestured to the laptop at the end of the table. "Connor can access them there for you."

Connor gave her the computer after he opened the first video. She moved down to the end of the table so she wouldn't disturb the ongoing interrogations.

Olivia watched and took notes on the notepad Connor set in front of her without her even asking for it. She'd fast-forwarded through several discussions when Jack finished his last interrogation and joined them in the room, followed by Devin, and finally Charlie. When the team stood together around the table, Olivia hit pause on the videos.

"What did you find?" Connor asked.

"They're all fighting over Maeve."

Devin nodded. "Yeah, it's been the theme throughout."

Olivia shook her head. "No. Their motivations have been the same. All of them. They might have described it slightly differently, but they all started fighting for the same reason. There is no way every guard on both sides would have been motivated by the same thing. What about the animosity between the clans? Or the encroachment of the East Coast pack on the West Coast's territory? Or the fact that the contract had been kept secret from them?

"All those reasons are strong motivation for starting the fight, but they all talked about Maeve in some form or fashion."

"So what do you think it means?" Jack asked.

"This might sound impossible, but it makes me wonder if the motivation was not their own."

Connor rested his hand on her shoulder. "You'll find in our world, anything is possible."

Devin stared off into the distance for a moment. "I agree. I think this is something Darcinda needs to be involved in. Maybe this is similar to what she already talked about with Phillip's wolf. Is she still with him?"

"Yeah, she's been talking to him and trying to coax his wolf out of hiding," Giz said.

"Have you been taping their session too?" Olivia asked.

One side of Giz's mouth quirked up. "Of course."

"I'd like to watch it, but I'm supposed to be meeting with Sullivan." She pulled out her phone and glanced at the time. "And I'm late."

"In the meantime, we'll talk to Darcinda and get her take on this," Devin said.

Olivia asked for directions to Sullivan's study and hurried to meet the alpha. Hopefully Darcinda would be able to shed some light on what was happening while Olivia met with Sullivan. He might even want to postpone their Maeve conversation so he could talk with Darcinda himself.

Olivia walked up to Sullivan's study door and knocked. No response. She knocked again a little harder, and the door swung open a crack.

"Sullivan?" Olivia pushed the door open slightly and found the study empty. A bookcase took up one side of the room, with a couch sitting to the side. A large desk sat in the center of the space with neat stacks of paperwork piled on it. Olivia began to close the door when she caught sight of a shoe on the other side of the desk. She pushed open the door and rushed around the desk.

Sullivan lay unconscious on the floor with a bloody knife lying next to his open hand. Olivia yelled for help before leaning down to push the knife out of the way.

She was a medical doctor, and even though she specialized in psychiatry, she still completed a rotation in the ER. She dropped to her knees and checked for a pulse. Weak and thready.

Blood had already stained the right side of Sullivan's shirt. She ripped open the buttons and bit back a gasp when she saw the wound in his side. Looking around the room until she saw a stack of hand towels by a small sink in the corner, she went over and grabbed them all before applying one to his side while she put pressure on the wound.

Footsteps pounded toward her, and she checked his pulse again. Nothing. He wasn't breathing, either. She started compressions just as Connor and several others ran into the room. More shouting and people running in and out. But she had to block them out so she didn't lose her rhythm.

Twenty-eight, twenty-nine, thirty.

Two breaths and she was back at the breakneck-speed compressions again. She would check his pulse after this second round.

Connor knelt down across from her. "I'll take over for the next round so you can tell Darcinda what happened."

She nodded and kept count until she finished the thirty compressions. Two breaths and then she checked him for breathing. Nothing.

"Go!"

He leaned over and started the pattern again. A hand gripped her shoulder and she moved out of the way for Darcinda.

"What happened?"

"I found him like this. He has a knife wound in his right side. His pulse was weak when I first got here, and then it stopped."

"How do you know it's a knife wound?" Darcinda asked as she put her hands out, making sure not to block Connor, who was still doing compressions.

"Because of the knife, right there." Olivia glanced over to where she had pushed the knife. "It's gone."

Devin barked orders behind her about searching everyone.

Darcinda closed her eyes, and light came pouring out of her palms and flowing into Sullivan. Connor stopped the compressions and gave him two breaths before checking his pulse. "He's breathing."

Darcinda kept the energy flowing. "If this was just a knife wound, I could repair it, but there's something toxic in his system. My guess is the knife is cursed somehow. I've sent out a telepathic call to my fellow healers. I'm going to need their help."

"Is he going to be okay?" Connor asked.

Darcinda gazed at him for a moment. "It's too early to tell. Olivia, what can you tell me about the knife?"

Olivia closed her eyes briefly, blocking out the craziness going on in the room so she could try to visualize the knife. "It's silver and it had a long blade." She opened her eyes. "Maybe as long as my hand, so five or six inches?"

"Anything else?" Darcinda asked.

"It had some sort of markings on the handle, but I didn't have a chance to study it. I was too busy checking on Sullivan."

"That's okay. Did you touch it?"

"Yes. I pushed it out of the way when I knelt down next to the alpha."

"And how are your hands feeling right now?"

Now that she thought about it, her left hand did feel weird. "The left one's tingling a little."

Connor reached for her, practically picking her up before rushing her to the sink and sticking her hands under water. "Wash your hands, Olivia. Hot water. Use the soap."

She scrubbed her hands as he leaned over her. When she had rinsed them, he told her to do it again and then a third time.

After she dried her hands, he grabbed them, checking them over. "I'm okay, Connor."

When they turned back to the room, it had been cleared of all the excess people and Devin stood next to the door, leaving Jack standing guard over Sullivan and Darcinda.

"How did you get Jonathan to leave the room?" Connor asked.

"I told him to help Charlie and Giz round up the suspects," Devin said.

Connor frowned. "He's one of the biggest suspects."

Devin nodded. "Agreed, but he doesn't think that and it got him out of the way."

Darcinda still knelt over Sullivan, one hand over his side, the other over his chest. "He's stable for the moment, but if faerie reinforcements don't show up soon, I'm going to need to tap into some energy. Devin, your elf powers will do nicely."

"You got it. Let me know when you need me and I'll trade places with Jack so he's guarding the door."

Olivia could feel the tension rolling off Connor in waves.

"Who the hell would do this?"

"We're going to find out," Jack said. "And make them pay."

"We've got an entire house full of wolves as suspects. We're going to need to narrow this down fast," Devin said. "Olivia, did you notice anything?"

Olivia looked over at Sullivan's desk, which was now covered with scattered papers from all the people who had been in and out of the room in the past few minutes. "I think you can narrow it down. When I first came into the room, Sullivan's desk was neat. The whole room was neat, actually. Sullivan was lying exactly the way you see him now. He didn't put up any sort of fight. So it had to have been someone Sullivan trusted for them to get the drop on him, right?"

Connor nodded. "Right."

"And now the knife is gone. Someone who came into the room took it. But why did they take it now instead of taking it when they first stabbed him?"

Darcinda spoke up. "They left it in him, because if it had stayed in his body, Sullivan would already be dead."

"It was lying right next to Sullivan's hand. He must have pulled it out himself," Olivia said.

Darcinda glanced over her shoulder at the door. "Devin, I need some of your juice now."

Jack hurried over to guard the door while Devin knelt down next to Darcinda.

"Lay your hands on top of mine."

Devin did as instructed, and the glow coming from Darcinda's palms brightened. After a while Giz opened the door and ushered in two women. One carried a carpetbag like Mary Poppins. The other lugged a large leather-bound book.

Olivia reached for Connor's hand and grasped it. He gazed down at her with a mix of emotions flashing across his face—anger, frustration, and determination.

They would find out who did this, and Sullivan would live. He had to.

Sometimes calm and rational need to be thrown out the window.

CHAPTER 25

Connor seethed. There was no other word to describe it. He seethed with anger at whoever did this. And he seethed with anger at himself for not protecting Sully.

Sully couldn't die. He was too good a man. Too good an alpha. And the clan needed him. Connor was convinced of it. And while many in the clan wanted to ostracize Connor and Jack, it didn't mean he didn't want the clan to survive. Until Sully took over a year ago, the clan was dying a slow death fueled by hatred and closed-mindedness. And someone obviously wanted to return to the old ways.

Enough to stab Sullivan with a cursed blade.

As soon as the other healers arrived, they had moved Sullivan into his bedroom, which luckily could be reached through the back door of the study.

The three women continued to work, kicking everyone out of the bedroom, so the team moved next door to Sullivan's office as their strategy room. It allowed them to be close at hand if the healers needed anything, with the added benefit of being able to protect Sullivan.

Unfortunately, Sullivan didn't have any cameras in his private office and living quarters so they couldn't check cameras to see who had come in and out of the room. So Devin conferred with Charlie and Giz, who had already made a list of people who were in the room during the crisis.

Sullivan's advisors, Victor and Jonathan, had been there, along with some of Sullivan's guards. Even Callahan and Maeve had been there. Connor had caught a glimpse of Jonathan, but not the others since he hadn't been paying attention at the time, first keeping Sullivan alive until healing help arrived, and then making sure Olivia was okay.

Olivia was amazing. She stayed calm in the midst of the crisis and now sat with Devin and Jack, going over the list of suspects. She hadn't even taken a moment to change her clothes, because dark stains — Sully's blood — still dotted the lower arms of her jacket.

Connor's attention moved to the frighteningly wide pool of drying blood on the floor by Sullivan's desk. Evidence of how appalling this crisis had become.

For once Jonathan was actually performing his role as chief of security. All the suspects had been detained in the large dining room.

Of course Jonathan didn't yet know he was one of them. Given Jonathan's ego, Connor wasn't surprised. Charlie and Giz were watching over the group.

The door from Sullivan's bedroom opened and Darcinda walked into the study while everyone got up and moved to join her. Her face didn't give much away, although she looked drained, more than likely from earlier when she gave their alpha her energy.

"How is he?" Connor asked.

"Better. He's stabilized, but it would help a lot if we knew more about the knife."

"I'm sorry," Olivia said. "I've been trying to remember what it looks like in more detail, but no luck. If one of my colleagues were here I would have them try some hypnotherapy to see if it could pull up the memory."

Darcinda held up her hand. "I have my own version of hypnotherapy. Would you be open to it?"

Connor darted a glance at Olivia. "Will she be safe?"

"Of course," Darcinda responded.

Olivia nodded, and Darcinda led her over to the couch, where they both sat down.

"Okay," Darcinda said, "I'm going to touch the top of your head." Darcinda laid her hands on her head while Olivia kept her eyes on Connor. He managed to smile at her even though this whole messing-with-her-mind thing made him nervous.

"Close your eyes, Olivia."

She closed them.

"I want you to think back to when you walked into this room earlier today, before you found Sullivan. What did you see?"

"Nothing. The room was empty, so I looked around the room, at his bookcase and his desk." She gasped.

"What's wrong?" Connor asked.

"I'm okay. I can *see* the room in my mind, like I'm watching a movie."

"You're fine, Olivia. When did you realize something was wrong?"

"I started to leave and saw the edge of a shoe by the desk. I ran around the desk and found Sullivan lying on the ground with blood covering his right side."

"And where was the knife?"

"By his outstretched hand."

"Look at the knife now, Olivia. Can you see it?"

"Yes. Don't let go of me." Olivia opened her eyes. "I need a pencil and paper."

Connor hurried over to the desk, found paper and a pen, and rushed back over to the couch to hand them to Olivia. She sketched a symbol on the paper, an intricate, woven design. She then drew the shape of the knife around it.

Darcinda removed her hands. "Are you okay?"

"Yes! In fact, it was a bit of a rush." She handed the paper to Darcinda. "Have you seen this before?"

"No, but Melinda is the expert on curses and ancient languages. Now that we have this, we can fashion a cure for him and restore him to health. Before I go, let me check your hands and make sure the magic from the knife is gone."

Darcinda held her hands out over Olivia's. "Feels fine. The magic dissipated already."

Darcinda left the room, and everyone let out a collective sigh of relief.

"So do we go tell everyone about Sullivan?" Olivia asked.

Devin shook his head. "I don't think we should share the good news yet. In fact, I think we should tell them it's touch-and-go right now."

"You took the words right out of my mouth," Connor said as Jack nodded next to him.

"Because?" Olivia asked.

"Because if they think Sullivan is in danger of dying, they won't try to come after him again."

Olivia said, "Right. And it might help with the interrogations if the tension is ramped up as well."

Devin grinned at her. "Keep this up, Dr. Jennings, and I'm going to recruit you for the team."

There was a knock at the door. Jack cracked it a little to check out the visitor, then opened it to Sharon, who rolled a cart into the room. On the top shelf sat a tray of sandwiches and bottles of water. The bottom shelf held Connor's duffel bag and some folded clothes.

"I thought you could use some food," she said. "And I brought changes of clothes for Connor and Olivia."

Devin set the tray of food and water on the desk.

Sharon glanced at the stained carpet and went pale.

Olivia walked over to her. "Thank you so much, Sharon. You're so thoughtful."

Sharon hesitated before continuing. "How is Sullivan doing?"

"It's still too early to tell," Devin answered.

Sharon cleared her throat. "If you'll excuse me, I'm going to take sandwiches to everyone in the dining room too."

Connor pulled the stack of clothes off the lower shelf for Olivia and handed them to her before lifting out his own bag so Sharon could take the cart with her as she left.

"You'll feel better after you change," Connor said as Olivia continued to just stand there. "There's a bathroom through the door on your left."

Olivia went inside and shut the door. Connor dumped his bag on the couch and unzipped it before pulling out a long sleeve T-shirt and exchanging it for the bloody one he wore.

A few minutes later, Olivia walked out wearing a fresh blouse that actually fit her and her hair all tidied up into its tight bun.

"Come eat something."

"I'm not very hungry."

"None of us are, but we haven't had anything to eat or drink since breakfast, and we need to keep up our strength."

Devin took sandwiches and drinks to the healers in the bedroom before the four of them sat down and each ate a sandwich, discussing next steps. A few minutes later, Sharon joined them again.

"How are things going in the dining room?" Olivia asked.

"Quiet in there for the most part. Maeve and Callahan are in a small side room per your request. But..." She hesitated.

"But what?"

"But Jonathan and Victor are calling an emergency meeting of the pack council. Charlie asked me to let you know they're supposed to arrive here within the hour."

Connor glanced at his brother, whose scowl probably matched his own. Why wasn't Connor surprised his father would instigate something like this? Sullivan wasn't dead, for Fate's sake, but they were lining up like vultures for the carcass.

"Not what we need right now," Devin said as Sharon picked up the tray and left the room.

We're going to attend Jonathan's council meeting whether he likes it or not, Connor said to Jack through their link.

Damn straight, Jack agreed.

"Whatever you two are plotting, I want in," Olivia said.

Connor shook his head while Jack gave Olivia a friendly nudge. She was freakishly intuitive. And he was falling for her, hard.

Thirty minutes later he stood in the conference room with Olivia on one side and Jack on the other, facing the wolf council, who watched them with varying degrees of anxiety. The council consisted of Sullivan's two advisors and eight other members of the clan, and normally Sullivan as their leader. Only today Callahan sat in Sullivan's chair.

What. The. Hell.

Before Connor could yank the cocky bastard from the chair, the door opened and Julia walked into the room carrying a briefcase.

Jack strode over to her side. "What are you doing here?"

Victor, the other senior advisor, spoke before Julia could answer Jack's question. "Why are these females in attendance?"

Time to let them know who she really was. Olivia spoke. "I'm Dr. Olivia Jennings. Sullivan asked me to help counsel him with pack matters."

Julia spoke up as well. "I'm Julia Cole, Sullivan's attorney."

Jonathan shook his head. "We have a pack attorney."

"I'm not the pack's attorney. I'm Sullivan's attorney, retained by him for some contract work."

"And I don't understand why this means you should be in attendance," Jonathan persisted.

Jack took a step toward Julia, but she held up her hand to stop him. "I think I know what this meeting is about, which means I do need to be here. How is Sullivan doing?" Julia asked.

Which Connor found ironic, since no one else in the room had thought to ask that very pertinent question.

"The healers are still working with him, but they don't know when he'll wake up," Connor said.

Jonathan stood. "Since Sullivan is incapacitated, we need someone to lead until he is well again."

Victor nodded. "I agree. It makes sense to have one of the advisors lead."

Julia spoke up. "As I suspected, I do need to be here. Normally it might be the case to have the council decide who the interim leader is, but not in this situation. A few days ago, Sullivan drew up a lineage agreement," Julia answered.

"What's that?" one of the council members asked.

"It's a document naming his successor as alpha in the event he does not have progeny and/or is killed or incapable of performing his duties as alpha."

"And how do you know about this?" Jonathan demanded.

"Because I helped draft it."

"How is this even legal?" Callahan frowned.

Julia didn't cower under his stare. "I can assure you, it's legal. There is precedent in pack law for this type of document. In fact it was routinely done centuries ago, when violence threatened packs."

"You're an outsider," Jonathan said. "How do we know you didn't forge these documents?"

A voice answered from the doorway. "She didn't do it alone. I helped." Everyone turned to see Godfrey standing in the door. An assistant district attorney in San Diego, Godfrey was an excellent lawyer. He was also a high-level member of the West Coast pack.

Godfrey continued. "Sullivan wanted two people to witness this so there wouldn't be any argument about its legitimacy."

"Well, don't keep us in suspense. Who did Sullivan choose as his successor?" Callahan asked.

"Dawson."

Connor would swear Jonathan's chest puffed out a little bit. He glanced over at his brother, unable to keep his eyebrows from shooting up. This was the last thing the pack needed right now.

"I will lead the way Sullivan would want me to until he is able to return," Jonathan announced.

Godfrey interrupted him. "I'm sorry, I wasn't clear a moment ago. Sullivan didn't select you, Jonathan. He selected your son."

Connor's stomach dropped. Jack was going to hate being alpha, even if it was just for a day. And why did Godfrey have a calculating gleam in his eye? Connor knew he wasn't one of Jonathan's biggest fans.

Jonathan crossed his arms in front of him. "Jack has not been an active pack member for years now. How can he successfully lead this pack?"

Wow. This was a new low for Jonathan. Throwing his own son—the one he supposedly actually cared about—under the bus.

Godfrey held up his hand. "Wait. You didn't let me finish. He put Connor in charge."

What the hell? Connor's stomach didn't just drop this time, it twisted into a knot. Olivia had been wrong in her evaluation of Sullivan's sanity. Their alpha had lost his damn mind.

The room erupted into chaos, and he wanted nothing more than to leave and never look back. But he couldn't. For some reason Sullivan had put him in charge, and he would not let him down.

Godfrey called for quiet. "You might as well not waste your time on questioning the legitimacy of this contract. It is legal and binding."

"I'm not arguing whether the document is legal and binding," Victor said. "I'm saying the wolf assigned as successor is not suitable."

Angry voices erupted in the room again, and Godfrey held up his hand to silence everyone. "You've made a serious allegation. Why would Connor not be suitable?"

Silence.

Finally Victor responded. "Because he shouldn't even be here. He's an abomination. The wolf spirit is assigned to each of us individually. But these two share a spirit."

"Which has nothing to do with their fitness to lead this pack," Godfrey countered.

Connor listened to Victor spew his poison while his father stood there silently. This was exactly what Connor had dealt with his whole life, endless backhanded insults. But this? This was blatant, and in his face, and he wasn't going to take it anymore.

Olivia gaped at the emotional train wreck happening right in front of her. Good Lord, this was like a tawdry courtroom reality show. Only there wasn't a snarky judge putting any of these pack members in their place.

She had been forcing herself to stand back and let them talk, telling herself it wasn't her place to speak. But she glanced over at Connor's face, and even though he tried to hide it, she could see the pain in his eyes. It pierced her heart.

And that flicker of emotion in reaction to the council's rejection was enough to wake up the dragon in her once again. It was time to take off her calm, rational doctor persona and kick some wolf ass.

"You're assuming Connor is even willing to lead you," she announced before looking around at the surprised faces. Did they not think the human female had a voice?

"Why would he, or Jack, for that matter, want to be a part of this pack, let alone lead you? A pack who treats them like they are less than."

She didn't wait for an answer from the council members. In fact, she didn't want one.

"No one, human or supernatural, wants to be less than. And the ironic thing is, both Connor and Jack are worth more than all of you put together. They came here to defend your pack. The pack that's treated them like pariahs since the day they were born. But they did their job to protect you."

The twins' father scowled at her. "You have no say here."

She was done with the intimidation tactics. "And yet I'm going to keep talking."

Chin up, she centered herself again and continued. "I have spent years treating people who as children were abused mentally, physically, and emotionally by the very people who should have loved them. I can see that same kind of pure selfishness and lack of a soul is present in your world as well."

"Excuse me?" Jonathan Dawson sputtered, looking around the room for support from his fellow pack members.

But for Olivia, there would be no condescension or righteous indignation allowed. "No, I'm not going to excuse you for anything. You punished your sons for being born. What kind of a person, being, werewolf, whatever you call yourself, does that?"

She plowed on. "You were their *father*. *Were*, because after the way you treated them, you don't have the right to be called father anymore. You were supposed to protect them and love them regardless. Instead you used some ridiculous superstition as an excuse to ignore and condemn them. And to top it off, you ostracized them from the pack. And now you challenge your alpha's choice of leader? Your son has been chosen. You should be proud."

Olivia clenched her fists. "I don't know what might have happened to you in your past to make you this way, and since I'm not treating you as a patient, I honestly could care less.

"And I find it ironic that this grappling for power is happening when the blood is still fresh on the carpet. This should be about the pack, and protecting it, and finding out who attacked Sullivan—not your ego. Grow a pair and be a real man or wolf or whatever you call yourself." She glared at Callahan and the other advisors. "And that goes for the rest of you as well."

Everyone started talking at once, but she turned and stalked out of the room, because in that moment she didn't care. She could actually feel the anger inside of her coalesce like lava under her skin, threatening to erupt again. She barely stopped herself from running down the hall, instead speed-walking out the back door leading to the patio. She needed to be outside, away from the dysfunction, and the closed-mindedness, and the never-ending drama.

She walked in a circle on the large patio for a couple of minutes to calm herself down. And as the anger seeped away, it was replaced with regret and embarrassment.

What had she done? Her outburst was totally inappropriate. What was *wrong* with her? She was going to lose her license if she kept running amok. It was as if her id had come out and decided to throw a nonstop party while ego and superego were taking the day off.

And what must everyone think of her now? This was not how she handled things. She was a professional. She couldn't afford to lose her objectivity when everyone else was mired in emotion.

"Olivia?"

Olivia's heart sped up at the sound of Connor's voice behind her. She couldn't convince herself to turn around to face him.

"I can't believe you did that."

She cringed. "I know. I'm sorry. I—"

Warm hands landed on her shoulders and he turned her around. "What in the world are you apologizing for?"

"Because I shouldn't have said anything. It wasn't any of my busine—"

Connor put his fingers over her lips for a moment, silencing her. "You were amazing."

She studied his eyes, trying to gauge if he was being sincere. "Really?"

"Hell, yeah. You don't know how many times I've imagined saying the same kinds of things to my father."

"Why didn't you?" she asked before she could stop herself.

Connor glanced away, shrugging. "Good question. I guess I didn't see the point."

Olivia didn't like his answer. It sounded like a cop-out to her. But before she could say anything, he spoke again.

"I can tell by that raised eyebrow of yours that you are going to call 'bullshit' on what I just said." He sighed. "The truth is, there's always been a part of me who believed the crazy crap they spewed. Maybe I am some sort of curse."

She placed her hands on either side of his face, her fingertips resting on his stubble. His normal crooked grin was missing, along with the light in his green eyes. Eyes showing the vulnerability he normally hid from everyone behind his cocky persona.

"Connor Dawson, I don't ever want to hear you say those things again. You have every right to be on this earth with the rest of us. The only issue I see is your crappy father."

The right corner of his mouth turned up, and a spark flared in his eyes. A spark that started her heart thumping like a bass drummer with no rhythm.

Before she could even begin to calm her erratic breathing, he leaned down and kissed her. Holy crap, the man could kiss!

Soft lips, gentle pressure, and teasing flicks of his tongue, and she wanted nothing more than to be closer to him. Her hands still rested on his face, and she pulled him to her and welcomed him in. Olivia had kissed and been kissed before, but she had never been savored, explored, revered.

After a few more delicious moments, he backed away and sucked in a deep breath. It was then she realized she hadn't taken a breath in a while either. She sucked air into her lungs as he stared at her hard.

"*Damn*," he growled.

Her thoughts exactly.

"There they are," a voice called out from behind them.

Olivia turned as Julia strode toward them like a woman on a mission, with Jack barely keeping up with her.

Before Olivia could say anything, Julia threw her arms around her in a rib-cracking hug.

Julia finally let her go and smiled. "Thank you."

"I didn't do anything."

"You stood up for both Jack and Connor in there. Thank you."

Julia gripped Olivia's hands but let go quickly. "Ouch."

Jack was by Julia's side in a heartbeat. "I told you to take it easy with your hand. We should have gotten some ice for it."

"What happened?" Connor asked.

"I punched Victor."

Connor chuckled. "I can't wait to hear this."

Jack grimaced. "After you both left the room, they all started arguing about the legitimacy of you running the pack. Julia tried to argue the documents were binding and Victor dismissed her. Before I could tear him a new one, she walked over and punched him in the face."

"He didn't just dismiss me. He said you and Connor weren't true wolves. I couldn't let him get away with it. They kicked us out of the room after that, and Godfrey took over the discussion."

Jack gently examined Julia's hand. "It doesn't look broken. You've got a great hook."

"Just because I'm a lefty doesn't mean I can't punch. It'll be fine. In a day or two the swelling will go down just like the last time I did this."

Olivia gaped at her. "You mean you go around punching people on a regular basis?"

"No. The last time was an extenuating circumstance. She tried to hurt Jack."

"Should we have talked about this in one of your sessions?"

"I couldn't exactly tell you about it since it involved a siren and mind control."

Siren? Someone needed to explain this siren fixation.

Jack cupped Julia's face. "You are wild and crazy, Julia Cole."

Julia hugged him. "I love you, and I'm not letting anyone treat you like dirt. Life's too short, Jack, to let small-minded bigots win."

Jack stared hard at Julia. "You're right. Life *is* too short." He dropped to his knee.

Olivia slapped a hand over her mouth.

Jack reached for Julia's right hand. "I've been trying to think of the perfect way to ask you this, but I don't want to wait any longer...because life *is* too short. For some reason you love me even though I'm cranky and half the time I don't know the right words to say. But I love you so much. You opened my heart, and I want to spend the rest of my life with you. Will you marry me?"

Tears spilled down Julia's face as she went down on her knees in front of him. "It's about time you asked. Of course I'll marry you." She grabbed Jack's face and kissed him.

Olivia's tears spilled over, and she glanced over at Connor to see a huge grin on his face, his eyes looking suspiciously moist.

"Where's the ring?" Connor asked hoarsely.

Jack groaned. "I don't have it with me."

Julia peppered Jack's face with kisses. "It's okay. It probably wouldn't fit my hand right now anyway. If I had known you were going to propose—"

"You wouldn't have punched him?" Jack asked.

"No. I would have punched him with my right hand."

Olivia laughed. "Congratulations, you two!"

Jack and Julia helped each other up and then hugs and back slaps were exchanged all around. After a few minutes of happiness, reality brought them plummeting to earth.

"I wonder how things are going in the meeting," Julia said.

Connor frowned at her. "I can't believe you didn't try to convince Sully to name someone else as his successor. Why didn't he choose Jack?"

"It's not my place to tell Sullivan what to do. I was there to help draw up the contract. You'll have to ask Sullivan why."

Olivia took his hand. "I think you need to stop asking, 'Why me?' and instead ask, 'Why not me?'"

"We'll find out soon enough what happened," Connor said.

"You're still in charge," a baritone voice announced from the lodge's back door. Godfrey walked toward them a moment later.

"How many more people are going to invade this patio?" Connor grumbled.

Godfrey shrugged. "You'd better get used to it for a while. You're going to be leading this crazy pack. I don't know if you consider it a good thing or not after the way you've been treated, but I think it's a win. We have to change the old ways and superstitions or this pack will never survive. We don't need someone undermining Sullivan's rule while he's recuperating."

Olivia squeezed Connor's hand. She knew he could do this, and if she needed to keep telling him so until he believed it, she would.

Connor squared his shoulders. "Let's go set some ground rules."

Handling adversity is the true test of a good leader.

CHAPTER 26

Connor stood at the head of the conference room table, the council members sitting silently on either side. He was done with feeling less than, as Olivia had said. She stood at the back of the room watching, along with Julia, Jack, and Godfrey. Connor first looked each council member in the eye, finishing with Jonathan and Victor, before he spoke.

"You have made it abundantly clear that you don't want me here. But it isn't your choice to make. Our alpha has chosen me to lead for him. And I will lead you to the best of my ability until he's able to stand in front of you again.

"First order of business is to find out who attacked Sullivan. Everyone waiting in the dining room as well as this room will be interviewed about this matter."

Connor's last words made several people sit up straighter and others frown. Good. Maybe now they'd realize he meant business.

"Any questions?"

Silence.

"Someone will be here shortly to interview each of you."

Connor started to leave, but a voice stopped him.

"Alpha," one of the council members spoke. "Not all of us agree that you should be ostracized. We'll follow you."

Several members nodded in support.

The knot lodged in Connor's stomach since Godfrey's earlier announcement loosened slightly. He wouldn't have to fight the entire council to get things done.

"Thank you."

He walked out of the room, followed by Jack, Julia, Olivia, and Godfrey. "Okay, where's the rest of the team?" he asked.

"Devin is guarding Sullivan. Charlie is watching the dining room, and Giz is ready to start the interviews," Jack said.

"Godfrey and Julia, will you stick around and help with the interviews? You might pick up something," Connor said.

They both nodded.

"Also, before we start the questioning, I think we should find out if Darcinda was able to translate the symbol on the knife. Whoever attacked Sullivan will know what it means, and we need to go into these interviews with as much knowledge as possible."

Connor continued. "Then I think we triage the interviews. First up, everyone Sullivan trusted enough that they could get close enough to attack him before he could put up a fight."

"I would say the two advisors first," Godfrey said.

"Agreed."

"What about Callahan?" Jack asked.

Connor frowned. "I'm sure he's hip-deep in this somehow, so we definitely question him as well. I just don't think he could have caught Sullivan off guard. Sully doesn't trust him."

"Maybe he's using someone else to do his dirty work," Jack said. "Like Maeve."

Olivia shook her head. "I can't imagine Maeve attacking Sullivan."

"You have to admit, though, that all the weird stuff happening around here is centered on her," Connor said.

Olivia rested her hand on his arm. "Let me talk to her, then. If you take her into an interrogation room for questioning, I don't think you'll get anything out of her."

"She could be dangerous. I know you see a scared woman, but she's also a wolf, and she is powerful."

"Then have someone waiting right outside the door while I talk to her. At the very least, if Callahan is involved, she may be able to shed some light on things."

Connor's wolf paced a bit under his skin. He didn't like the idea of Olivia getting more involved, but after watching her stand up to the council today, Connor didn't think she would give in without a fight. He was still in awe at her defense of him. She was a tigress, and his wolf was more than fine with that. "Okay, but there will be someone standing right outside the door when you talk to her."

Olivia winked up at him. "Yes, Alpha."

His brother and Godfrey chuckled behind him, but he chose to ignore them. If he was alone with Olivia, he would remove that cheeky grin with a kiss. After their kiss a few minutes ago, he was lucky he had been able to stand in front of the council and think straight. He would be exploring their relationship—yes, he actually was no longer afraid to use the R word—as soon as they solved this case and Sullivan was back on his feet.

The group joined Devin in Sullivan's study and asked Darcinda to join them.

"How is Sullivan doing?" Jack asked.

Darcinda gave them a thumbs-up. "Much better. He's out of the woods, but we're keeping him in a magically induced coma to help clear the curse from his system."

Everyone breathed a collective sigh of relief, and Devin reminded them this news should not leave the room. They didn't want anyone coming after Sullivan again if they thought he was recuperating.

"Can we wake him up and ask him who stabbed him?" Jack asked.

Darcinda shook her head. "I wouldn't advise it yet. He's still weak, and he needs to recuperate before we try to wake him."

"Have you figured out what the symbol on the knife means?" Connor asked.

"It's an ancient curse. We believe its origins come from the Lunadorium."

Godfrey frowned. "I thought it was just a myth."

"What are we talking about?" Devin asked.

Darcinda nodded toward Godfrey to continue. "I learned about the Lunadorium as a child through wolf witch stories told by my grandmother."

Darcinda picked up the story. "Legend has it that centuries ago a line of witches mated with wolves and the result was the Lunadorium. The knife Olivia drew for us would have been used during ceremonial sacrifices. The symbol on the blade drained the sacrifice of its powers, allowing for a swift death."

"How kind of them," Olivia remarked.

Darcinda shrugged. "They would have believed they were being humane."

"So what does this mean?" Connor asked. "Do we have Lunadorium in our clan who are intent on killing Sullivan? And for what purpose?"

"Maybe they want someone from their group to be in control," Julia said.

"We haven't located the knife," Devin said. "We searched everyone once we knew the knife was missing, but by then whoever took it must have stashed it somewhere."

Connor tapped his hand against his leg. There had to be some way to find that knife. "If the knife is magical, can you create some sort of locating spell to find it? Like a magic divining rod?"

Darcinda's eyes widened. "Possibly, but the spell would be hampered by distance."

"I think the knife is still in the lodge. We've kept everyone here since the attack," Devin said.

"It would also be hampered by whatever it was hidden in. If they used a metal like lead to block it, we won't be able to find it."

"Let's try anyway. Sullivan takes first priority, but can you take care of the locator spell?" Connor said.

"I'm on it," Darcinda said before going back to the other room.

"In the meantime, let's start the interviews," Connor said.

Olivia walked into the small sitting room where Maeve had been staying for the past few hours. She nodded at Charlie, stationed just outside the door, before she closed it. When Maeve caught sight of her, she rushed over to Olivia. Her eyes were red-rimmed.

"How is Sullivan?" she asked.

"He's still unconscious," Olivia said. It was the truth, but she felt guilty for not telling her Sullivan was going to be okay, especially when Maeve crumpled a little bit.

"My fault," she whispered.

Olivia put her arm around her shoulders and led her to the couch. "Why don't we sit down for a bit? Tell me why you think it's your fault."

Maeve shook her head. "I can't get the picture of Sullivan lying on the ground out of my mind."

So she was going to ignore Olivia's question, but Olivia would try again later. "It's a terrible image."

Maeve swallowed. "Except you didn't fall apart when you saw him. You were helping him. I couldn't move. I froze."

"How did you end up in the room?" Olivia asked gently.

"My father was talking to me, and we heard you yell. Father ran to see what was happening, and I followed him." She shuddered. "I wish I hadn't gone into the room."

Olivia brushed Maeve's hair behind her shoulder so she could see her face better. "What was your father talking to you about?"

Maeve glanced away. "He asked what Sullivan and I had talked about. If I…"

"If you what?"

Maeve jerked to her feet and began to pace. "If I had screwed it up. Father is convinced I'll say or do something to make Sullivan not want me and then he'll void the contract."

"Is that why you keep saying it's your fault?"

Maeve spun away from her and returned to her manic pacing. Olivia started to ask the question again, but she stopped when she saw Maeve's shirt had ridden up, uncovering her lower back and revealing a dark mark.

"Maeve. Are you hurt?"

Maeve's eyebrows drew together. "What do you mean?"

"What is that on your lower back?"

Maeve jerked her shirt down. "Nothing."

Olivia tried to keep her voice calm when what she really wanted to do was scream. "Please, Maeve. I'm here to help you. Let me see."

"I'm not supposed to show anyone."

"I understand, but I want to help if I can."

Maeve pulled up the shirt, and Olivia was able to breathe again when she saw the dark mark wasn't a bruise, but the edge of a tattoo. But when Maeve pulled up her shirt and exposed the whole tattoo, Olivia's breath caught again. The design was eerily familiar. While not identical, it had the same characteristics as the symbol on the knife.

Maeve turned to look at her. Was she the one behind all of this?

Olivia cleared her throat and smiled. "It's an intricate design. Does it mean anything?"

Maeve shrugged. "Father said it's the West Coast pack's symbol. He wanted me to get it done so Sullivan would see how serious I am about being his wife."

Olivia's stomach turned.

Maeve frowned. "I can see by your face that you're upset."

Olivia held up her hands. "No—"

Maeve interrupted her. "I don't blame you. My father had me branded like a cow."

"I'm sorry." Olivia held out her hand, and Maeve walked over and grasped it. What did the symbol mean? And why would Callahan have her tattooed with it? Was he behind all this?

"Maeve, I'd like to introduce you to someone. Her name is Darcinda, and she's a faerie."

"Father said I shouldn't talk to the faeries."

Which meant they should definitely talk to the faeries. "I don't know why just talking to someone could possibly be wrong. Do you trust me not to hurt you?"

Maeve studied her for a moment before nodding.

It was time to see a faerie about a tattoo.

Confession is good for the soul. . .
if you have one, that is.

CHAPTER 27

Connor took a deep breath as he stood in Sullivan's study with Olivia, Devin, Julia, and Godfrey. They had just started interviewing the others when Olivia came in to tell him about Maeve. Darcinda was with Maeve now, and Connor had immediately sent Jack to get Callahan so they could have a little chat with him.

That had been a while ago. And still no Jack and no Callahan.

Jack, what's going on? Connor relayed to him.

We can't find Callahan.

"Callahan's missing?" Connor said out loud, and everyone around him tensed. *How could that happen? Keep looking.*

"We lost Callahan?" Devin asked.

"They're searching for him now, but yeah, he somehow slipped out, which means he basically just confessed to being involved in Sullivan's attack."

"Someone inside must have helped him escape," Godfrey said.

"And that someone is probably the same person who

got close enough to stab Sullivan." Connor growled. "So damn close!"

"And he knew it, which is why he left," Devin said.

Olivia frowned. "Without his daughter."

"Are you surprised?" Connor shrugged.

"No. It's actually a blessing for Maeve. I wonder how things are going with her and Darcinda?" As if in answer to Olivia's question, the door opened and Darcinda came into the room alone. "Where's Maeve?"

"Maeve's fine. Melinda is with her. You were right to be concerned about the tattoo, Olivia. It's another symbol from the Lunadorium."

"What does it mean?" Connor asked.

"It's hard to explain, but it's a symbol that loosely translates to the word 'tenfold.' It amplifies powers."

"And it's on Maeve because?"

Darcinda's eyes widened. "Because she's very powerful, and she doesn't know it."

Devin frowned. "How is that possible?"

"Because the power lives in Maeve's wolf. I need to spend some more time with her, but if I'm not mistaken, her wolf is an empath."

"She absorbs others' emotions," Olivia said.

"And why would Callahan want her to absorb others' emotions?" Godfrey asked.

"Good question," Darcinda said. "Powerful empaths don't just absorb emotions, they also have the ability to project them, and the symbol makes her wolf very dangerous to those around her."

"Good God! Don't you see?" Olivia threw her arms out. "Callahan turned her into an emotional time bomb. It's why all the guards had the same motive for fighting, and why the other guard tried to kidnap Maeve. She projected her fears to them."

"Actually, she probably projected to their wolves, and they took over."

"Damn. That is scary," Godfrey said.

"So what the hell is Callahan's motivation?" Connor asked. "If he planned to kill Sullivan all along, what was the point of the marriage contract to begin with? If he wanted to control this pack, why wouldn't he wait until after Sullivan and Maeve were mated and then kill him?"

Devin spoke. "Maybe his only intent was to destroy Sullivan, although it seems like a really convoluted way to do it, especially now that the contract is null and void."

Julia shook her head. "The contract isn't null and void."

"What do you mean, Julia?" Devin asked.

"I can't believe I didn't think of this before, but when I reviewed the contract, I saw a paragraph referring to transferability. If Sullivan dies before the mating ceremony, Sullivan's successor would be allowed to fulfill the contract as well."

"How is that kind of misogynistic crap legal?" Olivia blurted. "Are we just supposed to pass Maeve around like a piece of meat?"

Julia grimaced. "It's couched in some legalese making it sound like both parties must agree to it, but we know how it would have turned out."

"Which brings us full circle to someone helping Callahan in exchange for the promise of becoming alpha and getting Maeve in the bargain," Connor said. He wished Jack was here, because odds were Jonathan was the guilty party.

"Well, we can't wait for Sullivan to wake up," Godfrey said. "The guilty party might bolt like Callahan did."

Connor crossed his arms. "So let's bluff our way through this. Darcinda, did the locator spell work?"

"Not yet. I think the knife has to be hidden in something capable of blocking its energy signature."

"When Olivia touched the knife, it left magical residue on her," Connor continued.

"Yes, but as I explained, it dissipates rather quickly."

"What if the person who stabbed Sullivan doesn't know that?"

Devin nodded slowly. "Good thinking, Alpha."

Connor turned to Darcinda. "Are you up for a little con?"

Darcinda's eyes danced. "Absolutely."

Half an hour later the conference room was full of anxious wolves. Between the council members, two advisors, and the guards who were detained after the attack on Sullivan, the room was packed. The team stood spaced out around the room to mitigate any issues. Olivia and Julia had insisted on being there, and Godfrey stayed close to them, ready to defend and/or hustle them out of the room if things got too crazy.

Darcinda stood next to Godfrey holding a stone bowl with wisps of smoke rising and circling from the top. Connor remained silent for a few more drawn-out moments, ratcheting up the tension, which could only help when they set the trap.

Jonathan was the first to break the silence. "Why are we all here? Has something happened to the alpha?"

Connor turned to face him. "Sullivan is still unconscious. As I stated earlier, we need to determine who will be charged with his attack."

Victor spoke up. "I would think the answer is obvious. Callahan has escaped. He must be guilty. We should be out searching for him instead of being locked in here."

Several others agreed with him.

Connor held up his hand to quiet them. "I agree we need to go after Callahan, but we need to first determine who he was working with."

A couple of angry growls and murmurs filled the room until one of the council members, the same one who had spoken up to support Connor earlier, called for quiet. "Why do you think someone's helping Callahan?"

Connor appreciated having at least one person willing to listen. Now they could continue with the performance. "Because Sullivan didn't fight against his attacker, which means whoever did it was someone he trusted. Callahan would never have gotten close enough to stab him."

Sparks popped up in the air from the bowl Darcinda held, causing several people to jump.

"Sorry about that," she said.

Connor schooled his face as Darcinda walked over to him. She should get extra points for that bit of theater.

"Why is the faerie here?" Jonathan asked.

"We've come up with a way to determine who the traitor is in our midst. The knife used on Sullivan was infused with magic, and anyone who touched it will still have residual magic on their skin." Connor held his hand above the bowl, and the smoke remained the same. Connor beckoned to Olivia. "Olivia touched the knife when she found Sullivan. Show them."

Darcinda held out the bowl and Olivia held her hands over the top. The smoke turned from white to red. But when Olivia pulled her hands away the smoke faded to white.

"Now that Callahan is on the run, we can't waste any more time. We're asking everyone in the room to be tested."

Connor watched the group. Everyone put their hands up on the table—except Victor and Jonathan.

"This is ridiculous!" Victor said. "We're wasting valuable time. Callahan needs to be stopped. Did it ever occur to you that the person working with him is his daughter?"

Jonathan frowned. "Let's be done with this already."

Darcinda walked to one side and started testing hands while each held their hands over the smoking bowl willingly. Darcinda then went over to Jonathan and Victor's side of the table. Connor held his breath until Jonathan lifted his hands from beneath the table to be tested. The smoke stayed white. Victor pushed up out of his chair and stepped away from the bowl. Charlie and Jack moved closer to him.

"Is there a problem, advisor?" Connor asked.

Jonathan stood as well. "What have you done, Victor?"

Victor growled. "Something you didn't have the guts to do yourself. I tried to rid us of an alpha who would destroy everything Morgan built."

Jonathan growled back. "By working with Callahan? How does that make it better? Morgan and Callahan fought for the past twenty-five years. They hated each other. Why would you trust him?"

"Because he promised I could be alpha of the West Coast pack! But Sullivan won't die! Shoot him, stab him, it's like he's a damn cat with nine lives instead of a wolf."

"You shot him?" Jonathan yelled. "When did you shoot him? Who's guarding him now?"

Connor held up his hand. "He was shot last week."

Jonathan gaped at the news before scowling at Victor. "And you assumed you would be chosen to succeed Sullivan?"

Victor barked out a hard laugh. "You can't honestly think they would have chosen you, Jonathan. You're nothing but a self-righteous prick. Nobody can stand you. The council would have chosen me over you, and then I would have been alpha. And Callahan sweetened the deal by giving me his daughter."

Connor heard twin gasps behind him, but he didn't dare turn to see what Julia and Olivia were doing. Godfrey could keep them from attacking. Hopefully.

Connor wanted so badly to tell Victor how Callahan had set him up to fail with Maeve as a ticking emotional time bomb, but he didn't want anyone to lash out at her. He knew firsthand what it was like to be shunned due to fear and ignorance, but it didn't mean he wouldn't make the bastard suffer.

"Thanks for the confession, Victor. Especially since this"—he pointed to the bowl—"was all smoke and mirrors."

Darcinda threw the bowl up in the air and it disappeared in a flash of light.

"Any magical energy you had on your hands has dissipated by now. This test wouldn't have revealed anything."

Victor bared his wolf teeth and lunged at Connor. Jonathan turned and punched Victor in the face before flipping him over and wrenching his hands behind him. Jack was there seconds later and secured Victor's hands with a band, pulling him away from the table.

Connor looked at the stunned group in front of him and nodded to Jonathan. "Now we go after Callahan."

Sometimes you don't realize your true strength until you're forced to use it.

CHAPTER 28

Three days later and still no sign of Callahan. After further investigation, they had discovered two of his guards were missing as well. Connor glanced at the various stacks of data, charts, and maps littering the conference table and pinned to the walls. At this point the bastard could be anywhere. Hell, he could even be out of the country. But something in his gut told Connor he wasn't far away. Callahan struck him as a sore loser, which meant he was not going to let sleeping dogs lie.

Connor chuckled at his pathetic pun. He hadn't gotten much sleep in the past few days. He'd been overseeing the manhunt with Devin and dealing with not only the West Coast pack council, but also the East Coast pack, who were reeling from Callahan's actions. They had offered the guards who arrived with Callahan to help with the manhunt as well.

Devin would be arriving shortly to help with coordinating the teams. Last night Connor sent him, Charlie, and Jack home to get a good night's sleep and spend time with their mates. He thought about Olivia.

The stubborn woman was still at the lodge. She refused to leave Maeve, who had fallen apart when the truth came out about Callahan.

On the one hand, he had a basic, bordering on primal, need to keep her close. On the other, they hadn't managed a moment alone together. And he needed them to be alone and together very soon.

A sharp knock on the door made him glance up. Darcinda stood in the opening with a big grin.

"Please tell me you have good news."

"He's awake. Is that good enough for you?"

Connor let out a little whoop. "How's he doing? Does he remember anything?"

"Oh, yeah. He started making demands the minute he woke up. I told him everyone was okay, because he wouldn't settle down until I did, but for the rest of his demands, I ignored him. I checked him over and got him to eat some broth. He grumbled about wanting a steak. Said he was starving."

"Good sign."

"Yes. I told him he can't get out of bed yet, but I would let him have some visitors. He's asking for you. He has a million questions, so be prepared. And fair warning. If he gets too tired, I'm kicking you out."

"Got it." Connor walked with Darcinda to Sullivan's bedroom, but stopped outside when he heard Sullivan talking.

"Get me something to eat, please. Soup, sandwich, something. She's not here right now, and I won't tell her if you help a starving wolf out."

Darcinda rolled her eyes. "This one is a trouble-maker. Why are the bossy ones always such bad patients?"

Connor shrugged before Darcinda opened the door. Sullivan sat propped up in bed, his hair wet and wearing a new T-shirt.

"Here's a visitor for you," she announced. "We'll leave you two alone. If you behave yourself and stay in bed, I'll have Sharon make you some food in a little bit, even though you tried to get Melinda to sneak you some when my back was turned."

Sullivan gave her a big smile. "Yes, ma'am."

Darcinda snorted. "Your smile isn't going to work on me. You're still restricted to bed rest until I say otherwise."

The two faeries left, shutting the door behind them.

Connor walked up to the bed. "It's about damn time you woke up, Sleeping Beauty."

Sullivan chuckled. "I'm glad to be awake. I understand there's been some excitement going on around here."

"A bit of an understatement."

"Sorry I got stabbed and missed out on the fun."

Connor frowned. "I would deeply appreciate if you don't do it again. Do you remember what happened?"

"Oh, yeah. Darcinda said you figured out Victor was behind it."

"Yeah. Him and Callahan. We're still looking for Callahan."

"Where's Maeve?" Sullivan asked.

"She's still here. She didn't take the news of her father well."

Sullivan scooted up farther in the bed. "Pull over a chair and sit down. I need you to bring me up to speed on everything."

Fifteen minutes later Connor took a breath. Sullivan had been peppering him with questions while Connor filled him in on everything, including the ongoing manhunt.

Darcinda walked in with a tray. "Lunch is served."

"Thank the Fates," Sullivan groaned.

"I have a chicken sandwich and potato salad for you, Connor."

"Sounds wonderful."

Darcinda turned to Sullivan. "And I have some more beef broth and some Jell-O for you."

Sullivan's mouth fell open, and Darcinda laughed out loud. "I couldn't resist. I brought the same for you."

Connor chuckled.

"But once you finish eating, you're taking a rest," Darcinda said.

When Sullivan looked like he was going to argue, Darcinda backed away—with the tray—as if to leave the room.

"Wait! Okay, I give in."

She set the tray down on the side table. "Excellent. Fifteen more minutes and then I'll kick Connor out of the room."

They dug into the food, Sullivan moaning at the first taste of his sandwich. Connor was hungry himself, so they ate in silence for a few minutes.

Sullivan rested against the pillows and gave Connor a hard stare. "You've got something else on your mind. I can see it on your face. Spit it out."

Connor set their empty plates on the table and sat back down. Did he really want to get into this right now with Sully? But he needed to know. "Why me?"

Sullivan's expression told him he understood what he meant. "Because of your drive, and your passion, and your stubbornness. I knew if anyone could take on this pack, it would be you. And I wasn't wrong. Based on what you told me just now, you are doing a damn fine job as alpha."

"I can't ever fill your shoes."

Sullivan shrugged. "I don't expect you to fill my shoes, I expect you to fill your own. Did you do what you thought was best?"

"Yes."

"Then it's all you can do."

Connor swallowed around the lump in his throat. "This experience has changed me, that's for damn sure."

"I don't think just being alpha has changed you. I'm thinking a strong, stubborn woman has played a part in it too."

"You've been in a coma. How do you know so much?"

Sullivan shrugged. "I'm gifted that way."

Olivia picked at her salad. It was good, like all the food Sharon made, but she wasn't very hungry. The last few days had been stressful for everyone involved. Connor had been working nonstop in his role as alpha, and Olivia hadn't been able to spend any alone time with him.

She wanted to talk to him about their future, if there was a future. Or maybe *future* was too big and scary a word. Maybe they could start by talking about The Kiss. And then relive The Kiss. That would definitely work for her. But she knew now was not the time to broach it. Connor was busy coordinating all the efforts to find Callahan.

And then there was Maeve.

She had retreated into her thick, seemingly impenetrable shell when she found out what her father had done. Before they had been able to explain about her powers, Maeve had holed up in the bedroom Sharon assigned to her. And she didn't seem interested in emerging anytime soon. Even Olivia's attempts to simply chat with her had been met with little to no response.

Olivia had called her service and either postponed

sessions or moved her more critical patients' sessions scheduled for the week to two other psychiatrists in the practice. She felt guilty about it, but since she never took time off, they were both more than happy to help out. Plus, she was distracted, and her patients needed her undivided attention.

She had been camping out the past couple days at the lodge. She told herself it was to watch over Maeve, but if she was being honest, she was also watching over Connor. He had been given a huge responsibility, which he was handling well, but it didn't mean she was willing to walk away from him.

Darcinda walked into the dining room with an empty tray and set it down before plopping down beside Olivia.

"Sullivan is awake."

"Thank God. How's he doing?"

"Bossy, but good. He is resting right now, but when he wakes up—and I don't expect him to be asleep for long—he's asked to see Maeve."

Olivia sighed. "I haven't been able to get Maeve to come out of her room in days. Maybe seeing Sullivan is okay will convince her."

"Yes. I'll be there too, so we can try some tag-team healing with her."

"Sounds like a plan," Olivia said as she pushed away from the table.

Five minutes later Olivia knocked on Maeve's door.

"I'm not hungry," Maeve called out.

Olivia opened her door and peeked inside. "And I'm not here with food."

Maeve sat in the chair next to the window. The same place Olivia had found her the last couple times she visited. "Hello, Maeve."

Maeve straightened from her slumped position. "Olivia."

"I've got some good news to share. Sullivan is awake."

Maeve's eyes widened. "He's okay?"

"Yes, and he wants to see you."

Her wide eyes filled with tears. "I can't see him."

"Why not?"

But Maeve shook her head and wouldn't answer.

Olivia took a step toward her. Time for some tough love. "Maeve, Sullivan has asked to see you. In fact, you're one of the first people he asked to see since he woke up. I think you owe it to yourself and to him to honor his request."

Maeve blinked up at her, and Olivia waited, and waited some more, until Maeve finally stood up. She ran her fingers through her hair and walked with Olivia out of her room—small victory—and down the hall.

When they reached Sullivan's room, Maeve stopped, turning to look at Olivia, her eyes huge, pupils wide.

Olivia squeezed her hand. "Everything's going to be fine."

Olivia knocked lightly on the door, and Darcinda opened it, saying cheerfully, "Perfect timing. He's awake and asking for Maeve."

They walked into the room and found Sullivan propped up in bed. He was a little pale, but otherwise looked great for someone who'd been unconscious for days.

"Maeve, Olivia. It's good to see you."

"And it's good to see you awake," Olivia replied when Maeve stood there and simply stared.

"I understand you found me and saved my life."

Olivia shrugged. "It wasn't just me. It was a team effort."

"Well, thank you."

Sullivan watched Maeve, who stood mute next to her. "How are you doing, Maeve?"

Maeve blinked as a tear slid down her face. "I'm sorry."

Sullivan frowned. "For what?"

"This is all my fault. My father said I was cursed. That I made people do bad things. But I didn't want anything bad to happen to you, I swear!"

Olivia wrapped her arm around Maeve's shoulders. "This isn't your fault, Maeve. Your father lied to you."

"Olivia's right," Sullivan said. "I don't blame you for this."

She turned to Olivia. "No, you don't understand. That guard attacking us was my fault."

Darcinda walked over and stood in front of Maeve. "What were you thinking about the night you were attacked?"

Maeve's eyebrows drew together. "What do you mean?"

"Were you upset? Was your wolf upset?"

"Yes. I was so nervous. I felt like I was on display. And I wanted someone to just want me for me. Why doesn't anyone want *me*?"

Olivia managed to keep her emotions in check during Maeve's outburst while Darcinda kept talking to Maeve.

"And then the guards started fighting over you, and Phillip tried to kidnap you."

Maeve nodded.

Darcinda placed her hands on Maeve's shoulders. "Here's the truth. You are special. Your wolf is empathic. And it has been sharing its fears and emotions with other wolves."

"So it *is* my fault!"

"Did you do it on purpose?" Olivia asked.

"No."

"Then how can it be your fault?" Olivia pushed.

"He almost died—"

Sullivan interrupted her. "This is not your fault, Maeve."

"He's right," Olivia said. "Your wolf did not compel anyone to stab Sullivan. Victor did it so he could take over as alpha. Your father bargained with him to do it."

Maeve took in a shuddering breath. "How do I control my wolf?"

"The tattoo your father forced you to get is an amplifier for your power," Darcinda said. "For now I can put a dampening spell on it while I figure out a way to remove the ink. But it's hard to remove a permanent magical marking."

Maeve wiped her tears away. "The tattoo isn't p-permanent. I h-had the artist apply it with henna."

Darcinda beamed. "Henna I can work with."

"I wasn't going to let my father brand me permanently."

"Good for you," Olivia said, glad to see this tiny spark of defiance in Maeve.

Maeve gave a deep sigh. "Plus he made me cover up my birthmark. He said it was ugly, but I didn't want to hide it."

Darcinda gestured for Maeve to turn around, then pulled up the back of Maeve's shirt and held her hand over the tattoo. "It shouldn't take long to remove it."

"Then what?" Maeve asked.

"Then we work with your wolf to manage its empathic abilities naturally," Darcinda said. "If your wolf feels safe, it won't strike out."

"I don't know what it's like to feel safe."

Sullivan spoke up. "You have a safe place with our pack, Maeve. You are more than welcome to stay here, but it's your choice to make."

Olivia held Maeve's hand. "And if you decide to stay, I'll be here for you as well. We can work on letting your fears go."

"Okay. I want to stay here for now."

"There we go. All gone," Darcinda said, pulling her hand away from Maeve's back. The tattoo had vanished, leaving behind a deep plum birthmark in the shape of a crescent moon split in the middle.

"What the hell?" Sullivan exclaimed.

Olivia looked over at the alpha. He had gone from slightly pale to white.

Darcinda rushed around the bed. "What's wrong?"

"I'm fine," Sullivan choked out. "Maeve, how long have you had your mark?"

"My whole life, why?"

Sullivan threw back the covers. "I need to show her something, faerie. Don't try and stop me." He stood on shaky legs and lowered the waistband of his pajama pants to show an identical tattoo on his hip.

Maeve's eyes widened. "What does that mean?"

"It's called the alpha's mark. I have this mark, as did my father, and his father, and so on for generations."

"So I got this from my father."

Sullivan pulled up his pants. "No. This mark is only found on the West Coast pack."

Holy crap. Olivia glanced over at Darcinda, who had obviously caught on to what Sullivan was saying.

"How old are you, Maeve?"

"Twenty-four. I'll be twenty-five in a month."

Sullivan nodded to himself. "I'm thirty-five. When I was ten, my father visited the East Coast pack to work on a treaty with them. I remember because he missed my birthday party that year, and he came home early from the talks. Something had happened to cause the meetings to be suspended. Father wouldn't talk about it, but our two packs have been on the outs ever since."

He stared directly at Maeve. "I think we're brother and sister. Our birthmarks mean we have the same biological father."

Maeve slapped her hand over her mouth and didn't say anything for a moment. Olivia and Darcinda stood silently, letting the girl absorb what Sullivan told her.

Maeve blew out a hard breath. "It makes sense. Father…Callahan…barely tolerated me for most of my life. Mother died when I was born, and I always thought Father blamed me for her death. *I* blamed me for her death."

Sullivan shook his head. "You've been paying the price for something that happened before you were born, between two spiteful, egotistical men. But now we have a chance to get to know each other. I was alone and now I have family again."

Maeve blinked, and more tears trickled down her cheek. "I've never had a family. Not a real one. I used to wonder if my mother would have loved me if she had lived."

Olivia's eyelids burned.

Sullivan held out his arms to her. "She would have loved you. How could she not?"

Maeve walked into his arms and laid her head against her big brother's chest. Sullivan looked up at Olivia and Darcinda with tears in his eyes.

Fear is a controlling bitch.

CHAPTER 29

Olivia felt too wilted, too emotionally drained, to put her doctor's hat on, but she needed to leave the hat off for a while anyway.

She left Sullivan's room to give him and Maeve some time alone. Even though she got to witness a happy ending, Maeve still had hard work ahead for both her and her wolf.

But Olivia had promised to help, and now Sullivan had pulled her into his protective arms, Maeve finally had someone she could lean on. She couldn't wait to tell Connor what happened, and practically jogged to the conference room to spend a few minutes with him. But it was empty.

She walked down the hall and ran into Sharon. "Have you seen Connor?"

"He went out back to get some air."

"Thanks." Olivia walked out on the patio and found it deserted. Maybe he had gone for a walk. She stepped off the stone patio and walked a short distance into the woods. Up until this point she hadn't ventured into the woods due to her anxiety, but it didn't bother her too much as long as she could look back and see the house.

Olivia stopped at a small bluff. She took a deep breath of the fragrant forest air and, after a couple of minutes, she turned to go back to the lodge when a hand slapped over her mouth and she was jerked back against a solid chest. She clawed at the arm wrapped around her chest and tried to scream around the large hand clamped over her mouth.

"Shut up," he growled, his hot breath hitting the side of her face, before he picked her up and jogged farther into the woods.

No! She dug her nails into his arm, and he growled again, showing her a mouthful of long, sharp teeth. When she saw his eyes glow, her brain short-circuited as if she just touched a live wire. He started running then, easily loping along as if he wasn't carrying a full-grown woman.

She wasn't sure how long he ran, but he finally came to an abrupt halt and let her go. She dropped to the ground, her teeth clacking together at the impact.

She scrambled away from him, and he shook his head. "You're not going to get away from me, but I'm going to let you try. My wolf loves the chase."

"Why?" she choked out.

"Because Callahan wants revenge on the wolf who thought he could be alpha. And you're going to serve as the message. Callahan told me to watch for an uptight bitch with glasses, and when you came strolling out of the house, I knew the Fates smiled down on me."

His face started to elongate into a snout as his voice went guttural. "Run, or I'll gut you."

Olivia jerked upright and took off running. The woods closed in around her, and she shoved away the branches as they tore her clothes and scratched her skin.

The monsters had finally found her.

He laughed behind her, getting closer and closer, no matter how hard she ran.

Olivia couldn't breathe. She was going to die, but she stumbled onward.

"I'm going to carve a message on you for your alpha lover to find because Callahan doesn't want him to die yet. He wants him to suffer first."

She tripped over a root and sprawled flat on the ground and he circled her.

He transitioned in the blink of an eye into a large brown wolf. He bared his teeth, and saliva dripped from his fangs while he advanced on her.

The wolf launched himself at her, and she screamed, flinging her arms up as if they might somehow provide some semblance of protection.

Before the wolf touched her, it was thrown off to the side by a gray wolf. The two huge animals rolled across the ground, snapping and snarling and fighting with now-bloody teeth and claws. Their growls shook the ground, and she made herself small by pulling in her legs and wrapping her arms around them. She couldn't move, but she couldn't look away either.

She should be running. She should leave and never return to this place where her monsters had emerged from the recesses of her terror, brought to life in bloody Technicolor before her eyes.

The brown wolf who attacked her lunged for the gray wolf, but the gray was too fast. He twisted and wrapped his jaws around the brown wolf's neck, biting down and then jerking the wolf to the side. Olivia cringed at the sound of its neck snapping. The gray wolf dropped the carcass and turned to her. She looked up into glowing green eyes. She knew those eyes.

Connor's eyes.

No, no, no. She rested her forehead on her knees and tried to imagine she was in her apartment, sitting in her soft chair, but the ground was too hard and the smell of dirt and pine choked her every time she sucked in shallow breaths. *No, no, no, no.* She was going to hyperventilate if she didn't slow her breathing down.

But was that such a bad thing? She would pass out from too little oxygen and escape the monsters.

Connor was the monster.

"Olivia."

She jerked at the sound of his voice and looked up at him.

He crouched in front of her, holding his hands up, palm out, in front of his naked chest. "It's okay. You're going to be okay now."

She shook her head.

"Are you hurt?"

She shook her head again, because she couldn't remember how to speak.

"Okay. We need to move, Olivia. I want to get you somewhere safe."

Words finally bubbled up in her brain and she whispered them. "Nowhere safe."

He frowned. "Wait here for a moment. Do you see through the trees there? That's a box with clothes in it. I'm going to put on some clothes and then we're getting out of here."

She saw the box. And saw the dead wolf, who had morphed back into his human shape, the man's neck twisted at an odd angle.

She rested her forehead on her knees again.

No. Her head hurt, and she didn't want to talk anymore.

Connor ran over to the box as fast as he could. He didn't want to leave Olivia alone for long. He grabbed some clothes and quickly pulled them on. Luckily, there were some shoes. Even though they were a size too big, they'd do.

He flashed back to the absolute terror on Olivia's face when she saw his wolf.

Connor called out to Jack through their link.

Connor! Are you okay? Giz just called us and said the security feed showed someone grabbing Olivia and carrying her away.

Yeah, he called me and told me what was going on, and I ran after them. But I lost my phone in the woods when I transitioned. We're a couple miles south of the lodge. I only heard a little bit of the conversation before I attacked him, but that damn wolf chased and taunted her. I'm pretty sure he's one of Callahan's guards. They put a hit out on her to punish me.

We're only a couple miles from the lodge, Jack said. *We'll meet you there.*

I'm not taking Olivia back there. The damn wolf practically walked up to the house and snatched her. I'm not risking her again. You guys need to keep looking for Callahan. If you capture him, we can stop him from coming after Olivia.

Where are you going to go?

We're not very far from the Demon Burrow. I'm taking her to McHenry.

Connor hurried back to where Olivia sat huddled in a tight ball, her forehead still on her knees.

"Olivia."

She jerked again at his voice, and his heart felt like it was caught in a vise.

"I'm going to take you somewhere safe."

She shook her head again and again, like the pendulum in a grandfather clock. "Maeve told me you can't hide from a wolf."

Damn it. "We're not hiding. But we are going somewhere wolves don't go."

She stared at him.

He kept talking. "We're going to a friend. He's a demon who lives on land you don't want to venture on unless you're invited."

"And we're showing up unannounced?"

She had to glom onto that part. "It'll be fine."

He reached for her, but she cowered away from him. His lungs burned as he held in his wolf's howl. He held up his hands in a gesture of surrender, and she got to her feet and wobbled slightly before righting herself.

"The demon burrow is a few miles east. Do you think you can walk there?"

She nodded.

They walked along in silence for a bit. Connor could see Olivia's energy was waning, but when he asked her if she wanted to stop or needed help, she kept shaking her head and backing away from him.

He despised the fear in her eyes, especially when he knew he'd contributed to it. He was one of the monsters now. He didn't know if she would ever be able to trust him again, but this wasn't about him. It was about protecting her. She was all that mattered now.

Connor's wolf started to pace. He could feel the energy from the barrier protecting the demon burrow from the rest of the forest. While it wouldn't stop supernaturals, it did stop humans from accidentally wandering onto demon land.

"We're getting close to the magical barrier we're going to have to walk through. It's going to sting a little bit, but you'll be fine once you make it through."

She nodded again, still not asking any questions, which made his concern ratchet up a notch. Olivia was always curious. She was shutting down even further.

He stopped in front of the barrier and had Olivia

walk through first while he followed close behind. She rubbed her hands over her arms, more than likely to try to ward off the tingling sensation. He held up his hands without touching her to get her to walk along with him.

After another few minutes, they entered a courtyard. With the log house on one side and a forge and a workshop on the other, the place still looked the same as the last time Connor was there.

The large man walked out of the workshop and stared at them for a moment.

"It's good to see you, McHenry," Connor said.

"And you as well, Connor."

"We need to stay here for a while, if you'll have us. This is Olivia."

McHenry bowed his head slightly. "Hello, lass. Welcome." To his credit, he didn't act like anything was amiss, even though Olivia looked like she was ready to fall over.

She stood for a moment and stared up at him in silence. Olivia was rarely silent.

McHenry breached the awkward silence. "Let's get you settled in my house. How's a warm bath sound?"

She blew out a fractured breath as they trooped into the house. "Please."

McHenry gave her a friendly smile as he led her up the stairs to a guest room. Connor waited at the bottom of the stairs for McHenry to return a few minutes later.

"She's settlin' in upstairs. Give her some time to calm down a bit. She's damn near ready to jump out of her skin."

"I'm not surprised. She's been through a helluva lot in these past few days." Connor gave McHenry an abbreviated version of the attack.

"What is it with you wolves, that you keep bringing beautiful women into my forest?"

"It was the only place I could think where the wolves wouldn't come after her. They aren't going to want to piss you and the rest of your demon clan off. Too risky."

McHenry nodded thoughtfully. "Very true. I can be a bit hotheaded."

"Except Julia would say your bark is much worse than your bite."

"How are Julia and your brother?"

"Recently engaged."

"I had hoped your brother would screw it up and I could sweep in and take Julia for my own."

"Not gonna happen. He's actually not so much of a cranky bastard anymore."

"I'm happy for both of them. Julia does have a way about her."

"Yes, she does."

"And what is this one's story?" McHenry asked.

"She's a doctor, a psychiatrist, who we brought in to help with a pack issue. But things got out of hand."

"Her red hair reminds me of my homeland."

"Don't even think about it, demon," Connor barked.

McHenry laughed. "Another wolf bites the dust."

Connor shook his head. "Nope. We're just friends." If that...especially now.

"Are you saying it out loud to convince me or yourself?"

"After what she's been through, the last thing she wants to do is mate with a wolf."

"And what does your wolf have to say about it?" McHenry asked.

"He's not too happy, but he's not in charge."

"She can stay here until you get your pack under control. But don't be surprised if I win her over with my charm."

A growl erupted before Connor could stop it.

McHenry's eyebrows rose over twinkling eyes. "Glad to see your wolf isn't in charge."

Olivia sighed as she leaned back against the high sides of the claw-foot tub. She had never been in this type of tub before, but she was enjoying every second of it. Her tightened muscles uncoiled along her shoulders and down her lower back, more and more the longer she relaxed in the warm water. She had been surprised when McHenry had offered her some lavender soap to use.

He was a burly man with a beard and a bit of a Scottish accent. She got the impression that only men lived in the house, but she wasn't going to spend too much time thinking about it. She reached for the bar and ran it along her arm, the lather bubbling up along with a calming scent.

Connor said she would be safe here, and she wanted to believe him. The logical part of her brain knew he would never hurt her, but the emotional, phobic side of the equation wanted to run far away from him. She inhaled slowly through her nose, counting to three before exhaling. How many times had she told her patients about this breathing technique? More often than she could count, but it worked, which was what mattered.

After a few minutes of calming breaths, she finished washing up, reluctantly climbed out of the tub, and dried off before wrapping the towel around her. When McHenry showed her the bathroom, she literally dumped her clothes on the floor and climbed into the tub while it filled up with warm water. She hadn't even spared a moment to look at herself. Now she stood in front of the mirror and cringed.

Her hair on the one side had come out of her bun and hung in wet tendrils down her back and over one shoulder. A small twig was tangled in her hair, as were several ragged leaf pieces.

Olivia attempted to pull the pins out of her bun and cursed at how her hair had twisted itself into knots. She wrenched open the vanity drawer and found the pair of scissors she now held in her hand.

Did she dare?

Why the hell not? She unfolded her bun and ran the scissors across it, snipping, and then snipped again. Her hair fell in chunks onto the floor. She combed her fingers through her hair, which was now a chin-length bob. She would have to see a real hairdresser to clean it up, but actually it didn't look too shabby.

Olivia cleaned up the mess and then put on the robe McHenry left for her. She practically swam in it, even after rolling up the sleeves, but it would do for now. She was so tired she could barely focus, even with her glasses on.

She padded out of the bathroom over to the bed and ran her finger over the intricate quilt pattern before turning the covers back. Before she could collapse on the bed, someone knocked lightly on the door.

"Come in."

Connor peeked his head in and grinned that ridiculous grin of his that made her heart speed up. She quickly squashed her reaction when she remembered what he could turn into.

"Just want to see how you're doing."

"Much better. I'm just going to lie down for a bit."

His eyes tightened on her. "You cut your hair."

She raised her fingers to the ends of her newly shorn hair. "It was a tangled mess."

"I'm sorry, Olivia."

"It's just hair. It was weighing me down. Besides, I

wore it up all the time. I don't know why I bothered to keep it long to begin with." Why was she babbling?

"I'm sorry about more than your hair. I wish we had never brought you into all this. If I could take it back, I would in a heartbeat."

"I know you would."

He took a step toward her, and she flinched before she could stop herself.

Connor froze. "Here's some chamomile tea in case you need something to help you relax."

He held it out to her, but she couldn't get her hands to lift. So he set the cup on the dresser.

"Thank you. You're a good ma-man."

"It's okay. I'm a man and a wolf. And neither of us plan to hurt you. I'm sorry you were pulled into this mess. That you had to relive what happened to you. That you had to see me fight and kill in wolf form. But not every werewolf is bad."

She nodded. "I know. At least my logical self knows. Just like I know there are bad and good people too. But the little girl in me…"

"Sees us as monsters, and I can't blame you. I won't let Callahan hurt you again, Olivia. Why don't you lie down and rest for a bit? Hopefully we'll hear something from Jack soon and this will all be over."

He backed away from her and shut the door behind him.

She looked like a lost little girl in McHenry's giant bathrobe. The last thing he wanted to do was leave her, but she needed to get some sleep, and she wouldn't feel safe with him in the room.

He jogged down the stairs toward the kitchen, where he heard someone banging pots and pans. Connor walked into the room and found McHenry pulling items out of cupboards.

"What are you cooking?" Connor asked.

"Trying to figure out what to make for dinner. Jamie and Andrew are out on a supply run, so we don't have much to work with."

"How are your nephews?"

"Good. Jamie is still workin' through some things, but he's alive thanks to you and your team. How's the lass doing?"

"She's resting."

"And how are you doing?" McHenry pulled out a bottle from the cupboard and set it on the table with two glasses.

"I'm fine."

"You don't look fine, wolf. Sit down and have a drink with me."

Connor sat, and McHenry poured amber liquid in both glasses, before handing one to him. "This is the good stuff, so don't go chuggin' it, now."

Connor took a sip and put it down on the table.

"How can I help?" McHenry asked.

"You already are helping. You let us stay here when we have wolves after us. I'm hoping Jack and the rest of the team will find Callahan soon. After that, Olivia will be happy to be far away from this and me."

"She's in shock right now. I'm sure things will get better."

Connor took another drink before responding. "It's not just what happened today. As a child she was lost in the woods for days. She still has night terrors about it. Until recently the only thing she remembered from it were flashes of hair and teeth and glowing eyes. But she had a flash not too long ago of a wolf."

McHenry nodded. "The Fates are tricky. And today she was attacked by a werewolf."

"And she saw me turn into the thing that haunts her."

"You aren't what haunts her, Connor. It's her fear."

He shrugged. "Either way, she doesn't want me near her. How do I get past that?"

"If you care about her, you'll find a way."

A scream had Connor out of his chair and running for the stairs with McHenry right behind him. He launched himself up the stairs and had the door open to Olivia's room in seconds.

She sat upright in bed, pulling at her neck like the last time she had a night terror. It was as if him talking about them with McHenry had brought on an episode.

He walked closer to the bed. "Olivia, wake up. It's Connor."

Olivia's glazed eyes cleared and she looked at him. And screamed louder. The screams pierced his chest like razor blades. Connor backed away from the bed and McHenry stepped around him.

"Lass, it's okay. You're safe."

Olivia blinked at the sound of McHenry's deep voice and the screams finally subsided. Connor stood back and let McHenry comfort the woman he ached to comfort himself.

But this wasn't about him. It was about Olivia and keeping her safe. It was what mattered now, his own feelings be damned.

There is nothing rational about a phobia.

CHAPTER 30

Olivia frowned at herself in the mirror. She was wearing a flannel shirt and a pair of sweatpants, both too big for her, but she couldn't keep wearing the robe.

She walked out of the bedroom and found McHenry in the hall waiting for her. He took in her clothes. "Still too big on you, but they'll do for now. My nephew Jamie is smaller, so I raided his closet."

Olivia looked down the hall but they were alone.

"He's making dinner for us right now. He wanted to give you some space."

She nodded while her eyes and throat burned. She felt so bad about her reaction earlier, but when she saw Connor, her terror latched on harder.

McHenry gazed at her for a moment before responding. "You know, lass, there's nothing wrong with crying. It's cathartic. Or punching something, as long as you don't punch my walls, that is."

Olivia felt the corners of her mouth quirk up.

McHenry gave her one firm nod. "There you go. You've still got a sense of humor in you. All is not lost."

"Is that your professional opinion?"

McHenry grinned. "Not like yours. Connor told me you're a psychiatrist."

"A psychiatrist who can't get over her own phobias."

"You're being too hard on yourself. Come along with me to my workshop. I want to show you somethin'."

She followed him down the stairs and out the front door of the house to his workshop. She gaped at the space. It was a blacksmith forge with several work-stations and various metals stacked throughout the space. But there was also something magical about it, and her skin tingled as she turned in a circle to take it all in.

"This is amazing."

"Thank you. Metals are a part of me. As an earth demon, I feel the magic channeled from the earth into the metals, and I fashion them into things. There's something calming about working with my hands. Do you want to help me with a project?"

When she nodded, he showed her how to file down the rough spots on a curved piece of metal. They worked in companionable silence for a while. McHenry was right. the work gave her something to concentrate on instead of her frayed nerves and guilty feelings where Connor was concerned.

"You're doing a good job."

"What is this going to be?" Olivia asked.

"I don't know yet. The metal hasn't finished speakin' to me."

"Thank you for letting me help…and for earlier."

"You're welcome. I'm sorry you had to experience something so ugly."

She had to nod since her throat closed.

"Here's the thing, Olivia. I have met people over the years who might appear pretty on the outside, but they're ugly monsters on the inside. I'm sure you've seen the same thing in your line of work."

Olivia nodded again.

"In the supernatural world, the same can be said. But the twist is that some of us may look like monsters on the outside from time to time, but it doesn't mean we're ugly on the inside.

"What happened to you today was awful, and while I can't grow fangs and claws, I would have still destroyed anyone who did that to someone I loved. Connor feels the same way."

Loved?

"Connor can't love me."

"I can't speak for Connor. It might be too early for love, but he cares about you deeply. If you felt something for him before this happened, don't let someone else, human or wolf, come between you and an opportunity for happiness."

She looked up at the man towering next to her. "If you ever get tired of metals, you would make a great counselor."

McHenry chuckled. "I'll keep it in mind."

Connor let out a deep breath as he finished up the dishes and went upstairs. It was getting late, and Olivia had settled into her room. He'd been happy to see she was hungry at dinner and ate a full meal.

He had called Giz on the special phone they gave McHenry the last time they were here. He'd hoped to hear they had captured Callahan, but they still hadn't found him. Olivia deflated a bit after the call, but McHenry got her talking again, and the three of them had actually carried on a conversation. It was stilted at first, but after a bit Olivia actually looked up at him. And at one point she smiled at him.

He had never thought something as simple as a smile would make him feel like howling at the moon.

He walked down the hall to find McHenry standing outside Olivia's room holding a pillow and a blanket.

"What are you doing?"

"I figured you'd be campin' outside her door tonight. I thought to make things more comfortable for you."

"You do have a heart, McHenry."

McHenry handed him the bedding. "Don't be lettin' that get out."

Connor grinned as he stretched out on the floor. But he couldn't relax. His wolf hearing picked up on Olivia's restlessness as she tossed and turned in the bed.

His wolf whined. *I know how you're feeling, but she doesn't want us near her. She's still scared of us.* The whine turned to a growl.

Connor lay on the floor, staring at the ceiling, thinking about what had happened over the past few weeks. How could his life have changed so much in so short a time?

The bedroom door opened and Connor sat up. Olivia hovered in the doorway wearing a mammoth bathrobe. She wasn't wearing her glasses, and her newly shorn hair curved around the collar of the robe.

"Are you okay?"

"Yes." She sat down in the hall across from him. "I thought I heard you and McHenry out here earlier. Did McHenry put the wards on the house like he said he would?"

Connor nodded. "Yes. He put a ward to prevent anyone from getting into the house tonight."

"You don't have to sleep outside my door, Connor. I'm fine."

His wolf whined at her words. "Maybe *I'm* not fine. Maybe I want to be sure you're okay."

She sighed. "I lied. I'm not fine either. I know you're a good man, Connor. And I'm trying to work through what happened earlier today. I'm sorry I can't help my reactions to you. I know this probably seems irrational to you, but phobias don't care about being rational. They invite the irrational into your psyche to come in and take root. In my case it's been decades. And now what happened to me as a child played out again today."

Connor clenched his hands. "Did you see a wolf in your night terrors again?"

"Yes. I saw him, and I don't believe he's a product of my imagination anymore. I think he's real, down to the color of his eyes—one blue and one brown. I was definitely with a wolf while I was lost in the woods as a child."

His gut twisted. "I wish we had never brought you into this."

Olivia sighed again. "Here's the thing, Connor. I appreciate it, but this is not your fault. You didn't cause my mother's traffic accident, or the fact that I was thrown from the car. You didn't make Alex's stomach glow, which led to me learning paranormals exist. And you didn't force Callahan and Victor to try and kill Sullivan, or the wolf to attack me."

"He attacked you as a message to me," he reminded her.

"It still doesn't mean it's your fault. You're applying logic to a madman. And while it isn't a word I would normally use, it fits. Look what he did to Maeve."

"I'm still sorry."

"And I'm sorry your father treats you the way he does, and that you lost your mother, and that some of your clan is closed-minded and tried to ostracize you."

"You are an amazing person, Olivia Jennings."

"So are you. And thank you for saving me today. You're so willing to shoulder the blame, so I'm going to make sure you also accept the good you've done as well. For me and for the clan."

He leaned forward, and she cringed slightly. Her eyes filled with remorse and his wolf whined at her reaction.

"It's okay, Olivia. I know you can't help it. We'll stop Callahan and get you home soon."

Her eyes drooped a bit.

"Why don't you go back to bed? You need your rest."

"Why don't you come in and sleep on the chair?"

He thought about it, then shook his head. He didn't want her to wake up in the night and be frightened by him.

She stood without protest and trudged into the bedroom. He pulled the pillow and blanket over to the far wall he was leaning against and lay down.

A moment later, the bedroom door opened and Olivia came out with her own pillow and blanket, lying down on the other side of the hall to face Connor.

He sighed. "Stubborn woman. Go back to bed."

"No, stubborn man. Good night."

"Night, Liv." Lying across from her, even if it was on the floor, felt intimate, and the nickname just popped out.

She closed her eyes, and he watched her relax into the pillow. He appreciated the comforting words she'd said—was in awe of it after what she had been through—but if her psyche couldn't stand having him near her, it wouldn't matter in the long run.

*Live in the present
or your past will never let you out of its grasp.*

CHAPTER 31

Olivia had fallen asleep on the floor rather quickly. She was sure it was due to mental and physical exhaustion, or maybe it was because Connor was watching over her. Whatever the reason, she slept hard and opened her eyes hours later to see Connor dozing across from her.

She watched him for a few minutes. She'd never truly seen him at rest before. He normally bubbled with energy and responsibility. Taking care of everyone else while believing he wasn't worthy of the same consideration.

His eyelids moved a little bit, and she wondered if he was dreaming. What would it be like to dream of something good for a change?

He jerked in his sleep and she sat up at his anxious movement. Was he actually having a nightmare?"

"Connor. Wake up."

His opened his eyes—his glowing eyes—and she scooted away from him, slamming her back against the wall.

He smiled, and long, sharp teeth peeked out before he sat up. "Don't you look yummy this morning."

Her heart threatened to bust out of her chest. "Connor, what's wrong?"

"What's wrong?" He sighed. "Everything, really. I'm tired of all this"—he waved his hand between them—"of you. So much drama. And baggage. We mustn't forget the childhood baggage."

His indifference ripped at her. "I'm sorry."

He laughed. "Yes, you are."

She frowned at his cruel taunt.

Wait a minute.

Connor wasn't a monster.

He was the man who brought her chamomile tea when she was hurting, and cooked like a chef, and was willing to lead a clan who had ostracized him. He was confident and sexy one moment and vulnerable the next. He had an incredibly loving relationship with his brother, and was willing to challenge her and sacrifice himself for her.

This, whatever this was, was not Connor.

"Stop."

His eyebrows rose at her tone of voice. "Don't tell me you're actually going to grow a spine and stand up for yourself at this late date."

"Something's wrong with you, Connor. This isn't you."

"Maybe this *is* me and I've been fooling you all along. Which is pretty ironic if you think about it. You're trained to read people, and yet you can't tell who I really am. Didn't I tell you I'm not looking for a relationship? I don't want you. You should be used to it by now. Your mother left you, and Susan didn't want you either. Who wants a crazy kid to raise?"

Olivia stared at him for a moment. She had never told Connor about her aunt, so how did he know her name? And why would he say any of this? It didn't sound anything like what Connor would say. Instead, this was a recitation of all her own insecurities, her own fears.

This isn't real.

She had lived most of her life in terror. Now she was through with letting terror control her.

This isn't real.

This isn't real!

Olivia jerked awake and sucked in a deep breath, trying to keep her heart from shutting down. A glowing symbol floated above her, and she stared at it for a moment before it faded away.

She turned to Connor, where he lay across the hall from her, a glowing symbol floating above him as he thrashed on the floor.

What was happening? "Connor, wake up!"

He didn't respond, scowling as he rolled from his back to his side. Was he trapped in a dream like she'd been? Was the glowing symbol the cause?

She sat up and shook him slightly. When she touched him, images flashed in front of her eyes and she jerked away from him.

"McHenry!" Olivia yelled.

No response. Olivia got up and ran down the hall to McHenry's bedroom. She opened the door and saw the burly man lying in bed with the same glowing symbol floating over him as well.

Now what?

She ran to her room, tripping over the giant bathrobe, but somehow keeping herself upright. She yanked off the robe and pulled on the clothes McHenry gave her yesterday, and her glasses. She had to get help. Running down the stairs, she searched for the cell phone Connor used last night to call Tim. It sat on the kitchen table. She pushed the send button and it rang twice before someone answered.

"Hello?"

"Tim? It's Olivia, I need your help."

"What's wrong?"

Olivia quickly explained what had happened to her and described the symbols over Connor and McHenry.

"It sounds like a spell. Probably something from the Lunadorium, since Callahan is probably behind this."

"How do I break it?"

"How did you get out of the dream?"

"I realized it wasn't real. My fears and insecurities were keeping me in the dream."

"Connor and McHenry have to do the same. Or you have to find the source of the magic and nullify it. It has to be somewhere nearby. I'm sending help, but it will take an hour or more before they can arrive."

Olivia ran to the front of the house and peeked out the window. A glowing orb hovered in the middle of the courtyard, pulsing like a heartbeat. Apparently McHenry's wards kept people out, but not magic.

How could she stop it? And if she went outside by herself, who was waiting for her? Right now whoever was outside couldn't enter the house because of McHenry's wards. If she opened the door now, it might mean anyone could enter.

She would try to help Connor first. The flashes she saw earlier when she touched him made her wonder if she could access his dream and convince him it wasn't real. Olivia raced back upstairs and knelt down next to Connor.

She placed her hand on his shoulder and her muscles pulled taut before she ricocheted away from her place kneeling next to Connor and into a tunnel of blackness. Seconds later, light flooded her eyes and blinded her. She blinked a couple of times and found herself standing in what looked like a courtroom.

Connor stood in front of a raised judge's bench with three judges sitting side by side, glaring down at him. His father stood up front as well.

Jonathan spoke. "Your honors. The evidence of his guilt is ironclad. He was tasked to protect the human woman and he failed her. His own brother died because of him. Why should we allow him to continue to be a part of the pack?"

"Connor!" Olivia walked over to him.

He jerked away. "You're dead. You can't be here."

Olivia stepped up to him. "I'm not dead, Connor. This isn't real. You're not standing trial, and Jack is not dead."

Connor shook his head. "No. I saw you both die. I still have his blood on my hands. Yours too."

Olivia grabbed his arms. "I need you to fight this, Connor. You didn't let any of us down. And right now I need your help. Please!"

He hesitated, looking like he was going to protest again, so Olivia wrapped her arms around his neck and kissed him, pouring all her emotions into this dream kiss until he finally kissed her back.

He slipped his tongue into her mouth, and she sighed against him. When they finally broke the kiss, she opened her eyes and found him staring up at her in confusion from his prone position on the hall floor.

She glanced up in time to see the symbol fade above him.

"Olivia?"

She grinned. "Welcome back."

Olivia placed her hands on McHenry's shoulders again. Nothing happened. After she explained things to Connor, they had each tried to enter his dream, but they couldn't see anything the way she'd been able to with Connor.

"Now what? Do we wait for the team?"

"We can't wait for them. I don't know how long McHenry can stay in that state. I can feel his energy weakening, which means the wards are weakening as well."

"The glowing orb has to be what's causing it."

"Right. We have to get rid of the orb. Except we know it's a trap."

Nerves danced along Olivia's skin. "Yes. The question is, how many others does Callahan have with him?"

Connor walked over to the window and studied the courtyard. "We know he ran away with two guards, and I took care of one of them already."

"So if we're lucky, there are only one or two to take care of."

Connor nodded. "I'll go out there and take the orb out. If we can wake McHenry up, it would help even the odds."

"How are you going to do it?"

"Maybe if I interrupt the energy flow."

"Iron," Olivia said. "McHenry told me about different metals, and he said iron can nullify magic. He has iron in his shop."

"I'll run to his workshop and grab a strip of it."

Olivia shook her head. "They'll be waiting for you."

Connor placed his hands on her arms. "Olivia, I'm worried about McHenry, and if we don't do something soon and then the wards break, they're going to come into the house anyway."

She sucked in a breath. She had finally faced her fear. She wasn't going to let it gain a stranglehold on her again.

They went downstairs and stood in the entryway. Connor turned to her. "For right now, you're safe in the house. Don't come outside. I'll take care of the orb and whoever is out there, okay?"

"You do whatever you have to to survive, even if it means turning into your wolf. Got it?"

He saluted. "Yes, ma'am. Remember. Don't come outside."

Connor opened the door and dashed full bore across the courtyard to the workshop. Olivia held her breath as he wrenched open the door and ran inside, reemerging moments later. Tingles ran along Olivia's neck. This was too easy.

Olivia looked across the courtyard just as a wolf appeared, running toward Connor.

"Connor! Behind you!"

The wolf jumped, and Connor swung the metal pipe, hitting him in the side, the wolf and metal bar flying in opposite directions. The wolf jumped up and circled Connor, who looked for the metal bar. He couldn't take on the wolf in his current form without a weapon.

The wolf's glowing eyes pulsed in the same rhythm as the orb in the courtyard. Was the wolf getting power from the orb?

"Change!" Olivia yelled as the wolf advanced on Connor.

Connor transitioned into his gray wolf, and the lupines circled for a moment before launching at each other with claws and teeth. Movement to the right caught Olivia's eye. Callahan stood at the edge of the courtyard watching the fight. The light in his glowing human eyes also pulsed in time with the orb.

She needed to stop them or Connor wouldn't stand a chance against both of them, especially if they were supercharged with magic. The iron bar lay three feet from the porch of the house. She could race out, grab it, and go for the orb while they were distracted.

The wolf viciously attacked Connor, raking his chest with its claws. Connor staggered back. *Move away from the orb, Connor. Move away!* Olivia screamed in her mind. As if he heard her, the fighting moved toward the workshop, and Callahan still seemed to be in a trance as he continued to watch the fighting.

She glanced again at the iron bar lying on the ground, focusing on that one thing as she raced out of the house and down the porch steps. She picked up the metal—God, it was heavy—before running and swinging the bar like a baseball bat, slicing the orb through the middle, and it sparked before disappearing.

"No!" Callahan yelled close behind her. His yell morphed into a growl.

Olivia spun, using her momentum to swing the bar and land a solid hit to Callahan's wolf's head. Before he could recover, she lifted the metal and slammed it down hard on the top of his head again. The wolf lurched to the side and lay on the ground. Was he dead?

A thud sounded beside her, and Olivia brought the bar up to her shoulder preparing to attack again. But Connor's wolf stood next to an unconscious one.

She could have sworn he sported a wolfy grin. She dropped the bar and held out her hand to him. He gazed up at her with his glowing green eyes, hesitating.

"It's okay." She needed to somehow let him know she wasn't scared of his wolf anymore.

He padded over to her slowly and bent his head down, as if bowing to her. She rested her hand on his head, enjoying his soft fur as she stroked his ears. Then she knelt down and placed her hands on each side of his long face before noticing the blood matted in his hair.

"I'm sorry you're hurt. Let's get you cleaned up."

Connor bumped his nose under her hand, and she laughed at his shameless bid for more petting. Of course she obliged him.

A moment later the front door of the house banged open and McHenry burst outside, eyes wild, looking around the courtyard.

"Well, now. Did I miss all the fun?"

Take charge of your own life,
or you'll always be living in a world of "what if."

CHAPTER 32

Olivia walked out onto the porch. She could still hear McHenry blustering inside, complaining about the team showing up. Devin, Charlie, Tim, and Jack had arrived and taken care of Callahan and the other wolf. Darcinda also came along in the event someone was injured, and was checking Connor over now. McHenry had stormed into the house at the sight of her, muttering about damn faeries.

Before Connor went upstairs, he made sure she was okay and then said silly words like…now that this was over, she could go back to the way things were and not have to deal with them anymore.

And the more he said, the more she realized it was a form of goodbye. A farewell speech.

Well, she wasn't ready to say goodbye.

She wanted him. She was tired of being alone. Of trying to control every part of her life so she wouldn't get hurt. How could she let him know she wasn't scared of him anymore?

After she had rejected him so profoundly? And cringed when he came near her?

She had been scared and lost, and he had done nothing since she met him but protect and comfort her. She wanted to be a part of his life. To be his.

Which was the scariest thought of all. To open herself to another person. To let him in and bare her soul. A once-upon-a-time fragile soul she had shored up for a new future, a future not plagued with phobias, but full of possibilities.

So Olivia began formulating a plan. The first step of her plan was having a word with one of the team. She needed a favor, and she hoped someone could help her. But who to approach?

She weighed the pros and cons in her mind and decided on Tim. As if he read her mind, the front door opened and Tim came out on the porch.

"There you are. I wanted to see how you're doing."

"I'm good, Tim."

He gave her a crooked grin.

"What?"

"I haven't been called Tim in years."

Olivia smiled back at him. "Well, you probably should get used to it, since I'm not going to call you Giz."

"So I'm going to be seeing you around then?"

"If I get my way, you are," Olivia said. "About my sticking around...I could use your help with something."

"Name it."

She cleared her throat. If she could stand up to her fears, she could ask a simple question. "Do you have any condoms?"

His eyes actually bugged out—there was no other word for it—and then he blushed. "Out of all the questions you could have asked me, that is the last one I would have expected."

Olivia's face heated too. "Well...I don't know if you heard Connor earlier, but he was talking about me leaving here and things going back to normal. And…"

"And what?" he prompted.

"And I've done normal. It's highly overrated. I'm more than fine with paranormal. So I've decided to stage a coup. It's time for some action…" Ugh. Bad word choice after her request.

Tim's eyes danced. "Hence the condom."

Olivia grinned. "Exactly. I'm going to show Connor what he'll be missing if he lets me go."

"I knew you were perfect for him. Told him so, too."

"You did?"

"Yep. He's a stubborn one. Be ready for a battle."

"I'm ready."

Tim pulled out his wallet and fished out a foil-wrapped square. "Here you go. Good luck."

Olivia tucked the condom in her shirt pocket and went inside. Step one complete.

Step two of her plan was now in play. Olivia was going to have a word or two with another male, one Connor Dawson. She dashed up the stairs and stopped outside the open bedroom door. Darcinda stood at the end of the bed where Connor sat buttoning up his shirt.

"Thanks for healing me. Normally I can heal claw marks on my own."

Darcinda nodded while she replaced some items in a bag. "The wolf was channeling dark magic at the time he clawed you. Your body just needed a little help."

"How is the patient doing?" Olivia asked.

"He'll survive. Are you feeling okay?"

"I'm good."

Darcinda picked up her bag and walked over to Olivia, squeezing her arm on her way out the door and winking. *Go get him,* she mouthed.

Olivia wanted to laugh out loud, she was so excited. Did she have a determined expression that gave her away? Maybe it was a good thing. Determined on the outside and the inside.

Darcinda walked out of the room and shut the door.

Connor stood up. "Is everything under control downstairs?"

"McHenry is blustering about being invaded, but I think he's actually happy to see everyone—except Darcinda. What's with those two, anyway?"

"I'm not sure."

"Well Callahan was ranting about how Morgan Ross destroyed his life so he planned to destroy his son and his clan. He is truly unbalanced. McHenry wonders if some of it has to do with him using dark magic. Charlie, Devin, and Tim are going to leave in a little while to deliver the two prisoners to the Tribunal so they can stand trial. Jack is going to stay here with us until we're ready to leave."

Connor opened his mouth, but Olivia held up her hand stopping him. "I don't want to talk about Callahan anymore."

Connor's eyebrows rose. "What do you want to talk about?"

"You, me…us."

He sighed. "I can't be with you."

"Why not?" she asked.

"Because I won't continue to expose you to this. The terrors, the bloodshed, I won't let you be hurt anymore."

"You saved me, Connor."

"I was there. You saved yourself. Hell, you saved me and McHenry too."

"I'm not talking about today. I'm talking about since I met you."

His eyes flared. "Olivia—"

She plowed on. "I want to be with you, Connor. Yes, you told me you aren't looking for a relationship, but I think you should give us a chance. I feel down in my bones we're supposed to be together."

He stared at her hard. Was he going to reject her?

"I like this side of you."

Her heart tap-danced in her chest. "I've decided to speak up. Objective listening is overrated. Sometimes you have to take action."

"Is that so?"

"Yes." She moved closer to him and rose up on her toes to nip at his chin, and he reared back slightly.

"You sure about this, Liv?"

Her toes curled at the sound of his nickname for her. "Definitely."

Connor's mouth curved up on the side right before he wrapped his arms around her and kissed her. She gasped, and his tongue slipped inside her mouth. She welcomed him in and then her tongue joined the party. She had missed being in his arms, feeling him caress and cherish her. How could she have ever backed away from him?

But at the time her reaction was not about him, but about her. Her inability to let go of the past. Her paralyzing fear. Her unwillingness to let go of control. Well, control didn't mean security, and it sure didn't mean happiness.

So, in this moment, and in many future moments, she would tell control to go stuff itself.

She giggled, and Connor pulled back to look down at her.

"Are you laughing?"

"Maybe."

"Then I am definitely doing this wrong."

She rested her hands on his face, rubbing her fingers along his scruff. "The one thing you can be sure of is you were doing it right."

His grin kicked up a notch, dimples and all, and she couldn't help but smile right back at him.

"I forgot how big your ego is. The last thing I should do is feed it."

Connor reached down and picked her up, cradling her against his chest. "My self-esteem took a real blow this week. I could use some emotional props right now."

She groaned and laid her head against his chest. "You're going to use all my psychological terms against me, aren't you?"

"A man's got to fight fire with fire."

"Stop talking and kiss me, Connor."

He laid her down on the bed. "Yes, ma'am."

He settled on top of her and kissed her like a man on a mission. Lips, tongue, light nips, and her insides fluttered before growing warm and melting like caramel spreading across every part he touched.

She nipped his chin again, and he growled before pushing away from her, eyes wide.

"I'm sorry."

Olivia cupped the side of his face. "Don't apologize, Connor. I'm okay. I'll let you know if anything scares me."

He nodded.

"Now get back down here before we have to start all over again."

His eyes danced. "You make it sound like starting again is a bad thing."

She laughed, and he took off her glasses before lying down and starting to nibble her neck, and then moving on to her earlobe. She almost levitated off the bed, and she felt him grin against her neck. "Score one for wolf man."

"Wolf man has too many clothes on." She gripped the bottom of his shirt and pulled it over his head, not bothering with the buttons.

And then it was time to explore. She ran her fingers over his abs and up onto his pecs. The pictures in her anatomy books never looked like this. Nor had the number of lovers she could count on less than one hand.

"I'm not going to be the only one doing show-and-tell, Liv." He reached for her shirt, and she stopped him so she could pull out the condom. His eyes widened for a moment before he went back to the task of helping her out of the flannel shirt while she pushed off her jogging pants.

Heat rushed to her face when she remembered she didn't have underwear or a bra on. While she had been with a very few lovers, she was sure the same could not be said for Connor. But when she met his eyes, she saw appreciation and heat. His green eyes seemed lit from within.

"Holy Fates. You are amazing," he whispered as he stroked his fingers down her neck to her collarbone and finally — finally! — to her chest, where he drew random patterns over her breasts, finding all the spots that made her breath hitch. It was like he was an artist and she was his canvas, his clay, whatever medium he wanted to use. Her cells tingled and popped like champagne bubbles.

How could he cause this much feeling with just his fingertips?

Then he slowly ran his fingers down to her belly and circled her belly button once, twice, before heading south. With his wickedly talented fingers it didn't take long for her champagne nerves to overflow in a mad burst.

She moaned, and he covered her mouth with his own, letting his tongue do some exploring. When he finally pulled away, her muscles had liquefied, and she simply lay there looking up at him.

But just to be sure, she blinked once, twice, three times. Yes, he was still there. This wasn't a dream.

"That was beautiful." When she didn't respond, Connor chuckled low in his throat. "You okay?"

"More than."

"You do look quite relaxed right now." The cocky man had the nerve to preen.

Olivia stretched like a cat in the sun. "Then you better get to work on waking me up."

While she stretched, his gaze traveled her body in a new type of caress. He reached for his own pants and pushed them off.

Holy hell, the man was glorious...and he was all hers. Now it was her turn to run her hands over his hard body and explore every delicious inch of him. And before long they were both the opposite of relaxed. Olivia helped Connor with the condom, and he climbed up her body and held himself up and over her with his arms.

"Are you ready, Liv? I want you so much."

A tear escaped, and he brushed it off her cheek with his thumb.

"I'm okay, Connor. More than okay. Please don't stop."

He lay down on her, and her body cradled his. Skin to skin. Connor worked his way inside, gently at first, until Olivia surged up and took all of him inside her.

Connor moaned, and gentle flew out the window as they both lost control. Coordinated movements quickly turned into a frenzied release.

Afterward they lay wrapped in each other's arms, trying to catch their breath. Olivia snuggled against him and he raised his arm to wrap it around her. A plum mark caught her attention and she sat up.

"Connor, what's that?"

He shrugged. "Nothing."

She pushed up his arm again. "That's not nothing. It looks like a birthmark."

"So?"

Her eyes widened. "It's exactly like the alpha mark."

"What are you talking about?"

"I haven't had a chance to tell you, what with everything else that's happened. Sullivan has a birthmark in the shape of a crescent moon with a horizontal split in the middle cutting it into two halves. He said it's the mark passed through the generations, only to those born to an alpha. We found out Maeve has one just like it, which means they're brother and sister."

Connor nodded. "So that's why Callahan said Morgan Ross wanted to ruin his family."

"Yes. And your mark looks like the bottom half of their mark." She sat up straighter. "Does Jack have a mark too?"

"Yes, it faces up."

"Two halves of a whole," she said, straddling his waist. "Do you know what this means? Sullivan may be your brother, and Maeve your sister."

Connor gaped at her. "Hell."

"Would it be a bad thing?"

"Morgan could be our father. He was a sadistic bastard. But Jonathan didn't exactly win father of the year." He frowned. "Do you think Jonathan knows and that's why he hates us?"

"Possibly. But I don't think it makes his treatment of you less horrible."

"No. But it would make more sense if his anger was due to his animosity toward Morgan. He sure hated our mother. I always thought he blamed her for having twins. Damn. I need to talk to Jack about all this."

She rubbed his chest, wanting to soothe him. "Of course you do. And you don't need to tell anyone else about it if you and Jack don't want to. I won't say anything."

He nodded and tucked her against him. She rested her head on his chest, and listened to his erratic heartbeat. She rubbed his stomach until he calmed down after a couple of minutes.

"I'm sorry I sprang that on you. Are you okay?"

"With you in my arms? Definitely."

"What can I do to make it better?"

His heart picked up speed again. "I can think of a couple things, but we have to be creative since we don't have any more condoms."

"Yeah. Tim only had the one."

Connor picked her up a little bit so he could look her in the eye. "Did you just say you got the condom from Giz?"

"Well, yes. I decided to seduce you, and I knew you didn't have any, and I didn't have any since we both ran for our life with nothing and have been wearing borrowed clothes. I didn't bother asking Devin since Alex is pregnant. And I didn't ask Charlie or Jack since they're both in committed relationships and I didn't think they would be carrying a hook-up condom in their wallet. Which left McHenry and Tim. I went to Tim first, and he gave me one."

Connor shook his head, groaning.

"You're upset because I asked him for a condom?" Olivia asked.

"No, I'm upset because he knows you had to seduce me, and if Giz knows, they'll all know, and I'm never going to live it down."

"I'm sure the guys will only pick on you a little bit."

"It's not the guys I need to worry about. Do you know what Alex and Julia are going to do with this?"

Olivia bit her lip to keep from laughing. "I'm sorry, Connor."

A little distraction was in order. She leaned down and kissed his chest, and then got her teeth and tongue involved to aid in the goal. He pulled her up so he could kiss her, and then flipped them over so her back was on the bed and he moved down her body ever... so...slowly.

He looked up at her. "Don't think I didn't notice you just seduced me again."

She combed her fingers through his hair. "Think of it as therapy. I'm pushing you out of your comfort zone."

"Oh, woman, you have no idea what you've unleashed now."

She gasped when he ran his tongue south, leaving a shivering trail in its wake. "Show me."

And he did.

More than once.

The scariest thing of all is love.
But it can also be the most rewarding.

CHAPTER 33

Connor held Olivia's hand as they walked toward a small cabin at the edge of the woods.

He had been the one to make this happen, but now he worried that maybe he should have left well enough alone. When Olivia told him the wolf from her childhood had a blue eye and a brown eye, he had gone to Sullivan to help locate the wolf. There couldn't be too many wolves in their pack who fit the description, if he was from their pack at all.

Sullivan actually knew of a wolf who fit the description. Sullivan had reached out to him to see if he would meet with them, and then Connor broached the subject with Olivia.

She was doing so well now with her phobia, but he wanted her to find closure as well. Now they stood outside the cabin, and Olivia blew out a breath before she reached up and knocked on the door.

Connor squeezed her hand just as the door opened. A tall man greeted them. He had dark brown hair and different colored eyes, and he smiled at Olivia before giving Connor a brief nod.

"Hello, Olivia. I'm Marcus."

"Hello."

"I thought, since it's such a beautiful day, why don't we sit outside at the picnic table and talk, if that's okay?"

Olivia agreed, and Marcus led them to a wooden picnic table at the side of the house. Connor sat next to Olivia, and Marcus sat on the other side.

Olivia cleared her throat. "I want to thank you for saving me."

Marcus hesitated for a moment, as if gathering his thoughts. "I've wondered over the years what happened to you. I'm so glad you're happy."

"Would you tell me about what happened when you found me?"

Marcus paused for a moment, frowning slightly. "Thirty years ago I lost everything in my life. I didn't want to be human anymore, so I stayed in my wolf form. If anyone from the clan had found me back then, they would have killed me as a rogue.

"One evening I was wandering the woods looking for food when I heard a crash. I ran toward the sound and came across a car accident. I saw the woman in the front, and my wolf could tell she was already gone. When I turned to leave, I heard crying. I trotted down the embankment and found you at the bottom, sobbing. When you saw me, you screamed, so I scrambled back and watched you from a distance. I had enough sense to know you were in trouble, and I waited for other humans to show up.

"But no one came. You eventually cried yourself to sleep, and something just wouldn't let me leave you, so I bit down on the back of the jumper you were wearing and carried you to the cave I used as my home. A stream ran nearby, and I drank out of it. You mimicked me and got down on your belly and drank out of the stream as well. But when I tried to feed you, you wouldn't eat the raw meat from the animals I killed."

"After another day of you not eating, I knew you needed to be with other humans, so I carried you through the woods to the ranger station and left you there. When I went back into the woods, you started crying, so I sat at the edge of the trees watching until the door opened and a ranger ran out to help you."

Olivia nodded slowly, several times. She hadn't interrupted Marcus during his story, more than likely letting him weave it as he saw fit. Connor wanted to pull the man into a hug for what he did for her so many years ago.

After a moment she finally spoke. "Thank you for filling in the blanks for me. I don't remember much from that time."

Marcus frowned. "Alpha explained a little bit to me. I'm sorry I scared you so long ago."

Olivia leaned forward. "It's not your fault. I was only five years old and had no idea what was happening, so I turned you into a monster in my mind."

"You saved her," Connor said, his voice rough. "That's what mattered."

Marcus stared out across the yard for a moment before looking at them again. "Olivia saved me as well. After I left you at the ranger station, I started seeking out other humans in the woods. Just to see them, to listen to them talk. After a few months, I turned to human for the first time in years. I only spent time in human form for a little while, but I began craving it more and more. And over time I finally came to my senses and relearned how to live as both a wolf and as man. You did that."

A tear ran down Olivia's face, and Connor put his arm around her shoulder.

"And you made me into who I am today as well. I won't lie and tell you my fears from that event haven't troubled me for a long time, but they also influenced me to become a doctor to help people like me who suffer from phobias."

Marcus gave her a soft smile. "The Fates had plans for both of us."

He reached into his pocket and pulled out a picture, placing it on the table. A blond woman and a girl with pigtails and beautiful eyes, one blue and one brown, smiled back at them.

"If it wasn't for you, I would never have met Joanna, and we would not have our daughter, Trish. Trish wanted to meet you since I've told her stories since she was a baby about the magical little girl in the woods who saved me. But Joanna felt we needed some time alone. Would you like to come back and meet them?"

Now the tears flooded Olivia's face, and Connor had to blink away a few in his own eyes.

Olivia wiped her face. "I would love it. I hope it's okay to ask this, but would you show me your wolf? I...need to see it."

He stood and transitioned in front of Olivia into a large gray and black wolf with glowing eyes — one blue and one brown.

She let go of Connor and stood, walking up to the wolf and holding out her hand. He bumped his snout against it, and she rubbed her hand over his head.

She looked over her shoulder at Connor, beaming at him, and the last of the damn brittle walls around his heart shattered. She was his and he was hers.

He had never been so certain of anything.

They left a few minutes later after promising to return, and walked along the trail to the SUV.

As he drove the SUV down the long dirt drive

leading to the main road, he tried to calm down. He was so energized he wanted to howl it to the moon.

He loved her. He would cook a romantic meal tonight, and he would tell her then, when he could find the perfect words.

He loved her.

"I love you too, Connor."

He slammed his foot on the brake and a cloud of dust rose up around the SUV as he jammed the car into park. "What did you say?"

She smiled at him. "I said I love you too."

He gaped at her.

Her smile faded slightly. "Why are you looking at me that way? Normally when someone tells you they love you and you feel the same way, you tell them back."

Connor nodded. "Yes, you do. Except I didn't say it out loud, Olivia. I thought it."

She gaped at him. "No, you said it just now."

Stubborn woman. Don't argue with me.

"I am not stubborn. Wait…your mouth didn't move just now, but I heard you. What does that mean?"

It means you can hear my thoughts. That we're true mates.

Holy crap!

Connor laughed out loud. "Holy crap is right." He leaned over and kissed her. He didn't need perfect timing, or a special meal, or rehearsed words. He just needed to speak from his heart every damn time.

His wolf was appeased, *finally.* Him too for that matter. Love had a perfect way of calming both man and beast.

Don't run away from love.
Embrace it and let it strengthen you.

CHAPTER 34

Olivia spun around the dance floor, watching the other wedding guests having a blast.

Jack and Julia had continued their life-is-too-short mantra and planned their wedding in a month. The For Better or For Worse team took the short time frame in stride and created a perfect day for the bride and groom, who were currently out in the middle of the dance floor.

Julia had chosen a red gown instead of the traditional white, but Jack wore a tuxedo, as had Connor, his best man. Her man. He was dancing with Maeve.

Maeve laughed at something Connor said as he spun her. Both Connor and Jack had decided to tell Sullivan and Maeve the truth, and now the four of them were forging a family. Maeve had already made great strides toward finding herself as well.

And Olivia twirled around the floor with Tim, who surprised her with his dancing skills.

The rest of the team also had their wives on the dance floor. Even at six months pregnant, Alex busted a move with Devin.

Olivia would never have believed she could now be friends with both Alex and Julia, but they all had become a surrogate family for her, and she was finally coming into her own as well.

"Thank you," Olivia said.

"For what?" Tim asked.

"For the condom and for not telling the others."

"I didn't see the point of torturing him. But it doesn't mean I can't lord it over his ass as a threat if he's driving me crazy," Tim said as they made their way around the dance floor.

Olivia laughed.

"I'm glad things worked out for you and Connor."

"Me too."

"He's finally happy. Hell, all my teammates are, and it makes *me* happy."

"What about you, Tim? Do you have anyone special in your life?"

He shook his head as he spun her. "Not yet. And now that everyone has paired off, I'm in trouble. Alex is going to make it her mission to find me a match."

Olivia laughed again. "You're right. I'll see if I can convince her to take it easy on you, but I don't know how effective I'll be."

"I'll take any help I can get. She's already introduced me to two women tonight."

"You got it." They danced for another minute and then, per her request, Tim left her on the side of the dance floor while he went in search of some wedding cake.

After a few minutes Sullivan walked up and stood beside her, watching the dancers. His relaxed face tightened into a frown, and Olivia turned to see what was upsetting him. Maeve stood off to the side by the bar. Several young wolves were glancing her way and looked like they were trying to decide who would approach her. *Oh, boy...* Time to distract the over-protective older brother.

"Glad to see you here, Alpha."

"I wouldn't have missed it," Sullivan answered distractedly.

"Is the pack settling down?" Olivia asked.

"Yes," Sullivan said, finally taking his eyes off his sister to face Olivia. "It's been quite an upheaval, but we'll get there. Victor's betrayal impacted a lot of people. Godfrey has agreed to replace him as one of my advisors."

Olivia nodded emphatically. "Great choice."

"And Jonathan is stepping down too. I haven't said anything to Jack or Connor yet. I didn't want to upset anyone before the wedding."

"Who are you going to ask to fill his role?" Olivia asked, too curious to curb her tongue.

"I'm going to talk to Jack and Connor about both of them doing it. There's nothing in our laws saying I can only have two advisors."

"Another good choice, although you might have a fight on your hands."

"Probably, but we'll figure it out. Speaking of figuring things out, when are you going to make an honest wolf out of him?"

Olivia chuckled. "He already is an honest wolf."

Sullivan winked. "He is."

"And how are you really doing now that you know Connor and Jack are your brothers?"

"Good. Even though my—our—father was a horrible person, the twins and Maeve wouldn't be here if it weren't for him. I just wish he had been a semi-decent man so we could have been raised together. But I have them now, and I'm not letting them go."

"Good, because I think you all need each other. There is one thing that still bothers me about this whole thing. I don't understand why your father agreed to the marriage contract between you and Maeve."

"I asked Callahan about it when we interrogated him. I don't think Morgan knew Maeve was his daughter. The rift between the two alphas happened when Callahan caught my father with his wife. But Callahan didn't tell Morgan he was Maeve's father."

"And the twins?"

Sullivan sighed. "I think Morgan eventually figured out he was their father, which is why he refused to throw them out of the pack. So I guess in the end he did one thing right." He cleared his throat. "Enough about the past. I have a question for you. I've heard rumors that you and Connor are true mates."

"Yes. We just realized it when we could hear each other's thoughts."

Sullivan groaned. "You poor thing, he talks nonstop already. I can't imagine what it's like hearing him in your head too."

Warm arms wrapped around her from behind as Connor leaned down and kissed her cheek. "Is he bothering you?"

"No, I'm not bothering her," Sullivan answered. "I just want to make sure you're treating her well."

Connor's eyes sparked as Olivia peeked up at him. "I'm treating her very well. Do you want to dance, Liv?"

"Yes."

"I think I'm going to ask Sis to dance," Sullivan said before striding away.

And stop her admirers from approaching her, Olivia wagered. But she wasn't going to mention it to Connor. Poor Maeve had her hands full with three overprotective brothers.

Connor led her to the dance floor and pulled her

close. "This is more like it." He grinned down while twirling her.

"I'm so happy for Jack and Julia."

Connor glanced over at his twin. "Me too. He deserves happiness. We all do."

"Including Maeve and Sullivan," Olivia said.

"Now Sullivan knows we're related, he's getting awfully nosy."

Olivia laughed. "It's what families do, Connor. Look how Elena interrogated you when we went out to dinner the other night."

Connor widened his eyes in mock horror. "Now *that* is a strong, opinionated woman."

"Yes, she is."

"It's a good thing I like strong, opinionated women. And she's also a good friend who's looking out for you."

"As is your older brother."

"How do you always find a way to get your point across?"

"I'm smart and well trained."

Connor waggled his eyebrows. "You're turning me on right now. I'm thinking you could dress up like a sexy librarian tonight..."

"Nope. I'm thinking more along the line of Little Red Riding Hood."

Connor pulled her tighter to him. "Which makes me the Big Bad Wolf?"

"Yes."

He growled in her ear, and she shivered in anticipation.

"Where did that idea come from?" he asked.

She shrugged. "I thought maybe we'd try something new on the menu."

He laughed. "I love you, Olivia Jennings."

"And I love you, Connor Dawson."

He dipped her and then captured her lips smack dab in the middle of the dance floor, to the sounds of applause and catcalls.

And Olivia loved every minute of it.

THANKS!

Thank you for taking the time to read *For Better or For Wolf*. The next book in this series is *For Witch or For Poorer* and will focus on Giz, the tech guru of the team. I think you'll be surprised who he ends up with...

I love reaching out to my readers. By joining my newsletter, you will receive notices of new books, sales, exclusive content, and other bits of news about my books. Plus, you will receive free content by signing up at subscribe3.aejonesauthor.com or follow me on Twitter @aejonesauthor or Facebook at facebook.com/aejones.author1.

I hope you enjoyed the fourth book in the paranormal wedding planner series. Please consider telling your friends about it or posting a short review. Word of mouth is an author's best friend, and much appreciated. Thank you!

— AE

Books by AE Jones

Paranormal Wedding Planner Series

In Sickness and In Elf – Book 1
From This Fae Forward – Book 2
To Have and To Howl – Book 3
For Better or For Wolf – Book 4
For Witch or For Poorer – Book 5
Till Demon Do Us Part – Book 6 (coming soon)

The Realm Series (Mind Sweeper Spin Off)

Demons Will Be Demons – Book 1
Demons Are A Girl's Best Friend – Book 2
Demons Are Forever – Book 3

Mind Sweeper Series

Mind Sweeper – Book 1
The Fledgling – Book 2 (A Mind Sweeper Novella)
Shifter Wars – Book 3
The Pursuit – Book 4 (A Mind Sweeper Novella)
Sentinel Lost – Book 5

MIND SWEEPER FLASHBACK STORIES

Forget Me
Protect Me
Trust Me

Find all of AE Jones's latest releases on your favorite
online retailer or visit her website:
http://www.aejonesauthor.com

ABOUT THE AUTHOR

Growing up a TV junkie, AE Jones oftentimes rewrote endings of episodes in her head when she didn't like the outcome. She immersed herself in sci-fi and soap operas. But when *Buffy* hit the little screen, she knew her true love was paranormal. Now she spends her nights weaving stories about all variations of supernatural—their angst and their humor. After all, life is about both...whether you sport fangs or not.

AE won RWA's Golden Heart® Award for her paranormal manuscript, Mind Sweeper, which also was a RWA RITA® finalist for both First Book and Paranormal Romance. AE is also a recipient of the Booksellers' Best Award and is a National Readers' Choice Award Finalist, Holt Award of Merit Finalist and a Daphne du Maurier Finalist.

AE lives in Ohio surrounded by her eclectic family and friends who in no way resemble any characters in her books. *Honest.* Now her two cats are another story altogether.

Made in the
USA
Lexington, KY